'With every turn of the page, my eyebrows moved slightly further up my forehead. There was I, assuming the junior bar was crammed with the serious and the high-minded, where the only trace of ambition is the politest nudge . . . *BabyBarista* shows the eagles and eaglets with their talons out and their feathers up. It is a wonderful, racing read – well-drawn, smartly plotted and laugh out loud – and we all just have to pray that none of it is true. You'll never look at a young lawyer in the same way again' Jeremy Vine, broadcaster and journalist

'*BabyBarista* is a classic British comedy set in a world of vanity, egos and cut-throat ambition that puts even the acting profession into the shade. It's sassy, sexy and hilariously funny' Denise Welch, *Loose Women*

'*BabyBarista* provides an entertaining and highly amusing insight into the mysterious world of wigs and gowns. Right from the start the gloves are off and the fight for tenancy is no less dramatic than a top class boxing match. It's a terrific read which makes you both laugh and keep the pages turning. It also confirms what I've always suspected – that the courtroom is not so different from the boxing ring' Barry McGuigan MBE, former World Featherweight Boxing Champion

'Tim Kevan gets the whole legal eagle (and especially eaglet) scene bang to rights. His Machiavellian "Chambers" makes many an opium den and sadomasochistic brothel look like a vicars' tea party. Half-Darwinian struggle for power, half-dangerous liaisons – beyond any reasonable doubt fast, funny, and furious' Andy Martin, author of *Stealing the Wave*

'If you thought *This Life*, *North Square* or Sydney Carton gave barristers a bad name, you ain't seen nothing yet. *BabyBarista* is a worm's-eye view of the profession, and the angle is far from flattering. It is also sharp, acerbic, and almost illegally funny. There's the usual disclaimer about it being a work of fiction, but if you believe that, you should be a juror' Boris Starling, author of *Messiah*

BabyBarista
and The Art of War

BabyBarista
and The Art of War

TIM KEVAN

BLOOMSBURY

LONDON · BERLIN · NEW YORK

First published in Great Britain 2009

Copyright © 2009 by Tim Kevan

Every reasonable effort has been made to trace copyright holders
of material reproduced in this book. If any have been inadvertently
overlooked the publishers would be glad to hear from them.

The moral right of the author has been asserted

Bloomsbury Publishing, London, Berlin and New York

36 Soho Square, London W1D 3QY

A CIP catalogue record for this book is available from the British Library

ISBN 978 0 7475 9464 2
10 9 8 7 6 5 4 3 2 1

Typeset by Hewer Text UK Ltd, Edinburgh
Printed in Great Britain by Clays Ltd, St Ives plc

The paper this book is printed on is certified by the 1996 Forest Stewardship
Council A.C. (FSC). It is ancient-forest friendly. The printer holds
FSC chain of custody SGS-COC-2061

FSC Mixed Sources
Product group from well-managed
forests and other controlled sources
www.fsc.org Cert no. SGS-COC-2061
© 1996 Forest Stewardship Council

www.bloomsbury.com/timkevan

To Michelle and my parents
and in loving memory of Lorna Wilson

Lawyers, I suppose,
were children once.

Charles Lamb

We are the hollow men
We are the stuffed men
Leaning together
Headpiece filled with straw. Alas!
Our dried voices, when
We whisper together
Are quiet and meaningless
As wind in dry grass
Or rats' feet over broken glass
In our dry cellar . . .

T.S. Eliot

Contents

CAST

BabyBarista: A young Flashman meets Rumpole meets Francis Urquhart for the twenty-first century.

OldRuin: How a barrister should be. Dumbledore meets Clarence, the angel in *It's a Wonderful Life*. BabyB's redemption.

TheBoss: BabyB's first pupilmaster. Unscrupulous, spineless coward.

TopFirst: Fellow pupil and BabyB's main competition for tenancy.

BusyBody: Fellow pupil and a whirlwind of interference with a good heart.

Worrier: Fellow pupil carrying the details of the world on her shoulders.

UpTights: BabyB's pupilmistress for his second six months who was almost called BoTucks for the work she's had done. Insists on boundaries and personal space. Has 'issues'.

OldSmoothie: Think Peter Bowles in *To The Manor Born* and the Milk Tray Man, but not quite. Once successful barrister now put out to graze as a committee man.

TheBusker: Barrister of ten years' call with the integrity and decency of OldRuin. Very laid back in his approach to both court and life. Admired by BabyB.

Claire: BabyB's best friend and a pupil in another chambers. Think Scully from *X-Files*.

ThirdSix: Final pupil thrown into the mix halfway through BabyB's pupillage. He is on his third six-month pupillage.

TheVamp: Tenant in chambers and a walking innuendo.

HeadofChambers: Well meaning, pompous and out of touch.

HeadClerk: The real power in chambers. All seeing, all knowing.

FanciesHimself: Junior clerk who has a fling with BusyBody.

JudgeJewellery: Judge with penchant for stealing high-street trinkets.

ClichéClanger: Solicitor with a colourful use of the English language.

SlipperySlope: Solicitor skilled in the creative art of billing.

PROLOGUE

Sunday 1 October 2006
Day 0 (week 0): Jewel thief

It's the day before I start work and I've been clearing out my room at home. One thing upon which I stumbled was a note I made some ten years ago at school. It's a list entitled 'Careers':

England football captain. I wish.
Vet. Sticking hand in dark places.
Binman. Too smelly.
Solicitor. Yawn
Barrister. Silly clothes.
Doctor. Too many ill people.
Banker. Pushing money around.

Then at the end I'd scribbled, 'Jewel thief?'

CHAPTER I
OCTOBER: FIRST DAYS

The art of war is . . . a matter of life and death, a road
either to safety or to ruin. Hence it is a subject of
inquiry which can on no account be neglected.
Sun Tzu, *The Art of War*

Monday 2 October 2006
Day 1 (week 1): TheBoss

'Where's the strong ground coffee?' I asked, starting to panic slightly. I spent the summer working for Starbucks in preparation for today but it didn't seem to be standing me in any stead so far.

'Where you'd expect it to be. Over there.'

'And the filters?'

'Ah. We may have run out of those. You'll need to go to the kitchen on the second floor west for those.'

I took out the little map I'd been given and worked out where this was before making the dash across corridors and staircases. I arrived back, sweating, only to find that the kettle was now empty and needed re-boiling. Time was ticking and my stress levels were rising. Eventually it was all done and I made my way through to serve the coffee, albeit somewhat belatedly.

'Just put it down over there, young man.'

I did so and only just stopped myself from making a bow before withdrawing to my desk.

So there it is. My first day as a pupil barrister in chambers and this is truly the diary of a nobody. I've been warned about it by those who've gone before. 'Glorified coffee-maker' and 'underpaid photocopier' were the most common descriptions. Such is the ordeal through which the Bar Council continues to force its brightest and best. Interviews and offers might be sufficient for Goldman Sachs or McKinsey. Not so the Bar. Twelve months of four pupils fighting it out before chambers vote for which one of the four they want to take on as a tenant. A sort of upper-class reality show in microcosm where every one of your foibles will be analysed and where a blackball system exists so that if you annoy one person, you're out. As with *Big Brother*, you're playing to the lowest common denominator. Attempting to be as inoffensive as possible in the sound knowledge that it won't be the votes in favour that get you in but the lack of votes against. Sure, they'll go through the motions of checking my work and ticking the Bar Council's equal opportunities forms. But the crunch comes in the unsaid so-called 'Tennis Club Test' – would they have me in their club . . . or not. All of which for a comprehensive-school kid from north London might seem a little daunting were it not for the fact that I'd already had ivory tower practice for three years whilst studying law at Oxford. Still, as I sit here at my laptop in the corner of the office reflecting on my first day, I realise that the Bar takes that whole elitism to a new level. Not that I didn't know what I was letting myself in for, nor can I pretend that wasn't part of the attraction of it in the first place. That, and getting paid huge sums of money to prance around in silly clothes all day.

Anyway, after a sleepless night I'd rocked up at chambers at 8.30 a.m. on the dot. There were no signs telling new pupils where to go. Just a board with the names of the members of chambers below an ancient archway. The entrance hall was all old *Punch* cartoons and tatty leather armchairs and from there it went through to the clerks' room which in contrast looked more like a city traders' office with a collection of seven or eight computer screens and a bunch of people talking at top speed on the phone. I made my big entrance, the start of my new life, and was completely ignored by everyone in there. A couple looked up before resuming their conversations. The others didn't even acknowledge my presence at all. I stood there for a few minutes not wanting to interrupt before deciding to leave and try my entrance afresh. Ten minutes later I'd been around the block and was met by an immaculately dressed man in his fifties, with a paunch and a well-groomed, Richard Branson-type beard the same size as the bald patch on top of his head, as if one was somehow cancelling out the other. He looked at me in a slightly intimidating way and boomed, 'Where did you go, young man? Taking breaks before you've even started?'

'Er, no, Sir. Wasn't sure if I'd got the right place. Went to check.'

'Never call me Sir, Sir. My name is John. Head Clerk. You must be young Mr BabyBarista, Sir?'

'Yes, that's right – er – John.'

'Welcome aboard, Sir. We run a tight ship here in the clerks' room. Never forget to tell us where you are when you're not with your pupilmaster. We'll always have something else for you to be doing. Now, where is your pupilmaster?'

One of the junior clerks eventually got around to leading me up the bare stone stairs of chambers to a decent-sized room overlooking a large car park. I'd already checked out my pupilmaster online. I'll call him TheBoss. Educated at Winchester and Trinity College, Cambridge, he had a pretty traditional upper-middle-class barrister background. Upper second in law and then called to the Bar in the Middle Temple in 1986. He's therefore been a barrister for some eighteen years and I found with a bit more of a Google search that he is married with two kids. Official interests: chess and tennis.

Even on first meeting you could tell that he was a vain man and he was at that stage of life where he was just starting to lose his looks but hadn't quite come to terms with it yet. This was fairly obvious from the fact that he had clearly outgrown both his shirt and his suit trousers to the extent that they were beyond even 'fitted'. Up top, his dark hair was receding and where it still remained it was greying. All of which he seemed to be trying to hide with a kind of arrogant air, as if trying to tell the world that nothing could touch him, not even time itself.

He showed me my tiny desk, the size of a small laptop, and before even mentioning his work or anything like that he said, 'Now BabyBarista, let's get the important things out of the way first.'

He led me through to a poky little boxroom with a kettle, a sink and a fridge.

'I take my coffee on the hour but if I'm working hard, I'd like it more often. It's something you'll have to learn to judge. Now, I will provide you with the coffee beans and you will take it from there. Take the grinding slowly and make it as fine as possible. Increases the surface area you know. Gets that extra bit of flavour.'

He started to look animated. 'Then I insist on paper filters. Only the best as well. Can't be too careful these days. Lot of rubbish on the market. Once you've filtered then you're home and dry. Mugs are here and you'll provide the milk each morning. Semi-skimmed. Just a dash along with half a sugar. Get this right, BabyBarista, and you'll be destined for great things. Remember, it's all in the grind.'

This was no joke or amusing metaphor. He was absolutely serious. This would be the heart of my job. Then, as he led me back into the room grumbling about coffee-makers he'd had in the past, he went on, 'Oh, there's one more important thing I like to give my pupils.'

He rummaged in his desk and then handed me a strange little book entitled *The Art of War*, by Sun Tzu.

'Litigation is like war, BabyBarista. Read this and learn.'

Tuesday 3 October 2006
Day 2 (week 1): Political correctness day

It was political correctness day today. It started with the chat from TheBoss. He sat back in his swivel chair, put his feet on his huge old leather-topped desk – which stood in stark contrast to my tiny Ikea number – and clasped his hands together in front of him.

'Something I have to go through with you today, BabyBarista. We now have rules about sexual harassment at the Bar,' (as if it was all perfectly fine before that). 'I'm sure you understand, being an Oxford man,' (whatever that was meant to mean). 'Please remember that if you are ever feeling sexually harassed, you must not hesitate to report it to me.'

He then paused, for effect, and shifted a little awkwardly. 'I'm also bound to tell you, for the avoidance of any doubt that, if you believe that I am the one doing the sexual harassing then you must tell HeadofChambers immediately.'

All said deadpan and without even a hint of irony.

'Yes, of course,' I said. Certainly. I'll do that. Note to self. Must not forget.

Well, HeadofChambers was quite different. There are two men and two women doing this pupillage and we were all herded into his very grand room. Here, for the first time, I squared up to my competition for the year. On average only one in four gets taken on and there is no avoiding the fact that we are directly in competition for that place. It was hardly high noon at the OK Corral but there was definitely a lot of sizing up going on. The two women tried to be more subtle about it and one in particular appeared almost shy, but the other guy just came across as plain arrogant, like he already owned the place and was finding this whole induction process a distraction from his otherwise important business.

Two of the walls in the room were lined with law reports. Another had yet more old cartoons of long-dead lawyers, along with a painting of someone shooting on what was probably a Scottish grouse moor and a photograph of HeadofChambers in full hunting regalia astride his horse and raising a glass to the camera. It was quite a walk to get to the end of the room where HeadofChambers sat at his old wooden desk in front of a massive window which overlooked the courtyard below. We were told to sit at the conference table in front, as, no doubt, thousands of his clients had done over the years. He was how you might have imagined a barrister to look a hundred years ago. It was as if he had modelled himself on that image to such an extent that he had himself eventually become it, from his immaculate pin-striped suit to his slicked-back hair, which looked as if it had been flattened by forty years of wearing a bowler hat. He looked like a man for whom doubt had been cast away many years ago. As we entered his look was stern, despite the fact that he was clearly trying to take a slightly paternal tack with, 'Ah, the Baby Bar. Do come in and take a seat.'

After a brief introduction telling us that chambers had been founded some sixty years ago and that we were following in a fine tradition, he continued, 'Now. I've got to tell you this. Bar Council regulations and all that. Sexual harassment. Terrible mess. Hope it doesn't happen. But, if it does, I'm bound to inform you that you should report it either to your pupilmaster or to me. This is without reservation and you should be fully aware that we comply entirely with the Bar Council policy on this issue. I'm also bound to tell you that should you make any such complaint it will not be held against you in this chambers.'

So that was that and now we knew. Except it wasn't.

'However,' he looked up and peered at each of us over the top of his half-moon spectacles and then focused on the two women. 'I probably shouldn't say this, but it's meant in the most helpful way. Consider it practical advice from an old hand at the Bar. Bear in mind that whilst you are absolutely within your rights to make any such complaint, in fact more than within your rights, you must not forget also that there are consequences to every action. This is always the case and is no different here. Whatever you do has consequences whether you notice them or not. I can't say what they'd be in these circumstances but you have to be aware that not all chambers or barristers are as enlightened as us. Not that they'd actively discriminate against you in those circumstances. It's just that you should know that they would know. That's all.'

Welcome to the modern Bar.

Wednesday 4 October 2006
Day 3 (week 1): TopFirst

'So, how have you found your first few days?' I asked.

'Pretty easy really. Personal injury's not exactly very taxing intellectually, if you know what I mean.'

We were in the clerks' room and this was my first chat with TopFirst, the other guy pupil with the over-confident swagger. Today he was obviously on his best behaviour although he still seemed a bit of a swot. Got a first at Cambridge and even went on to do a master's. A little quiet, although I've been told that quiet is not a bad tactic for pupillage. Seems strange when you're training for such an ostensibly outgoing and independent profession that you spend the first year proving your abilities to slime up to the right people and keep out of the way of others. Yet TopFirst is quiet to the point of being aloof and has an almost aggressive air of cleverness. Physically he's tall and quite thin, but in a more rodenty than a chinless aristocratic way. Like one of the ferrets who took over Toad Hall. All dressed up and airs and graces and yet not quite making it. Let me be more clear. He's arrogant and pretentious. Two things which will no doubt serve him well at the Bar.

Thursday 5 October 2006
Day 4 (week 1): Lunch

So far, other than making coffee, I've been wholly occupied in trundling along behind TheBoss and meeting and greeting other pupils. It seems that the way he likes it done is to refuse to acknowledge my presence when he's with other barristers outside of chambers. We were at lunch yesterday in one of the halls and he greeted a number of his chums. Some had pupils and the only confirmation that I was not invisible was that there were perfunctory nods from them. A knowing look that says we're all in the same boat and it's not much fun. Raised eyebrows and at least the tiniest bit of human interaction.

Though I did at least learn an important lesson at lunch. Chat was about nothing in particular and after much thought I eventually came up with something designed to impress, only to find that TheBoss had decided to speak at the same time. Quick as a flash he looked at me and said pointedly, 'Sorry, after you,' with raised eyebrows. It wasn't the first time I'd noticed that his best put-downs are in the insincere courtesies he offers around.

'No, no,' I said. 'Sorry to interrupt.'

'No, I insist,' he replied. 'Go ahead.'

Well, I was lost for words by that point and could only manage some incoherent ramblings. TopFirst was sitting opposite and smirked into his soup. Round one to him.

Friday 6 October 2006
Day 5 (week 1): Library life

Found my first PupilSkive today. Time in the library. Pretty obvious really, though I had to be told about it by Claire, my best friend from Bar School and now a pupil in another chambers. 'Researching a point' is the general line to be taken. Found a whole collection of pupils wandering around the library, gossiping and looking as though they'd just been let out of jail. What would you give as the collective noun for such a gathering? A giggle? Certainly for some of them. They really are an earnest bunch as a whole. Not a little self-important too. Breathlessly talking about the merits of their respective pupilmasters and the cases that they're on. Then there's the revelling in the pomp of it all. Today, for example, I bumped into a friend and went to shake his hand and he corrected me. 'Barristers don't shake hands with each other.'

We'd all had that pointed out on the first day of pupillage but I'd noted that it was a custom often not followed, particularly by members of the Junior Bar. Next thing he'll be addressing me as his 'learned friend' over coffee. I mean, please. Give it up, won't you? It's a job, and a pretty menial one at that. But perhaps that's why they treat it so seriously since if they didn't they'd realise quite how they're being exploited. After one week, it seems clear to me that for less than the price of a junior coffee-maker in the local café (not even Starbucks), chambers gets itself a bunch of dogsbodies who will do all the inconvenient bits of paperwork, not complain at having to spend two hours poring over a photocopier and offer to make coffee or tea on an hourly basis. In the meantime, my contemporaries who went off to City solicitors are dealing with multi-million pound deals and flying off delivering papers to the Middle East whilst those in banking are swanning around on training courses in places like Geneva.

For me, I am off to Slough County Court on Monday. The glamour of the Bar. Though when I said this to my friend Claire as we sat in the library she replied, 'You should be so lucky, BabyB. I've spent the first week of pupillage babysitting for my pupilmistress' two-year-old son whilst she swans off to court.'

'So why do we do it?' I asked.

'Because you're too vain to get an ordinary job,' she replied.

'Easier to fail at the Bar and go to the stage than the other way round, you mean?'

'Exactly.'

'Whilst of course all you want is to save the world.'

'Naturally.' She pushed a few stray strands of her brown hair out of her eyes and smiled. 'Though quite how babysitting and coffee-making duties are going to help accomplish that I have no idea. But I've never asked you before. Why on earth did you choose the Bar?'

'You want the truth?'

'Why not.'

'It's pretty uncool.'

'Go on, try me.'

'To pay off the loans and credit card debts my mother's incurred getting me this far. Get her back on her feet. Put an end to the constant worry.'

I paused before adding quietly, 'I want to make her proud.'

Tuesday 10 October 2006
Day 7 (week 2): No-win, no-fee

TheBoss was actually stressed for once today and it was all over a no-win, no-fee agreement. Appropriately, it was a stress-at-work case which he'd assumed would settle which would have counted as a win and the fee would have followed. Except it didn't settle and was now promising to end up in a five-day bunfight at Central London County Court starting tomorrow. The first big problem was that until last night, truth be told, TheBoss really hadn't ever read the papers particularly carefully. It just seemed the sort of case which was going to settle. It was only late yesterday that he realised this was not so and started ploughing through the documents the other side had handed over months before. Needless to say, I received a late and rather abrupt phone call asking (i.e. instructing) me to get in early the next morning.

So, six o'clock this morning, bleary eyed, I crawled into chambers and started delving into the disclosure. By the time TheBoss arrived at half past eight I'd made a pretty good start and had managed to highlight a couple of good reasons why the other side might not be making the offers which TheBoss had anticipated. Factors other than work to suggest why the client might be stressed, such as a marriage break-up and massive debts. These certainly weren't fatal to the case but they were enough to get TheBoss worried. So, rather than getting any credit for spotting these points, it seems that all day I've been seen as the reason why TheBoss might be about to lose 'forty grand's worth of fees', as he kept muttering under his breath. As if it would have been somehow better to have made these discoveries in the middle of the trial.

With this much money at stake for TheBoss, one thing was clear. Settlement was a priority, and the quicker the better. His solicitor had even more riding on the case and so there was no resistance there. As for the client, the solicitor apparently gave him a call mentioning the difficulties that the other evidence might cause and, '. . . well, you do understand.' No, the client didn't really understand but what was he going to do, some eighteen hours before his big day in court?

So it settled and all's well that ends well as far as TheBoss and his beloved 'forty grand' were concerned. Afterwards, he turned to me and asked whether I'd been reading the little book by Sun Tzu, to which I replied, 'a little'.

'Remember what he said about fighting, BabyB. "To fight and conquer in all your battles is not supreme excellence; supreme excellence consists in breaking the enemy's resistance without fighting." '

What I'd say is, 'Never take on a lawyer on a no-win, no-fee basis.' Invest now in legal expenses insurance. Pay upfront. But whatever you do, don't let the lawyers start worrying about getting paid. However much they protest otherwise, it's there in their mind. Not even at the back of their mind. It's a big fat ugly screaming beast jumping up and down on their head telling them to settle whether you want to fight it or not.

Wednesday 11 October 2006
Day 8 (week 2): BusyBody

With the settlement under his belt, TheBoss didn't show today and apparently will be away the rest of the week. He figures that he's got his brief fee for the five-day trial and so at the very least after all that hard work he deserves a rest. By Jove, he's earned it. Not that I'm complaining. When TheBoss is away . . . BabyBarista goes to the library. Turns out there's quite a social scene already developed. A little pupil ecosystem all of its own. One of those places where the only work done is by this one librarian we call JobsWorth who sees it as his mission to seek out and find every nook or cranny which might be hiding a little collection of pupils and then to scowl and say, 'Can you either get back to work or leave please,' which is what he's forced to say since one of the pupils last year apparently reported him for swearing.

Claire was at the library this morning. I was on the top floor, which is usually empty, and was playing cricket with a couple of friends. As she strolled through the door, she caught us scarpering back to our desks, like rabbits in the headlights, thinking that JobsWorth had caught us red-handed.

'Good to see that the future of the legal profession is in safe hands,' she said. 'Coffee?'

Off at the nearest café, Claire looked relieved to be away from chambers.

'I've decided I can't stand my pupilmistress. Last week it was babysitting. This week she's making me teach her precocious little four-year-old brat to read.'

'What do the rest of chambers think about her using the place as a crèche?'

'So long as she continues paying them inordinate amounts of rent, they don't care what she does.'

'Even when she's completely taking the mickey?'

'Regardless, and anyway, she's played the militant-single-mum card so well that they'd all be terrified to question her right to do anything, I reckon. But hey, what's new with you?'

'Well, I've got myself a pretty straightforward plan to win over each of the sixty or so members of chambers one by one.'

'You and the rest of the pupil world. So how's it work?'

'Drawn up a spreadsheet and set myself a target of doing at least one piece of work for each of them by the time of the tenancy decision at the end of next September.'

'Geek.'

'You think I'm bad. You should see some of the others.'

'It's so sad we've got to do this, but I guess they'll be making their own little plans. I have to say, I don't like the sound of TopFirst.'

I then went on to tell her about meeting one of the girl pupils for the first time. Let me call her BusyBody. Boy oh boy is she that. This morning she collared me outside the clerks' room and boomed so that everyone and their dog could hear, 'Are you going to stand for election to the Young Barristers Committee of the Bar Council, BabyBarista?'

'Er . . .'

'Because if you're not, do you think you would support me?'

'Er . . .'

'Thank you, BabyBarista. I knew I could count on my core vote in chambers.'

She's a bundle of interfering energy who wants to boss and generally organise everyone on the planet, as well as wanting to know everyone's business and more. It's exhausting just watching her so I can't imagine what it must be like to be whizzing around inside her head. Needless to say she's been on every student committee and organising body you can imagine and was renowned even before arriving at Bar School. A human whirlwind, unable to sit still. Oh, and an overachiever on all fronts which makes it even more unbearable. She's the other one with the Cambridge first. Same college as TopFirst in fact, just the year below. Didn't have time for a master's. Life is short, particularly when you're BusyBody.

Not that she herself is short. More what you might call big-boned all round. Not massive or anything but I would say that she's as aware as anyone from the cut of her thigh that she's blatantly sitting on a genetic time bomb which will explode inside of her by her mid-twenties and add another five stone in the process. Perhaps it's the price she has to pay for having inherited her Italian mother's dark good looks, something which was evident from a photo which BusyBody has as her screensaver. Whatever the reason it leaves her very little time to find an unsuspecting husband, something she is just as transparently ambitious about, even on first meeting.

As I described her to Claire, I reflected on my first impression. On balance, I'm against.

Thursday 12 October 2006
Day 9 (week 2): Utter barristers

Today I'm feeling a little the worse for wear. Last night was my 'call night', the time when I was officially 'called to the Bar'. Technically called to the 'utter' Bar which apparently makes me an 'utter barrister'. Still sounds rude now. So we all queued up in Inner Temple Hall and were paraded in front of our families and various members of the great and the good to be officially made barristers and be given the right to wear the wig and gown.

The hall itself was all wood panels, coats of arms and ancient portraits, but none of that was as impressive as the hat that my mother arrived in. To say that it looked like a peacock would not be to do it justice, for in all aspects but for the fact that it did not have blood running through its veins, it did indeed appear to be a peacock. Claire, who had changed her usual black trouser suit for a jacket and skirt, thought it was all mightily amusing and kept telling me not to worry. Which would probably have been good advice were it not for the fact that her headgear had caught the attention of HeadofChambers who had sidled over to see who on earth it was sporting this grand design. Even that would have been OK if HeadofChambers had not felt the need to compensate for the air of silliness surrounding my mother by lecturing her on the significance of the ceremony. Even I, who had actually read about it beforehand, didn't quite understand it. Remember the scene in *Pulp Fiction* when they tried explaining Dutch marijuana laws? It basically came across as something along those lines, but centuries older. Let me give it a go. First, 'inner barristers' are students, as they sit at the inner tables in Hall. All simple so far. 'Utter' or 'outer' barristers are the juniors and QCs. I'm still there, just. Then, the next day the inner barristers trot off to court as utter barristers along with all their newly found QC buddies. But no. Once at court, they go back to being the inner Bar as they can plead from 'inside the bar' in court. I'm afraid I'm still none the wiser – a phrase incidentally that is worth mentioning in front of any lawyer just to hear them mutter back in an almost Pavlovian reaction, 'No, but hopefully at least better informed.'

Anyway, I'm glad we've got all that settled (just what TheBoss said on Tuesday).

Unfortunately the lecture from HeadofChambers took rather longer and even my poor mother, standing there keen to please, was starting to look a little exhausted. Eventually she broke and turned to his wife. 'It all sounds rather complicated to me,' she said. 'Are you another of these utter barrister thingies?'

'Er, no, actually. I run a hedge fund in the City.'

'Golly. Good for you. Although I wouldn't have thought there was much call for hedges in this urban wilderness. Do you do funds for flowers and other plants as well?'

Friday 13 October 2006
Day 10 (week 2): Worrier

With TheBoss away I'm slowly offering my services to different members of chambers. Yet I fear that BusyBody has the same idea. I'm kicking myself for even imagining that it was somehow original. It's obvious that this is one long lobbying session and there are, I guess, a very limited number of strategies which can be deployed. I shall have to endeavour to add a little originality in future.

The only pupil I haven't mentioned so far is someone I shall call Worrier. The most accurate way of describing her would be to say that she was almost beautiful. Not in a nearly way but as in just missed out. You see, in many ways she might be considered attractive. Blonde, slim and a certain symmetry to her face. It's just that, well. It's as if when they were creating Worrier they turned the dial to beautiful and then, just to be cruel, kept on turning. Turned a fatal notch too far and left her with a slightly freaky moonface dominated by her large eyes. Eyes which on a different face would undoubtedly be a plus but on this one are set so far apart that they give her a look which reminds you only of E.T. In itself an inconsequential detail, but as part of the whole something which completely skews her look. Maybe it is this which has determined the nervous tendencies which dominate her whole demeanour. I'm sure they will probably make her a good lawyer, but they can also drive you simply to wanting to shout, 'Stop! Enough is enough! No more worry. Just get on with it.' She carries the details of the world on her shoulders.

'Hi, BabyB. Sorry to disturb you. Can I ask you about a piece of work I've been set?'

'Of course.'

'It's just that when we're typing, do you put one or two spaces after a full stop? I mean I know it shouldn't matter and everything. It's, well, I've spent an hour trying to find out on Google and not managed to turn up anything and I wouldn't want to create a bad impression right at the start.'

For Worrier, no pebble is ever knowingly left unturned. Despite this, I like her and even see her as a potential ally.

Monday 16 October 2006
Day 11 (week 3): OldRuin

TheBoss was back with a vengeance today. He's got kids aged six and three and is already stumping up thousands in school and nursery fees. On top of that, according to a comment I picked up from HeadClerk on Friday, he has a wife with expensive tastes. 'He won't be able to afford not to be back in on Monday with the Christmas holiday his wife is demanding,' he chuckled. But despite his three days off he looked a little ragged when he strolled in this morning. Some comment mid-morning about the kids keeping him up. Not my place to ask so I just kept my head down.

Met TheBoss's room-mate for the first time today. I'll call him OldRuin. Apparently he was TheBoss's pupilmaster long ago. He lives somewhere down in Hampshire and has the air of a dilapidated country pile, gently harking back to better times but too modest to mention them. He's about sixty-five and has been practising for over forty years. Although in his time he was pretty successful, he apparently fell into the same trap as many barristers and spent what he earned and now can't afford to retire. He's a very charming man.

'I'm in my country clothes today, I'm afraid, BabyBarista,' he said, as if somehow this wasn't quite what was expected. In fact he looked the height of farmer fashion, with tweed jacket, elbow patches and cords, and I have to admit there was also the very slightest smell of mothballs although definitely not so much as to be in any way off-putting, but rather it just amplified the effect of his rustic charm. 'Although my wife used to call it my Bunburying outfit,' he continued. 'Always used to put it on when I claimed to be needed back home by mid-afternoon. Pleased her no end when she saw me reaching for the tweed rather than the old pinstripe. Got to the point where she'd put the tweed jacket out with my breakfast and sometimes even hide the suit just to encourage me to take the earlier train home.' He smiled and looked somewhat wistful and I didn't like to ask further about his wife.

What I liked about him most of all was that he was the very first person in chambers to offer to make me coffee.

I, of course, declined.

Tuesday 17 October 2006
Day 12 (week 3): Paranoia

Today I've done around £4,000-worth of work for TheBoss. Copying and pasting one of TheBoss's precedents and just changing a few minor details each time. He seemed very proud of this standard form document, as if it was somehow the magic which he added to the case. Hardly, though I can understand why he was concerned to try and justify some input, as once I'd got through the twenty sets of papers at £200 a shot, he didn't even check them. Straight back to the solicitors for processing.

TheBoss himself had important business. One of the few solicitors who provides him with any decent employment was in town today and expected the works. Lunch was therefore taken at 11.30 a.m. and TheBoss wasn't seen again until 5 p.m. Not surprising that he didn't check my drafting really, given the state he was in by that time. Made some snide remark about no amount of work he does being enough to please his wife, and left. District Line to Parsons Green.

For all their supposed independence, most barristers seem to live in a state of complete paranoia and spend so much time kowtowing to solicitors that their independence is worth even less than their pride.

Friday 20 October 2006
Day 15 (week 3): ClichéClanger

Last night I was working until about midnight on a skeleton argument for TheBoss's case today after he'd dumped it on me before swanning off mid-afternoon. All on behalf of an insurance company which wants to use a technicality to ensure a disabled old lady doesn't get the damages she deserves. So much for Atticus Finch.

But it did at least mean that I finally got to see him do some work today, and in the grand surroundings of the Lord Mayor's Court, no less. His opponent spent an hour setting out his grounds of appeal to the judge, who looked decidedly unimpressed. Then it was TheBoss's big moment. He stood up and offered up my skeleton argument. 'I've summarised my case in there, Your Honour. Do you have any questions?'

'No.'

Which was all there was to it. He won and got his costs, which at £3,000 worked out at over £200 a word on my reckoning. Another hard day at the coalface.

Fun to meet TheBoss's solicitor, though. I'm going to call him ClichéClanger. He's in his late fifties with a worldly air, a neatly trimmed beard and a hangdog slouch inside his old suit which makes him look like he was born with his hands in his pockets. But it is his language which truly distinguishes him with his wonderful habit of coming out with clichés which he has twisted in some tiny way in his own mind, occasionally adding a sprinkling of French just for good measure, for example:

'Well, we don't want to keep all our *oeufs* in one basket, now do we?'

'I mean, Rome wasn't built, you know, yesterday, was it?'

'No use locking the stable door, what with *chevals* around and everything.'

'I thought discretion being the better part of glory and all that.'

'We can't go counting one's *poulets* now, can we. Not until they're clucking.'

All in a broad Yorkshire accent of which Geoffrey Boycott would be proud.

Tuesday 24 October 2006
Day 17 (week 4): Bluffing

BusyBody is really starting to get on my nerves. I have taken to offering my services to at least one new member of chambers each day for an extra set of papers, but for the last two days in a row, they have mentioned in passing that BusyBody had already offered but that they'd bear it in mind in future. Maybe she spammed all of chambers with the offer. Maybe she's been round each person individually. Whatever it is, I hope she's annoying those members of chambers as much as she is me. This morning was just a good example.

'How's it going, BusyBody? Doing anything for lunch?'

'Oh. Too much on I'm afraid. My pupilmaster's working me non-stop.'

Absolutely no mention of the other work she's doing, although I have to admit that there's a certain cathartic pleasure in hearing a straightforward bare-faced lie and I give her credit for that. Something quite upfront and almost honest in the approach. No attempt to try and muddy the waters or to spin her activities in advance. Just straightforward denial. Anyway, we can both play at that game.

'Lucky you,' I answered. 'My pupilmaster's not giving me any work at all so I've had to ask the clerks if they can allocate me extra.'

That should get her going.

Wednesday 25 October 2006
Day 18 (week 4): State of the world

'It's terrible, you know,' said HeadofChambers at lunch as he tucked into his roast lamb.

'I don't know what the world's coming to,' replied TheBoss as he picked out the bones from his roast trout.

'It would never have happened twenty years ago,' Headof-Chambers continued.

'Even ten years ago. Extraordinary, really. Sometimes I just don't recognise the world we now live in.'

'To think that over half of our next door chambers's tenants are now non-Oxbridge.'

'Do you think it's catching?'

'It certainly seems to be.'

'Well I think we need to guard against it as a matter of top priority. Thin end of the wedge, you know.'

'Thick end more like.'

The wonderful modern Bar.

Thursday 26 October 2006
Day 19 (week 4): Criminal case

Looks like I will get to see my first criminal case next week. TheBoss appears to be the king of the returned brief at the moment and a privately paying road traffic prosecution just came through the doors. Causing death by dangerous driving. Essex businessman driving a Porsche down Marylebone Road at seven in the morning. Knocked over a middle-aged man who set off about ten yards from the official crossing. Seems like he has a pretty good defence as the client had the sun behind him and the man crossing was most likely dazzled. The main reason for the prosecution, it seems, is that there were skid marks on the road, and although there is no proof, there is a suggestion the client was speeding. It could end up boiling down to how well the two reconstruction experts perform on the day. Will be good to see TheBoss finally fight a case.

Friday 27 October 2006
Day 20 (week 4): Bailiffs

'BabyB, I'm in trouble.'

It was my mother and I was sitting at my desk. TheBoss scowled at the interruption and I scuttled outside of chambers to take the call.

'What's up?'

'I've got the bailiffs round, BabyB. They want to take all our stuff and also they say they've got an order to evict us from the house.'

I could hear the panic in her voice, and I imagined her pacing up and down the small hallway of our house, pulling one hand through her shoulder-length grey hair.

'What? How? Why?'

'It's the debts, BabyB. I thought it was best not to tell you at the time but they're far worse than you know.'

'How much worse?'

'More than you can imagine. Probably twice the value of the house.'

'But how did that happen?' I asked, completely shocked.

'It's been all I could do to keep us afloat after I lost my job.'

What she didn't mention was the crippling expense of putting her son through Oxford, Bar School and now pupillage.

'But how did you actually get the loans if the house was already fully mortgaged?'

'Very complicated. Borrowing from Peter to pay Paul.'

'And you didn't tell each of them about the other.'

'No.'

Oh. This was getting even more serious. Not only did we face the prospect of being kicked out on to the street, but there was also a real worry that it could even end up as a police issue.

'Look, don't panic. Tell them I'll be there in an hour and also, if you can, try and get your largest creditor on the phone.'

'OK, BabyB. I'm so sorry. Really didn't want to worry you and I felt so ashamed at the mess I've made.'

'Don't worry, I'll sort it out.'

Not that I had any idea whatsoever as to how I was going to do that. But first I had to get TheBoss's permission to leave chambers in the middle of the day. I returned to his room and told him that my mother was in trouble. He didn't look the slightest bit sympathetic and grudgingly allowed me to leave, though as I did he sneered, 'Can't go running home to Mummy when you have your own cases, you know.'

Once home, it seemed that when the bailiffs realised that there might be a legal dispute they had agreed to return the next day. My mother was in a state and it took a long time to calm her down. After that I rang up the manager of the loan company.

'You do realise that your mother has been taking out loans without properly declaring the extent of her debts?'

'Er, I'm looking into that,' I said, not wanting to incriminate her.

'And that that's a criminal offence?'

'So what can I do to make this better?'

'Only one way, Mr BabyBarista, and that's for you to raise the money. Either that or we evict you and report the matter to the police.'

'Well, that's impossible at present as I'm a pupil barrister living on the breadline. But this time next year I will be a tenant in these chambers and will certainly be in a position to start making repayments at that stage.'

I paused and gave him time to mull this over. 'How about,' I then suggested, 'that you transfer the whole of the debt into my name and you charge me a punitive rate of interest this year in return for deferring repayments until I am taken on as a tenant and agreeing not to report my mother.'

The manager considered the suggestion and then replied, 'I would be prepared to agree to that, though with the proviso that if you then default I retain the right to report your mother's dealings.'

He knew where to hit me hardest, but I had no option but to agree. The problem, of course, is that the prospect of tenancy is very far from the sure thing that I suggested and it may come back to bite me much harder this time next year.

I'll just have to make sure that doesn't happen.

Monday 30 October 2006
Day 21 (week 5): Spineless

TheBoss is spineless. He's a yellow coward of the very worst kind. He is a greedy, self-serving, scum-of-the-earth parasite who even gives his profession a bad name. He has so little spine that were it not for his stiff barrister wing collar, I don't know how he'd manage to stand up.

It was a criminal case today. They don't settle. They are a matter of justice one way or the other. The Crown against a particular private individual. The state enforcing the laws. The defender arriving and exercising the right to a fair trial. Innocent until proven guilty and all that. Even plea bargains don't exist in this country. So no settlements. At all.

Or so I thought. But I had underestimated even TheBoss's ingenuity in this respect. For once, he was at court an hour early. Met up with the client for the first time (two minutes) then with the reconstruction expert (three minutes). Then he was off 'to talk to his opponent'. I tagged along, despite his look of irritation.

The two barristers took themselves away from the rest of the crowd and started chatting.

'You're in TheVamp's chambers, aren't you?' the prosecutor asked TheBoss.

'That's right,' chuckled TheBoss. 'Everyone knows TheVamp.'

'Though legend has it that there remain at least a few who don't know her intimately.'

'Not that I've met any myself.'

'Nor me.'

'What was it the legal directory said this year? "Has quickly gained a reputation as an all-rounder." '

'That one certainly did the rounds.'

They both chuckled.

'So how long did you have the pleasure?' asked TheBoss.

'Longer than most, actually. As I remember it, a whole weekend. How about you?'

'Landed her as my pupil for a month, so you can imagine . . .'

'A month?'

'Well, there were a few of us vying to be her pupilmaster after we met her at the pre-pupillage drinks. So rather than limit it to two lots of six months, we divided her time twelve ways.'

'Nice.'

Well, that all led to a good quarter of an hour's worth of cruel gossip at her expense. Then it was down to business.

'So, any chance of reducing it to careless if we were to plead guilty?'

'Unlikely, but I could run it past them. Why? Is that an offer?'

'Let's just say that whilst I don't have any instructions, I'm sure I could bring him round to seeing sense if that was on offer.'

'OK. I'll make the call.'

Ten minutes later, the prosecutor had called the file handler at the Crown Prosecution Service, who very reluctantly had agreed to reduce the charge, '. . . in return for my buying her dinner this evening,' he smirked. 'It'll also give me the rest of the day off, which I could do with, actually. Quite a heavy weekend. Just got back from skiing.'

That was all TheBoss needed. Straight back to the client. Explained the risks of putting this in front of a jury. 'Notoriously unpredictable,' he said. 'Not that I don't think you've got a strong case. You have. Otherwise, we wouldn't have been fighting. But if you can in any way manage that risk before you enter that courtroom, I think we at least have to consider it.'

The client was, to put it mildly, reluctant. He had been advised by the last barrister that the case against him was hopeless.

'I entirely agree,' TheBoss said, as he stepped up his settlement mode a notch further. 'It's why I would never advise you to plead guilty to the charge made. But even if there's a ten per cent chance that you get yourself in front of a rogue jury – and I'm afraid they do exist – well . . . it's your call and I wouldn't like to seem like I'm trying to persuade you one way or the other . . . however, if the charge were merely careless driving, the most you're likely to get is a six-month ban. On the other hand, the full charge and a rogue jury and you're possibly looking at packing your toothbrush.'

This was simply beyond the pale. The man was innocent, of that I was absolutely sure. The other side's reconstruction report was a shambles and I'm not surprised that TheBoss's opponent was prepared to reduce the charge. It shouldn't even have got anywhere near a courtroom. I don't pretend to hold myself to the highest of standards and I don't think I have the naïve illusions of the Bar that many people may possess. Yet, even allowing for my already jaded image of the profession, I was ashamed.

Needless to say, it settled. The client only got a two-month ban, probably reflecting the fact that the judge had also read the papers and didn't think the client was guilty either. The terrible irony of this was that the client left the court raving about how great his 'brief' was and how he'd recommend him to all his mates. And to cap it, TheBoss left muttering sarcastically, 'Yeah, because I *so* want to build up a criminal hack's practice.'

Back in chambers by noon. Brief fee, £2,500.

CHAPTER 2

November: Faustian Pact

If you know the enemy and know yourself, you need not fear the result of a hundred battles.

Sun Tzu, *The Art of War*

Wednesday 1 November 2006
Day 23 (week 5): Big mistake

TheBoss was away yesterday with no explanation. Just simply didn't turn up. I could have gone to the clerks and exposed the fact that he hadn't even arranged anything else for me to do, but on balance I wouldn't have been doing myself any favours in anyone's book. Plus, this was an opportunity for TheBoss to owe me one. Even a small one. So to capitalise on this, I got stuck into one of the bigger sets of papers lying around his room. The date the papers came into chambers was back in June and the instructions sought a general advice as to the value of the claim for injury and loss of earnings. No urgency in any of the instructions and so, although four months seemed a pretty long time in which to be turning around a set of papers, I could understand at least that they might not have been top priority.

So, I settled into them, gently getting a feel for the case. It involved an accident on a British Navy ship back in September 2004. Looked pretty straightforward. In fact, liability appeared to have been admitted. Started writing the advice on the value of the claim which, with a loss of a career in the Navy, looked like it could be as much as half a million pounds.

Worked on it until lunch and then went off to meet a friend who was also doing pupillage. Pretty relaxed day all in all. Got chatting and what with one thing and another I mentioned the case.

'Have you issued yet?' he asked.

'No, why? No need at this stage. Might even settle and we've got until next September anyway.'

'No you haven't.'

'What?'

'Limitation. It's not three years when the accident occurs on a ship. It's two.'

'What?'

'No doubt about it. Had to deal with it in my first week. It's definitely two years.'

Oh.

This did not look good. At all. The first dilemma was who to tell and when. TheBoss was incommunicado. Should I call him at home? Would he actually be at home? Knowing TheBoss as I already did, I figured that there was at least a small chance that he was not. Should I phone his mobile and interrupt whatever he was doing? Or should I just ask the clerks or even OldRuin?

I went for a walk around the garden in Gray's Inn and took a few deep breaths. Maybe this was the opportunity I'd been waiting for. Maybe I could help TheBoss. One thing of which I was certain. I needed to give him a discreet heads up without alerting anyone else. I therefore left a message on his mobile yesterday afternoon. And yesterday evening. And this morning. But there has been no sign of him all day.

Thursday 2 November 2006
Day 24 (week 5): The return

TheBoss was back today with the only explanation given being 'trouble and strife'. OldRuin, uncharacteristically, was also around for the third day in a row. It meant that it wasn't going to be easy getting time alone with TheBoss without giving the game away. In fact it had to wait until mid-morning when OldRuin popped out to the loo and I asked TheBoss if it would be possible to talk to him in private.

'You got a problem with OldRuin?' he asked, in his usual slightly bullying way.

'No,' I replied. 'I think there's a problem with one of your sets of papers.'

'Yeah, that they haven't settled yet,' he chuckled, clearly thinking himself very smart and witty.

'I think you've missed limitation on one of your cases.'

'What do you mean? Which case? My papers? What?'

OldRuin then re-entered the room and I bowed my head. TheBoss glared but said nothing more. Eventually, he very unsubtly suggested I might like to join him for coffee on Chancery Lane. OldRuin looked at me conspiratorially. There was obviously something up, as such a gesture was wholly out of character from TheBoss. Nevertheless, a few minutes later we were indeed heading off to a café down the main legal thoroughfare in London.

'So, what are you talking about?' he asked as he tucked into the large doughnut he'd ordered to accompany his coffee.

'Just what I said. Your papers for the solicitors on the shipping case have passed limitation during the time they've been sitting on your shelf. It's an accident on a ship and you've only got two years.'

After a brief bout of Tourette's that shocked an old lady walking by, he started to think it through a little more carefully. True to character, his only form of defence was attack.

'What were you doing going through my private papers? You had no right.'

'I'm your pupil. That's my job.'

'You were only to touch papers that I told you about. There could be all sorts of confidential documents in there.'

'But you told me that I was to do as many of your sets of papers as I was able and that there was no need to ask you about them – just to get on with it.'

'I didn't mean go and cause this sort of trouble.'

By that point, I'd had enough. Even a pupil has a tipping point.

'I'm extremely sorry you feel that way,' I said, raising my head and catching his stare. My sudden bout of confidence appeared to unnerve him and he changed tack immediately.

'Anyway, I suppose I should also be grateful to you for spotting it. What do you think we can do about it?'

'Well, we haven't told the solicitors yet. That might be a start.'

'Who else knows, exactly, except you?'

'No one.' I hadn't wanted to involve my friend from the other chambers and so had refrained from saying anything else to him.

'Let's sit on it today. I'll try and think of a solution by tomorrow morning.'

And that was that.

Friday 3 November 2006
Day 25 (week 5): Faustian pact

Today I compromised myself. It is not the first time and will probably not be the last, given my initial impression of this mighty profession. But today I crossed a line that, until now, delineated the boundary between the bad and the wholly unacceptable.

TheBoss arrived this morning and put forward a solution: that I would forget that I had ever seen the papers. He would then write a short advice and print it off for his own records dated July 2006. This would include a gentle reminder about limitation. He would then change the records in chambers showing the papers had been returned in July along with the advice and a fee note. This was one of the advantages of giving members of chambers full access to their own parts of the system. Come Monday, he would ask the most junior clerk to phone the solicitors politely asking about the progress of the case. So long as he could show that the papers were not on his shelf, the responsibility would then lie with the solicitors.

TheBoss explained that he'd had a misconduct issue in the past and that if this came out it could be the end of his career. Also, it was only a tiny thing. Just amending the records. Not a big deal and ultimately it would be the insurance which would pay up, if anyone. Furthermore, the solicitors were in the wrong even if he hadn't sent an advice. It was just an adjunct to their primary liability in any event. All not a big deal. Just making things clear.

I have to admit that despite being shocked, in the heat of the moment I also saw this as an opportunity. I asked him how it might affect my pupillage.

'Only positively,' he replied.

The deal was done.

Monday 6 November 2006
Day 26 (week 6): JudgeJewellery

There's a vicious rumour going around about one of the district judges who I shall call JudgeJewellery. It apparently started with a barrister friend of hers and has been doing the rounds for weeks. It seems she unwisely confided to her garrulous friend that she has a penchant for stealing cheap jewellery from a certain high street shop I will call CheapnNasty. Whips it straight into her Gucci handbag and then she's away without anyone daring to accuse someone so glamorous of such petty theft. If that isn't enough, she then likes to show off her wares in court the next day like some sort of trophy. Sounds completely unreal but although the chain of Chinese whispers was fairly protracted, the gossip did come from reliable sources.

Today I was with a junior barrister called Teflon, so called apparently due to the fact that whatever trouble he gets into, none of it sticks. He was appearing in front of JudgeJewellery and she was certainly sporting some gaudy-looking earrings. Yet despite the fact that they clashed with her judicial uniform, she carried it off with enormous style. It's not merely that she is beautiful. She seems somehow to be above all the hustle and bustle of the arguments going on around her, easily reducing Teflon to rubble with one of her slightly amused smiles. All of which kind of makes even her pilfering seem kind of cool. Which of course it isn't. But hey. I don't think I'm the only male member of the Bar who is suffering from this mild, if somewhat inappropriate, infatuation.

When I got back from court TheBoss had left a set of papers on my desk with the instruction 'Email me the advice by tomorrow morning' scrawled on a Post-it note on top. Great. Just what I needed at six in the evening. Then, with impeccable timing, Worrier strolled in looking for help. Not that I wasn't pleased to see her. In fact I've already grown to like her very much, partially based on our mutual dislike of the other two goody-goodies. It's just that I already had work which would probably take me past midnight and Worrier's little queries never tended to be quick.

'I'm in a panic, BabyB. I've got to finish an advice by tomorrow morning and I'm completely stuck.'

'You and me both,' I replied.

'Oh, sorry.' She stopped in her tracks and looked slightly forlorn.

Immediately I felt bad for taking my impatience out on her.

'How can I help, Worrier?'

'Well, I've done a first draft. I just need someone to have a read through for me. But if you don't have the time . . .'

'Of course I have the time. Let's have a look.'

'It's quite long,' she warned.

'Let's see.'

She handed me the advice, looking slightly embarrassed.

'Worrier, it's forty-five pages long.'

'That's the problem, BabyB. I'm having difficulties working out what needs to go in.'

To leave Worrier to hand in that particular piece of work would have made her a laughing stock. To correct it would probably leave me getting a couple of hours' sleep at most. But I have to say Worrier really did look in a state, and as I looked at her again I heard myself saying, 'Pass it here. Let's see what we can do.'

Tuesday 7 November 2006
Day 27 (week 6): Sorted

Today TheBoss has been dealing with the fallout from his plan. Or to put it more accurately, the lack of fallout. He amended the entries on the system without a hitch. It wasn't designed to protect against corrupt barristers and so it was easy to do so without any trace. The junior clerk then made the call yesterday afternoon. This morning, the solicitor called TheBoss. Despite the calm in his voice, he was swivelling around nervously on his expensive orthopaedic chair. I only heard TheBoss's side of the conversation.

'I was wondering how the case was getting on.'
. . .
'Oh. Didn't you get my advice?'
. . .
'Oh. That's strange. It was sent back in July. I can dig out a copy and fax it over after this call.'

. . .

'No. Not at all. It would be my pleasure. Very strange. Must have been a problem with the post.'

. . .

'Oh, by the way, I assume you've issued by now?'

. . .

'What? Oh, no. Oh, no. Did you not realise that limitation for cases involving ships is two years? I did mention it in my advice but to be honest, I thought you'd know that anyway.'

. . .

'Hmm. I don't know what you can do at this stage. It's pretty serious. I'd certainly suggest that you report this to your professional indemnity insurers and seek their guidance before doing anything further.'

. . .

'No, no. I'm sure it must have been the postage. I wouldn't want you to start blaming your internal post.'

. . .

'Oh. It's my pleasure. If I can help you further with this, please just ask.'

Looking particularly smug, TheBoss turned to me and said, 'Some might say, BabyB, "Case closed".'

How worryingly easy it was. Makes you wonder.

Thursday 9 November 2006
Day 29 (week 6): Flirt

Pretty much back to normal now. TheBoss is his old arrogant self and I'm making coffees and photocopying. BusyBody's been at her worst today. Sniffing around our room under the pretence of researching through the law reports there. Worse though, was TheBoss's reaction to her presence.

'That's a nice blouse,' he kicked off with, to which BusyBody was all, 'Oh, do you like it. I just bought it at the weekend.' Then he followed up with more questions than he's asked of me in the last five weeks. 'Where are you from?', 'What university?', 'Ooh, what college?', right down to questions about parents and siblings. At first I just noticed that he was being peculiarly nice, but within about ten minutes it was obvious he was in full-on flirt mode. BusyBody of course was lapping it up and wasted no time in returning the compliments and looked positively reluctant to leave when the call came in from her own pupilmaster demanding her return.

After that performance I needed to get out and managed to persuade Claire to bunk off at 5 p.m. under the standard excuse of 'research in the library'. Then it was down to what has become our local wine bar, The Cheeky Monkey.

'So what's your pupilmistress had you doing this week?' I asked.

'Dry-cleaning Monday, food shopping Tuesday and then researching packages for her Christmas holiday today.'

'Still saving the world then.'

'Quite.'

'Well, you should be so lucky. Got to be better than drafting schedules of loss and photocopying duty.'

'Sometimes I do wonder.'

I then told her about what TheBoss had been up to and the fact that I had stood by.

'You fool, BabyB. Didn't you try to stop him?'

'I wish I'd had the courage. I really do. But it'd risk everything.'

She looked pensive and then came to a judgement. 'It's terrible, BabyB. You were put in an impossible position. I mean, what were you meant to do?' she asked rhetorically. 'Report him and end your chances of tenancy?' She looked concerned. 'I wouldn't mention it to anyone else if I were you. Let's just hope it all blows over.'

Friday 10 November 2006
Day 30 (week 6): Busker or Creep?

Today I had the pleasure of seeing two members of chambers against each other in court and they couldn't have been more different in every way.

First there was TheCreep who, despite the fact that he's only been in chambers for three years, carries himself as if he's a member of the House of Lords. I've heard him around chambers approaching QCs and asking them their thoughts on the latest ruling on a particular aspect of public policy. As if everyone goes round reading the law reports each day. He's desperate to be picked as a junior by one of these big beasts, but what he doesn't appear to realise is that they just find him irritating. Worse for him is that the clerks can't stand his airs and graces and go out of their way to put him in his place with tiny cases in grotty, far-flung courts. TheBusker, on the other hand, couldn't be less of a creep. He's ten years' call and about as laid back as it's possible for a barrister to be, almost to the point of seeming a little spaced on occasion.

Physically TheCreep is short and stocky and his brown hair is always neatly combed to the side. Though his suits are always immaculately pressed, they appear to be slightly too big, as if he's still hoping to grow into them. The way he holds himself has the air of a sergeant major on parade, as if he's always standing to attention, although again I wonder whether this is more a manifestation of him willing himself to be taller. TheBusker, on the other hand, is around six foot and quite slim and with a lazy slouch which makes even his tailored suits look slightly scruffy, as does his dishevelled mop of blond hair. But these differences aren't anywhere near as great as that between their courtroom styles with TheCreep all jumped up and stressed out and TheBusker only highlighting those difficulties with a laid-back style that is often more surfer dude than traditional barrister.

Today it was a building dispute and TheBusker was representing the dodgy building contractors. TheCreep had some particularly needy clients, which only exacerbated his brittle manner. With their obvious differences the two were grating against each other even before they got into court with TheCreep trying to have an argument with TheBusker in the robing room.

'I'm going to be asking for your Defence to be struck out as it doesn't comply with the Practice Direction,' he said.

'No worries, my friend, you can apply for what you like.'

'Yes, but do you agree that it doesn't comply?'

'Sorry, Creep. You're acting as though you think I might care.'

'Yes, but how are you going to answer it?'

'Oh. I'm sure I'll think of something.'

The more stressed TheCreep became, the more laid back was TheBusker. He had no notes and came across very much as if he'd only just read the papers on the train there (which I can confirm was true). It was only when we got into court that I realised how he had prospered at the Bar for so long despite (or perhaps because of) his approach.

TheCreep rose and spoke first. 'Your Honour, the Defence fails to comply with the Practice Direction and should be struck out. Unfortunately, m'learned friend has not provided me with an answer to this point . . .' He then set it out in characteristic length for the next twenty minutes. To which TheBusker simply got up and said, 'Your Honour. We're not here today to argue pleading points. We know that, you know that and I'm afraid to suggest that even m'learned friend might know that too.' Without even addressing the substance of the argument he sat down and smiled at TheCreep. The judge then spent the next half hour addressing all TheCreep's arguments before concluding in almost exactly the same terms as the submissions of TheBusker.

The same applied to the hearing proper. Whilst TheCreep was busily scribbling notes, shaking his head and making loud sighs to himself, TheBusker just sat back in his chair with his hands behind his head staring at each of the claimant's witnesses and not making a single note. Watching how they gave their evidence. Looking for a chink or foible in their character. Then he'd get up and ever so gently ask them questions which didn't even seem to be relevant, but which resulted in each of them being tripped up in one form or another. As for his closing submissions, they were again brief.

'Your Honour. It's clear the building work wasn't perfect. We'd be the first to admit to that. In fact we'd go so far as to express our regret in that respect. But nor was it sufficiently imperfect to be classified as negligence. M'learned friend has, quite properly I might add, made a lot of points today but, with respect, they were nitpicking. Thankfully, Your Honour, we do not yet live in a world where nitpickers rule the roost nor where courts of law award them damages.' After which he sat down and TheCreep's case was done for.

After we all left court, the colour in TheCreep's cheeks had risen as high as his limited height would allow and he petulantly fired at TheBusker, 'I don't think you take your cases seriously enough.'

'You're probably right,' TheBusker replied, only winding TheCreep up further. Then he added mischievously, 'But hey, do you think it'd be fair on the opposition if I did?'

'You only won today because of that mad cow of a judge,' said TheCreep moodily.

'You know,' said TheBusker, 'you're always complaining. Stuck in the murky details of life's little unfairnesses.' He paused and looked TheCreep in the eye. 'Just for once, why don't you look up to the horizon and admire the view. You know, like chill your boots a bit and hey, you never know what might happen. Judges may even start to listen.'

As we went back on the train without TheCreep who'd gone off in a huff, TheBusker commented, 'Less is always more, BabyB. Lets the judge think he's deciding. How did someone once put it? "Cast your bread upon the waters and it will return buttered."'

It was a cold day and I think both our minds wandered to hot buttered toast. Then he continued, 'The curse of lawyers, BabyB, is that they're trained to foresee problems in everything and so nothing can ever be simple. Just be careful that doesn't take over your life like our friend TheCreep.'

I do like TheBusker.

Tuesday 14 November 2006
Day 32 (week 7): OldSmoothie

Received a visit today from a member of chambers who I shall call OldSmoothie, not after the yoghurty fruit drink, but because of his oily self-confidence, which oozes from every pore. Think Peter Bowles in *To the Manor Born* and Milk Tray Man, but not quite there on either count. He's about fifty. He was made a QC five years ago, until which time he was moderately successful. Since then he has struggled for work, having fallen into the trap of being not good enough for the top work and too senior for the bread and butter. Some in that position go on to become judges. Others to become committee men for their golf clubs, their private members' clubs and, of course, their chambers. OldSmoothie was just such a man.

Today it was the pupillage committee and he wanted me to sift through the applications for mini-pupillage. His instructions were given in the mellifluous tone which he has no doubt used to good effect in court over the years:

'You're an Oxford man like myself. Figure I can ask you to do this properly without any complaint. Here's what I want. Plain and simple (just like your fellow pupil Worrier, I may add).'

I felt slightly protective about his taking Worrier's name in vain but I remained quiet and continued listening.

'Take out the following and then give me the rest. No sixth-formers looking for work experience. Definitely no one who's been to a polyversity or whatever they call themselves these days. Doesn't fool me. Preferably no one who didn't go to Oxbridge if possible. None of that second career old age nonsense. Oh, and no one called Wayne or Shane. Just wouldn't look good on the board.'

Reminded me of the story of a recruiter in the City who, having proclaimed how Napoleon wanted his generals to be lucky, randomly picked up half the application forms and threw them into the bin with the comment, 'We don't want the unlucky ones in this bank, now do we?'

Thursday 16 November 2006
Day 34 (week 7): Nuclear option

'I can't believe it,' said TheBoss today as he arrived into chambers. 'My case listed for tomorrow was meant to settle weeks ago. I'd have never said yes to it otherwise as I'm booked in for pheasant shooting in Devon from tomorrow morning.'

He said this as if the weight of the world was upon his shoulders. 'There's only one thing for it, I guess.'

'What's that?' I asked, curious as to how he was going to sort out a straight case of double-booking.

'The nuclear option.'

'Which is?'

'Contact the judge.'

'Oh.'

'Well, I won't actually talk to him myself. Fortunately one of the party is in his old chambers. I'll see if he can have a word.'

Sure enough, one phone call and a couple of hours later and a call came through from TheBoss's solicitor. He put it on loudspeaker, just to show off.

'I've just had the judge on the phone. Wants to know if the time estimate of one day is accurate. I think it is but I thought I'd better check with you.'

TheBoss smiled. He had his chance. 'I agree with you. I'd have thought a day was about right.'

My mouth dropped and he raised his eyebrows. He was definitely showing off. 'But you know,' he went on, 'you have to be very careful when a judge asks a question like that on a Thursday.'

'Why's that?' his solicitor asked.

'Sounds like he's trying to think of a way of getting out of the case. Maybe he wants a long weekend.'

'But we're fully prepared for trial. The client's all set and you've been briefed.'

Meaning of course that TheBoss would be paid whether the case went ahead or not. Brief delivered, fee due.

'You're right,' TheBoss said. 'Look, I'm keen for it to go ahead and to get stuck into the fight.' Then he added, almost as an afterthought, 'But it would be terrible after all this time and preparation to start off on the wrong foot with the judge. Just a thought.'

'Hmm. You might have a point. Thank you. It helps to have such sound, independent advice.'

'Oh, my pleasure.'

Come early afternoon a call came through from HeadClerk.

'Seems your case has just adjourned,' he said.

'Oh, I see,' TheBoss said, trying to sound surprised. 'That's a shame.'

'Quite. Full brief fee and no need even to turn up.'

'Well, I suppose when you put it like that . . .'

'Have a good time at the shoot, Sir.'

Friday 17 November 2006
Day 35 (week 7): Know the enemy

Met TopFirst's fiancée today for the first time. She had popped in to visit him for lunch and he took the opportunity to show her off to as many people as possible. If you met her, you'd understand why he'd want to do that. Unlike him, she's beautiful, modest and understated, which does make you wonder what she's doing with him. Maybe it's an academic thing as they were apparently sweethearts from Cambridge where, he loudly proclaimed today, she was the only person to get more academic prizes than him. No surprise, then, that she is now doing a doctorate. It all left me feeling that TopFirst has got to be one of the most smug and downright annoying people at the whole Bar. At the moment he seems to have everything going for him on all fronts and I'm struggling to imagine how I'm possibly going to compete when it comes to the final decision. The problem with all this stuff about knowing your enemy is that the more I get to know him, the more unassailable he appears.

Though maybe this is something which in itself I can use.

Monday 20 November 2006
Day 36 (week 8): Chambers tea

Chambers tea happens every afternoon at 4.30 p.m. on the dot. Despite the fact that we are now all on email, each member of chambers is called by the clerks and told that 'tea is served'. About fifteen people turn up in the main conference room each afternoon and it's always quite an occasion. The tea itself comes in an urn on a trolley which is pushed into the room with great ceremony by a junior clerk. Despite the fact that the members collectively earn enough to buy their own factory, the chocolate biscuits are always treated as a great delicacy, probably due to the fact that chambers only provides the cheaper plain biscuits for client conferences.

As a pupil, the lesson I learnt very early on was not to speak unless spoken to and even then to keep it as brief as possible. You've basically got a room full of egos sitting around on their own personal highs, usually after a day in court. Lets them wind down before getting back to their families. Lots of victories to report and anecdotes to regale and if anyone interrupts, never mind a pupil, then woe betide them. Which means that it's the politest tea party in the world and the phrase 'no, after you' can be heard at least a few times a minute.

Today, BusyBody learnt this lesson the hard way. HeadofChambers had been telling a story about some cross-examination in court today. '. . . At which point she burst into tears. A rare pleasure indeed.'

He paused, and thinking he'd finished and wanting to muscle in BusyBody started a follow-up story, 'I saw a similar thing . . .'

She got only this far since HeadofChambers had restarted at almost exactly the same time with, 'You know, it's funny how . . .'

BusyBody stopped in her tracks, still wanting to tell the story, and HeadofChambers took great pleasure in a bit of PupilSport.

'I'm very sorry, BusyBody. You were telling us how you saw something similar.'

'Yes, that's right. I went to the Old Bailey a couple of days ago and one of the barristers there was having a whale of a time with one of the witnesses . . .'

It was only at this point that BusyBody realised that all eyes were now on her and that if interrupting HeadofChambers was bad, not having an entertaining punchline to mitigate the interruption would be almost unforgivable. She suddenly looked a lot less confident. Meanwhile, HeadofChambers chased down his prey.

'Go on, BusyBody, do tell all. Sounds fascinating.'

'Well, er, yes, he was asking one question after another and getting all sorts of different answers. The witness didn't even seem to know what time of day it was. Must have been on drugs or something. Anyway, she started getting all flustered after a while . . .'

The mention of the word obviously reminded BusyBody of her own situation and her whimpering became disjointed. 'So, er, yes. As I was saying. The barrister was catching her out. Lots of details. Then. Well, er, he told her she was a liar and she denied it and started crying.'

She tailed off, defeated. 'It was very gripping.'

HeadofChambers was straight in with, 'I expect you had to be there, BusyBody.' Before adding, after an awkward silence from the whole room, 'And that is why pupils should always be seen and not heard.'

Tuesday 21 November 2006
Day 37 (week 8): Wigs and gowns

Today TheBoss and I went off to the High Court to get the stamp of approval on a consent order following another settlement and for the first time I wore my wig and gown into court. What on earth is that all about? I mean, if you're going to be dressing up in silly clothes there've got to be better options than something which went out of fashion over two hundred years ago. Why not go the whole hog and have say, Batman outfits for barristers and Robin ones for solicitors? I know I'd choose the caped crusader over someone with a horsehair wig in any fight. As for women, maybe Catwoman costumes would do on the basis that Wonder Woman would give an unfair advantage with the judges. Pupils, well, they could have red learner plates on their backs and then green ones for the first year of practice. Oh and if we're going to have things pinned on to us, then let's have a few adverts for good measure, tennis player style.

Still, for today I liked it. We waltzed into court and for just a second the flowing robes felt almost like a suit of armour all set for gladiatorial combat. Such a shame then that by the end of the hearing any dignity with which I had started was in tatters. You see, there I was. Sitting next to TheBoss. Nodding intelligently and making notes in all the right places when all of a sudden I got a terrible urge to sneeze. Well, as you can imagine I suppressed it immediately. Except it didn't go away. It was one of those sneaky little sneezes which slips around everything you throw at it and comes back even stronger for the next round. At one point I gave in to it and held my head back about to sneeze as the whole courtroom looked at me and then, as if it was just being mischievous, it went away without actually happening. But, you guessed it. It hadn't gone away. It'd just side-stepped for a minute and then was back in action and hit me without any warning with an almighty thunder. Boy, I think it was so loud that they could hear us all the way along in the Court of Appeal. In itself though, that would probably have been OK. I could just about have lived with that by burying my head in my notebook and imagining I wasn't there. The problem with this particular sneeze was that it had taken me unawares and on my first day of wearing my wig. The significance of this was that as my head was levered backwards I didn't have time even to consider that when it was triggered forward it would literally be bombs away. You guessed it. As I play it back in my mind it is all in slow motion, but at the time it happened in an instant. My wig was displaced from my head and sent flying, not onto the floor in front of me or anywhere so convenient. It went flying through the air only to land on the judge's desk, knocking over his jar of ink and his water glass and sending it all everywhere. Just when I thought it couldn't get any worse, after having wiped off most of the water and ink, the judge then peered down at me and asked, 'Mr BabyBarista. Do you have an application which you would like to make?'

You what? An application? It was like having to go round to the next door neighbour's and ask for your football back.

'Er, yes, My Lord. Can I have my wig back?'

'What's the magic word, Mr BabyBarista?'

'Please, My Lord. May I have my wig back?'

'You may.'

Friday 24 November 2006
Day 40 (week 8): Piffling

Today I went to Willesden County Court with OldSmoothie who was not at all happy when he saw the name of the judge. Apparently they fell out at university 'over a particularly strong-minded filly'. Whatever the details, there has been no love lost between them since and from the kick-off OldSmoothie was hitting the judge where it hurt most: his ego, addressing him as the more senior 'My Lord' rather than 'Your Honour' in reference to the high court judgeship he had failed to attain. Each time he said it (which was frequently), you could detect a slight twitch around the corner of the judge's mouth. To correct OldSmoothie would only highlight his point. Not to correct him left OldSmoothie getting away with an insult. All he was left with was to remind OldSmoothie that, for today, the upper hand was his.

'It must be a great comedown, OldSmoothie, to have had to come to Willesden and fight with the baby Bar on such a piffling case as this one.'

I don't know whether OldSmoothie had deliberately provoked such a remark but I wouldn't put it past him. He certainly seemed well prepared with his response.

'This case might be piffling to you, My Lord, but,' he paused for effect, 'I can hardly say the same for my client, who has a wife and

47

five children to feed on a salary which is less than a fifth that of a high court judge. Nor, I am bound to say, do I think the higher courts would find it, as you say,' he licked his lips, savouring the moment, 'piffling.'

The judge was lost for words. A careful man, not usually prone to losing his temper, he was also sufficiently honest to admit defeat, and we all saw him visibly crumple, his hands on the bench and shoulders hunched. Without giving any further time for a response, OldSmoothie continued, 'Of course, I'm sure such intemperate remarks were not intended and that we may still be able to proceed without any prejudice.'

The judge was snookered. If he passed the case to another judge, he would have to give a good reason and his remark would be exposed and if he continued and found against OldSmoothie's client, he would be appealed. So he took the only other option available and OldSmoothie returned victorious.

On the way back, OldSmoothie said to me, 'You've got UpTights as your pupilmistress in April, haven't you?'

'That's right. Why?'

'Good luck is all I'll say. That woman's got more edges than a broken [chamber] pot.'

Monday 27 November 2006
Day 41 (week 9): Ultimatum

'Mr BabyBarista.'

I recognised the voice immediately as belonging to the manager of the loan company whose debt I had agreed to take on last month. We'd been in touch several times in the previous few weeks finalising the contract, which was all signed off last Wednesday.

'Speaking.'

'I discovered something very interesting at the weekend, you know.'

'Oh, yes?'

'Just a little get-together for the Round Table but by complete coincidence one of the couples mentioned that their daughter had just finished her pupillage last year and is currently unemployed. Very high-risk year, they tell me.'

'Ah, well, I see, well . . .'

'Which is not what you led me to believe.'

I was stumped. In my panic to get my mother out of trouble last month I'd dug the hole even deeper.

'Let me cut to the chase, Mr BabyBarista. It seems to me that you're my only option of getting any money out of the loan I should never have made to your mother, so let's put it like this. Get the tenancy, pay back the loan and everything will be forgotten.'

'Yes, thank you. Thank you very much, yes . . .' I was all over the place.

'But, Mr BabyBarista, if that doesn't happen, not only will I be handing your mother's name over to the police, I shall be doing the same with yours as well as contacting your professional body. Good day.'

With which he put down the phone. I really need to get this tenancy.

Wednesday 29 November 2006
Day 43 (week 9): Showdown

On the face of it barristers employ their clerks, so strictly they are the bosses. But you'd never guess it to watch TheBoss and HeadClerk in action. For all his arrogance and pomposity, he is humility itself when HeadClerk walks through the door. This was particularly apparent when HeadClerk came round today.

'Time for a quick word, Sir?' There was an unusually pointed tone to the way he said 'Sir' which didn't bode well.

'Of course. Come in. Have a seat.'

'Actually, I won't if you don't mind. Bit of a rush today.' Ouch.

'So how can I help?' asked TheBoss.

'Just had a bit of an awkward conversation, Sir, with the senior partner of that firm you did the accident on a ship for.'

'Oh, yes?' TheBoss tried to look relaxed but couldn't help folding his arms and taking his feet off the table.

'Seems they didn't receive an advice you say you sent.' He emphasised the word 'say'.

'Well it certainly went out. Er, what do the computer records say?'

'Well, they say it was sent, which is strange, as I've never had any problem from this firm in the past.' His suspicions were at best thinly veiled. 'Anyway, Sir, they have demanded every detail as to when it was sent and where this was recorded so if you could give me a copy of anything you have, that would be most helpful.'

'Of course, of course.' TheBoss tried to wave him away as if it was an inconsequential detail. 'I'll look into it in a day or two.'

'Er, Sir, there is one thing I need to get clear before we proceed further with this.'

'What's that?'

'Well, I've never had any problems with our computer records before and the senior partner seemed so adamant and clear in what he was saying that . . . well . . .'

'What is it?'

'Well, I need to know from you that it was actually sent. Do you actually remember doing so?'

TheBoss didn't even flinch and had obviously been preparing himself for this question. 'Of course it was. I remember printing it off and putting it in with the papers myself.'

HeadClerk still didn't look completely satisfied but he clearly couldn't quite put his finger on what was wrong.

'Right you are, Sir. Just needed to check.'

CHAPTER 3
December: Sex Discrimination

In war, the way is to avoid what is strong and to strike at what is weak.

Sun Tzu, *The Art of War*

Friday 1 December 2006
Day 45 (week 9): Sex discrimination

TheBoss definitely has a full-on cringeworthy mid-life crisis going on. First it was the flirting with BusyBody. Then today he announces that he's just bought himself a Ferrari. 'Got a lot of grief from her indoors over this one you know. But, hey, I'm worth it.'

Hey. You're not. More like a Robin Reliant if you ask me.

It did mean that he was oozing smugness when Worrier came to visit this morning. She seemed embarrassed as she asked me in a whisper whether I was free for lunch as she needed some advice. I was touched that she had come to me, particularly as she's the only one of the pupils that I can foresee becoming a friend. But before I could even whisper back 'of course', TheBoss was all over it.

'What's the problem, Worrier?' he asked, flashing a large insincere smile.

'Er, well, actually, it's just something I wanted to ask BabyB about.'

'Anything about pupillage?'

'Er, well . . .' She hesitated too long.

'Well, please, allow me to help. I assure you that whatever it is will be taken in complete confidence.'

Yeah, right, I thought, but Worrier looked like she believed him. I tried to steer her away from giving him any revelations at all with,

'Well, lunch would be lovely. What time?' TheBoss got up from his chair and moved towards Worrier before sitting himself on the edge of his desk.

'Worrier, we're here to help. What exactly's bothering you?'

'Oh, it's probably nothing.'

'Well, let's see. Try me.'

I tried to warn her by catching her eye, but vulnerable as she was she appeared to have been taken in by his mock concern.

'It's OldSmoothie.'

'Ah,' said TheBoss. 'Being offensive again is he?'

'Well, it's just that I did some papers for him and he didn't like what I'd done so I gave it another try.'

'And he still didn't like it?'

She then started to blurt it out: 'He told me not to be so indecisive in my advices. That I needed to get to the point. Well, that was OK in itself. In fact I've often thought that myself. I just don't find it terribly easy.'

Like a cheap car salesman, TheBoss pulled a super-caring face and asked, 'So what did he then say, Worrier?'

'He told me that he didn't know how on earth I was going to cope with court. Maybe it's a girl thing, he said, and that he just wasn't quite getting it. Is it a girl thing? he demanded. Is that what it is?'

Now, it seemed to me that he could certainly have phrased his comments more diplomatically, but if you met Worrier, you'd know that he had a point – although it certainly isn't a 'girl thing'. But TheBoss was off on a completely different tangent.

'Worrier, despite all my years at the Bar I'm shocked to hear that such things go on. Really. You hear apocryphal stories but you don't actually think they happen in real life.'

'I know,' she whimpered.

'It must be terrible to be in your position and feel so powerless. You know, that's exactly why the Bar Council is so strict about this sort of thing. To avoid this abuse of power.'

'I know.'

'They're there to protect not only you but everyone like you around the country.' The thought of armies of little Worriers was an exhausting one.

'You're right.'

'And the biggest thing they have to fight against is fear. Fear instilled into the victims that somehow they will be punished if they complain. Classic battered wife syndrome.'

He paused, perhaps concerned that he might be pushing it just a little too far. 'You know, the real difficulty for you is that you're almost in a Catch-22.'

'Why's that?'

'Well, if you complain, you'll annoy OldSmoothie and potentially even HeadofChambers.'

'Exactly.' She brightened up. This was obviously what she wanted to hear. In fact I think all she wanted was a little reassurance.

However, he followed up with, 'But if you don't complain you may undermine your whole position. Fatally, even.'

'Because?'

'It's obvious, really. If you don't complain you give him carte blanche to bully, discriminate and otherwise demean you for the rest of the next year. He's hardly going to improve. Then, when you are finally pushed over the edge into complaining, it'll be held against you that you didn't say anything early on. They might even use that to question your whole account.'

'Oh. You're right.' She started to look even more worried than usual. 'So the only course is for me to complain to the Bar Council, you think.'

'Well,' TheBoss said, taking a more conciliatory tone. 'Perhaps there might be a compromise where you don't have to go nuclear at this stage but you can still record your unhappiness.'

'Really?' She looked hopeful.

'Perhaps,' he continued, 'you could simply start with complaining to HeadofChambers.'

'Oh. Yes, I suppose you might be right. That might work.'

'Although I'd be careful if I were you and I'd definitely take a dictaphone along in your pocket to record the conversation in case he comes out with anything else.'

'Oh thank you so much. You've been a real help.'

'Oh, my pleasure,' TheBoss replied.

As she left the room, I looked at TheBoss with what can only have been horror on my face and he said, 'Litigation, pupillage, life, BabyB, it's all war. Read the book. You fight or you die.'

Tuesday 5 December 2006
Day 47 (week 10): HotCake

Today I had a visit in chambers. Not work-related either. Actually, it couldn't have been more non-work-related. In fact it's something to which in many ways I'd rather not admit. My esteemed visitor was none other than my mother. In itself, you might say that's not so unusual. Nice that she's interested and all. With that I would agree. To a point. Even if she arrived without any notice whatsoever. Even that I could handle. But not, and when I say not I mean never, when she arrives in the middle of the afternoon carrying a hot cake which she's just baked. Nor when she proceeds to tell the whole clerks' room that she's worried that I've been 'working a little too hard' and thought that this might cheer me up. Is she mad?! I couldn't have been more mortified when I was called out of a conference with TheBoss to greet her. Worse still, OldSmoothie was around and spotted the comedy potential at my expense.

'Ah, BabyBarista, I see you have a guest. Do introduce us.'

'Er, OldSmoothie, this is my mum.'

'Delighted to meet you.' He extended his hand, all charm itself. 'And I see you've brought along a cake? Smells rather good, I must say.'

'Well, they do work you all very hard and poor BabyBarista. He's only young, you know. Hasn't even left home and he's thrown into this big grown-up world.'

'I quite agree. It's very tough on the little ones. We try to help them along, of course, but nothing can beat a mother's tender care.'

'Oh, I'm so glad you understand.'

'I certainly do. Now, you must come and join us at chambers tea where perhaps everyone can have a small taste of your wonderful culinary skills.'

'Oh. Do you think so? I wouldn't want to get in the way or anything.'

'I can assure you that you will be most welcome.'

No! Please! Just leave me alone and let me go and hide in the farthest corner of the library. No such luck and I simply had to smile wanly and trot along tied to my mother's apron strings. Literally. Which meant that chambers were merrily entertained by my mother for the whole of tea as she regaled them with the usual motherly embarrassing stories. Worse still, everyone now knows that I continue to live at home, which was something I'd hoped to keep hidden under my little horsehair wig, despite the fact that my pupil poverty is actually caused by them. All she could say afterwards was, 'Sorry, BabyB. I've embarrassed you, I can tell. It's just that I was worried about you, that's all.'

No answer to that.

Wednesday 6 December 2006
Day 48 (week 10): Killing the Mockingbird

'I had my meeting with HeadofChambers this morning,' began Worrier as she came into our room just before lunch. Her remarks were addressed to us both but it was TheBoss who replied.

'And? What did he say?'

'Discouraged me from doing anything at all.' She put on a particularly pompous voice and said, 'You know, my dear, I'm sure this can be sorted out informally with a word in the right ear.'

TheBoss raised his eyebrows. 'Did he say anything else?' he asked.

'Yes, he went further than that,' she replied and put her HeadofChambers voice back on. 'I can assure you that I say this with the very best of intent for your career. Be very careful where you take this. A woman can get a name for herself for causing trouble which it becomes impossible to lose in such a small world.'

'He actually used those words?'

'Oh there's more,' she said, rising slightly to the occasion with all the attention TheBoss was lavishing on her. Back to the voice again. 'I'm afraid, dear, you're going to have to get used to the rough and tumble of the Bar. It's only going to get worse once you're in court and throwing insults at each other across a courtroom. To survive in this job, you have to be tough. I'm sure OldSmoothie was only trying to help you.'

'That's extraordinary, given the nature of your complaint.'

'So what do you think I should do?' she asked TheBoss. 'I'm now completely confused. Though I did get it on tape as you suggested,' she added.

'Well, your choices are pretty clear. You can either make a

formal complaint to chambers or you can take it straight to the Bar Council and include HeadofChambers within that complaint.' He paused and let her mull this over before continuing, 'You know, my own view is that you should still avoid overstepping the mark and so maybe it'd be wise simply to formalise your complaint with chambers.'

Both TheBoss and I knew that to make such a complaint would be professional suicide. He had brought her to the edge of the cliff and was now giving her the choice of jumping.

'I'm not sure Worrier needs to go as far as that,' I attempted, but TheBoss interrupted me and gave me a dismissive wave of the hand. There was only one answer as far as he was concerned, but just to make sure he pushed her over the edge.

'The problem is, as I've mentioned before, if you do nothing now it may well come back to haunt you if things then get worse.'

This was indeed a winning argument and over the edge she went as I just stood by and watched.

By mid-afternoon it was the talk of chambers. Whilst I was supposedly making coffee I overheard one of the more senior barristers in chambers telling TheBoss, using the word 'foolhardy' and finishing with, 'Well, on her own head be it.'

Later I told Claire.

'Of all the people to do it to. Poor innocent Worrier wouldn't harm a soul.'

'I know.'

'But why? What has he got to gain?'

'Nothing. Nor is it because she's a woman or anything like that. I think with him it's just sport. Killing for killing's sake.' This was probably about right, although I still felt bad for not mentioning the book he had given me.

'He aims, he fires and down comes the mockingbird,' said Claire ruefully. Then she added, 'But why didn't you say anything?'

'I don't know. I tried,' I ventured, as Claire raised a sceptical eyebrow. I was silent. I felt and probably looked quite ashamed. Seeing my unease, Claire didn't pursue it further though I could tell she was disappointed. She ended the conversation with, 'It's terrible, this pupillage thing, and it's only going to get worse.'

The problem is that I fear TheBoss may have a point. Kill or be killed.

Thursday 7 December 2006
Day 49 (week 10): Solicitor party

Out to a party at a solicitors' firm this evening with TheBoss, who was feeling generous after another of his last-minute lucrative settlements.

'Now, BabyB,' said TheBoss. 'There's a pecking order at these sorts of things and you'd better get it right.' He paused for effect before continuing. 'Accident management companies chase ambulances, solicitors schmooze accident management companies and barristers fawn over solicitors. Fail to do that and you'll have no practice even to lose.'

Once there I ended up chatting to SlipperySlope, the senior partner. He's got all the airs and graces of a country squire but a suit with stripes that would have done Arthur Daley proud. Maybe a legal version of Boycie from *Only Fools and Horses* might be a way of imagining him. He oozed his way over to chat to TheBoss who then eventually dumped him on me. Looking for something to say, I commented on the plush surroundings of the large room at Somerset House which must have cost an arm and a leg, which I guess would be appropriate for a personal injury firm.

'How do SlipperySlope & Co. make the sort of money that can pay for a party like this out of personal injury cases?' I asked, going for the subtle approach.

'We're alchemists, BabyB. Making gold.'

'I see,' I replied, politely.

The champagne was starting to take effect and he warmed to his theme. 'You know how?'

'No.'

'Working forty-eight hours a day.' He chuckled at what must have been an in-joke.

'I don't think I understand.'

'It's simple. When each little action like a quick letter or a ten-second telephone call can be billed as six minutes, you can accumulate a lot of hours in a short amount of time.'

'Oh.' Silly me. Kind of reminds me of that joke about the lawyer who died aged forty and was standing before Saint Peter at the pearly gates:

'You know, I'll sue,' the lawyer says. 'I don't smoke or drink, I take regular exercise and above all, I'm only forty years old. There's no way I should be dead.'

So Saint Peter goes off and checks the records and replies, 'I'm afraid that according to your time sheets, your age is at least one hundred and thirty-five just by hours billed alone.'

Until this point the evening was going swimmingly. Until, that is, I stumbled across SlipperySlope's second-in-command at the firm who managed to corner me for a good twenty minutes and tell me about how important the firm was to chambers. In the end I just had to escape and made it to the serving area for some fresh air and away from the stench of smug drunken legalese.

'If that man over there has the same effect on me as he has on his opponents, I'm sure he could bore them all into settling just to save themselves from having to listen to him again,' I said to the two waitresses who were also taking a sneaky break.

'Er, yes. Well, that's one way of putting it,' replied one of the waitresses.

Maybe it was the champagne, or maybe it was simply because he was so dreadful, but I ploughed on.

'One way of putting it? Boy oh boy, if boring people to death was an Olympic sport he'd be its very own Steve Redgrave.'

'Well, er, that might be going a little far,' said the waitress again.

'A legend in his own time. The undisputed heavyweight, yes definitely heavyweight, champion of the world in boring the socks off anyone in his firing line.'

'Well, I see, er . . .'

'Anyway, enough of him. I'm BabyBarista. What are your names?'

'Well, my name is June Dawson and this here is, er, well, it's, er, Liz Waller.'

A little penny started dropping in my mind. Slowly at first. Waller, Waller, Waller. Sounded familiar. Then it all seemed like slow motion. Waller . . . The name of the second-in-command . . .

'Er . . . no relation, I hope?' I tailed off as I said it, not looking at all hopeful.

'I'm his wife,' and with that she stormed off and left me standing and fretting as to whether my foot-in-mouth disease had scuppered chambers' lucrative line of work with this particular firm of solicitors. As I hovered between coming up with an awkward apology and on the other hand simply letting it lie, fear and inertia got the better of me and I eventually left quietly and most definitely in shame. Not, it has to be said, my best day so far.

Monday 11 December 2006
Day 51 (week 11): UpTights

Had lunch with the person who will take over from TheBoss as my pupilmaster at the start of April. Well, pupilmistress to be exact. I shall call her UpTights. She's in her late forties with a civil and criminal practice. She's never married and has no kids (having always put career first) and is Very High Maintenance. Considered calling her BoTucks due to the work she's had done, which gives her a very peculiar 'Mother of Barbie' kind of look. But it's her attitude which defines her.

'The most important thing at the Bar is boundaries, BabyBarista.'

'Sorry?'

'Clearly defined boundaries between work and non-work.'

'Er, yes.'

'I will never ask you about your life outside chambers and you will reciprocate. Life here. Life outside. Separate. Is that clear?'

'Of course.' Crystal.

Ouch. And she barks her words in high, clipped military tones reminiscent of a cross between Margaret Thatcher in her poll tax years and a Dalek screaming 'Exterminate!' UpTights is definitely her name. Looks like there'll be big changes when I start with her in April.

'Unless you are in court, you will arrive into chambers at 8.30 a.m. and leave at 6 p.m., during which hours your time belongs to me. Time outside those hours does not exist as far as I am concerned. Understand?'

'Yes.' I got it the first time, thank you.

'And there'll be no skiving in the library, just so you know, although you will get thirty minutes between twelve thirty and one each day when you will disappear from sight.'

It seems she also has what the Americans might call 'personal space issues'.

'When you are in my room, you will not hover around my desk. Absolutely no hovering. Got it? No hovering.'

No hovering. Right. I think I got that too. Promises to be interesting. Particularly as somehow I have to get her onside before the tenancy decision in September. First thoughts revolve around the question of why she is so defensive. Barriers built over years of working with lecherous dinosaurs such as HeadofChambers and OldSmoothie? Resentment that the rest of the world seems happy? Or just plain nastiness? Whatever it is, there's plenty to be getting on with.

Later BusyBody was back in TheBoss's room again. I'm beginning to suspect that she's started flirting back. She stayed about an hour doing more 'research' at OldRuin's desk. I gave TheBoss fifteen minutes before he mentioned the Ferrari. He did it in ten.

Thursday 14 December 2006
Day 54 (week 11): Chambers party

It's the party season and this evening it was the official chambers drinks party. I was there simply to serve the drinks, as were the other three pupils. The most interesting thing about the evening was seeing what each of the spouses were like. HeadClerk's wife was the most glamorous by a country mile. OldSmoothie's wife was the most daunting and treated him like he was some over-aged naughty school boy in front of everybody all night. Which of course he is. TheBoss's wife was, well, noticeable only by her absence.

It was held in chambers' large meeting room and for two hours there was free-flowing champagne and canapés provided courtesy of Marks and Spencer. For just a short space of time it was almost as if everyone forgot their petty differences, of which, I have already discovered, there are many. But it wasn't long before the cliques started to regroup and the gossip flowed more freely than the champagne.

Interesting to see how badly UpTights gets on with OldSmoothie. They don't even seem to pretend to be polite. OldSmoothie strolled over to her in the middle of the party and looked her up and down in mock admiration before opening with a sarcastic, 'Nice work you've had done recently, UpTights. Is this what they call growing old ungracefully?'

'Maybe you should try dyeing those ever-receding silver wisps of yours, OldSmoothie. Looking a bit tired, I must say.'

'Not half as tired as your neck and wrists, UpTights. Shame your miracle doctors can't hide all the evidence.'

TheBoss spent quite some time talking to BusyBody about how she was enjoying pupillage as she quietly sipped away on the champagne in between rounds of serving. It was during their little flirtation that I overheard her getting stuck into me.

'Did you hear about what he said to the senior partner's wife at the party the other night?' she whispered just loud enough for me to hear standing nearby.

'Er, no. What happened exactly?'

'Well, I don't want to be indiscreet or anything but I guess it's right that you know since you do a lot of work for that firm. But, well . . .'

'Go, on. Don't worry, it won't go any further, I promise.'

Yeah, right! As if she believed that. She ploughed on, 'Well, I heard that he was rude about one of the partners in front of his wife. I mean, I'm sure he didn't mean it or anything but, well, I just thought you should know.'

Well thanks a bundle, Little Miss BusyBody the SuperGrass. I just hope it doesn't cause even more damage.

As for TopFirst, predictably he wasn't drinking. Says he's on a detox. More like a delife. There seems to be no chink in his armour at all. Poor Worrier is already out of the picture and BusyBody – despite obviously living up to her name and trying to undermine me – is likely to annoy just about everyone except TheBoss. But TopFirst unfortunately remains a complete conundrum. One thing I have noticed is that despite having a beautiful fiancée, his ego is so bloated that he can't seem to help being an almighty flirt with the opposite sex, and in the naffest way possible. I've seen him at it a few times, but perhaps the most cringeworthy example was today. He was ostentatiously carrying around a bowl full of sweets and as he approached TheVamp he bowed slightly, offered her the bowl and in his best Austin Powers voice delivered the lamest of all his lame lines, 'Jelly, Baby?'

Though he isn't at all fat, he certainly isn't what you might call athletic either and TheVamp immediately responded by patting him on the stomach and saying, 'Jelly belly, more like,' before leaving him standing slightly dazed.

Now by that point, although like most people I knew her by reputation, I still hadn't actually met TheVamp and so I slowly made my way in her direction. I have to admit that she's extremely attractive, though in a way Claire, who has met her a few times, has described as 'obvious'. I think she was referring to her style as much as her looks, with the short skirts, low-cut tops and bleach-blonde cropped hair. All of this she carries off, in my opinion, if not in Claire's, with a redeeming wit that comes through most of all in the form of innuendo, even on the most innocent of subjects. When she's on form, she's a twenty-first century, living, breathing Carry On film. When I eventually sidled up to her she was chatting to TheCreep, who despite the fact he was talking about one of his cases was looking almost furtive. TheVamp was out to embarrass him. 'BabyB, how nice to meet you. Do join us. Mr CreepyWeepy here was asking me to help him with his manual handling,' she coochie-cooed.

TheCreep fell for the bait and blushingly mumbled, 'Er, well. . . . er, yes, The Manual Handling Operations Regulations, to give them their full title.'

'Absolutely, Mr CreepyWeepy. Whatever you want to call it. I hope I helped?' she pouted.

He looked lost, and only managed a vague nod.

'Very sweet. Now Mr CreepyWeepy, run along, will you.'

With which she dismissed him with a wave of her little finger and gave me the full glare of her attention for all of ten minutes before moving on to her next victim.

Monday 18 December 2006
Day 56 (week 12): Trouble

'So, how's GavisconMan then?' Claire asked.

'Who?'

'You know, TheBoss. "Will settle anything in under five minutes."'

'Too true in his case, I'm afraid.'

'How about your pupilmistress?'

It was all going swimmingly until I told Claire that TheVamp was coming along. She'd popped round mid-afternoon and asked what I was up to later. Call me naïve, but I had foreseen no trouble. But hey, I'm a guy and therefore genetically blind to such things. I say that because even before TheVamp arrived, Claire had started huffing about having to meet up with 'TheTramp'. 'She's had every male member of your chambers who's single, BabyB, along with half the married ones, I wouldn't wonder.'

'That's a bit harsh. I know she's a flirt, but . . .'

'She's more than a flirt, BabyB. Believe me, I can tell. That woman is trouble.'

Given that there's nothing between Claire and me, I didn't see what the problem was. Despite this, I could feel Claire bristling for a fight within a few minutes of TheVamp arriving and after about half an hour she eventually stropped off claiming to have a dinner engagement that she hadn't mentioned until that moment.

'Very nice little friend you have there, BabyB,' TheVamp commented.

'Drinking buddy throughout Bar School. Much needed.'

'Pretty keen on you, I'd say.'

'Oh, no. You've got the wrong end of the stick with that one. Definitely just friends. Never been anything between us except a very small thing early on.'

With that, TheVamp switched to her flirt mode. 'Oh, BabyB, a very small thing indeed? Don't be so modest.'

Well, if she wanted to add a notch to her barrister's wig (or maybe a curl?), who was I to argue?

'Come on BabyB, where are we going next? You're young enough to be trendy. What bars do you know?'

Young enough to be poverty stricken, more like. The only late-night place that I knew was a Spanish bar just off Tottenham Court Road where you had to say the owner's name after ringing the door bell to be let in as part of a kind of 'open sesame' routine. Girls dancing salsa, couples eating Spanish beans and old men playing cards out the back. Not a place I'd think of taking a fellow member of chambers to try and impress her. But hey, it was TheVamp and she was demanding late-night drinking, and despite my reservations it went down pretty well.

So well, in fact, that I ended up having breakfast with her the next morning. Actually about four hours after arriving back in. I was definitely still drunk and was glad I didn't have to go to court.

TheVamp, on the other hand, was moaning that she had a big trial starting in a couple of hours and not only had she not yet read the papers but worse, her vision was still so blurred that she wasn't actually able to start.

'Don't worry, BabyB. I can do these cases with my eyes shut. I'll just get the client to tell me what happened in his own words beforehand. Always good to hear it from the horse's mouth. Should be enough.'

Yet she was positively steaming alcohol from her pores and I didn't think that any amount of perfume or extra-strong mints was going to mask that. Whilst she was rushing around making coffee and downing glasses of water, I sat there like a lemon not really knowing what to say.

'Now BabyB,' she said. 'That was a great evening last night, but if we're going to be friends let's get one thing clear. This isn't the start of anything. Not even the start of the start of anything. I'm a free agent and will continue to be. All very enjoyable and everything, but it goes no further.'

Fine by me. In the meantime, I just hope that after the half hour it would have taken her to get to court she didn't look even a fraction as rough as when she left the house. Sometimes having a wig and gown to hide beneath can be rather helpful.

Tuesday 19 December 2006
Day 57 (week 12): Hard disks

TheBoss received a letter today from the solicitors in the case involving the accident on the ship. It sought formal pre-action disclosure of chambers' computer records and access to the hard disk. His first reaction was to rant against the ways of the modern world, with some of his choice lines being:

'Things are far too accountable these days.' (Meaning: 'How dare they question my word, even if it was a lie.')

'People have no respect.' (Meaning: 'Whatever I've done wrong, people should still know their place.')

'What right do solicitors have to be questioning a barrister in such a way?' (Meaning: 'What happened to good, old-fashioned deference and, for good measure, immunity from suit?')

After anger he moved straight on to fear and it was at that point that HeadClerk came in for a chat.

'You know, I've read what they're after and since we have absolutely nothing to hide, I would suggest that we give them what they want, wouldn't you agree?'

TheBoss was in an impossible position and looked caught in the headlights. He couldn't very well disagree since it would give the game away in an instant. Eventually, the best stalling he could manage was, 'Well, in principle I would completely agree with that approach. However, I'm not sure we can do that under the Data Protection Act. Have to be very careful, you know, these days.'

HeadClerk rightly looked sceptical. TheBoss was possibly the very last person on the planet to be sensitive to other people's data protection rights, and each one of us in the room was aware of that. No sooner had the words passed his lips than you could see on his face the realisation that HeadClerk had smoked him out. As he stood on the open plain with a big guilty sign on his forehead, he decided that the only option was retreat. 'Although I doubt very much that that'll cause much of a problem. Yes, you're right. Let's give them what they want. Nothing to hide, after all.'

HeadClerk replied with a slightly curt and almost sceptical 'Quite', before making his exit. Once he had gone, TheBoss went into something of a panic, despite the fact that he tried to play it cool in front of me. 'Yeah, these computer experts. What do they know anyway?' He laughed nervously to himself.

I slunk off to make some coffee whilst surreptitiously putting my ear to the door. He immediately rang his IT friend for advice. 'But would a computer expert be able to find out that the records had been changed retrospectively?'

'. . .'

'What do you mean it's unclear? How am I supposed to know the exact computer system we use? Or even how thorough their expert's going to be?'

When I arrived back with coffee, he couldn't sit still for a second. Getting up, walking around the room. Mumbling. Thankfully, as he had become unbearable, he left early. The irony is that whilst TheBoss is still slightly uncertain as to what the computer expert will find, I am in no doubt. He will uncover the fraud. It's what they do. How they make their money. As simple as that. I was naïve even to have been a passive accomplice. On balance, though, I have decided that TheBoss won't mention the fact that I knew about it. Involving one's pupil in a potentially criminal act would only exacerbate his already precarious position. I will therefore sit tight.

Thursday 21 December 2006
Day 59 (week 12): One down . . .

TheBoss has now gone off on his expensive holiday in Barbados.

'Should keep Her Indoors happy,' he said as he whisked out of chambers this morning. He's away now until 8 January. You might think that means pupil freedom, but sadly this has turned out not to be the case. Not only has he left me about twenty sets of papers to plough through but he has also asked another barrister to check that I 'have enough to do'. So much for Christmas spirit extending to pupils. Not that this has affected TopFirst, who has managed to scrape a week away and still enhance his reputation, since he's to be best man at the wedding of a friend who just happens to be the son of a judge.

Worrier came to see me today and asked if I had time for a drink after work. Of course I did. She looked absolutely lost, but that wasn't something particularly unusual for Worrier.

'BabyB, after all that I've been through, they've now gone and dismissed my complaint. I just can't believe it.'

This came as no surprise, but I was beginning to feel like a passive accomplice to the crime also.

'Oh, Worrier, that's terrible. I'm so sorry.'

'I just feel sick to the stomach, BabyB. I've had enough of their pompous sexist ways. I'm really starting to doubt if the whole thing is really for me.'

'Don't think like that. At least you stuck to your guns. Didn't lower yourself to their own compromised standards.'

'I guess you're right, BabyB.' Then just to make me feel worse, she added, 'Thanks anyway for all your support.'

I felt terrible for Worrier, but it did also make me wonder once again whether TheBoss really had a point. Particularly with the loan company's threats hanging over my mother's head.

Wednesday 27 December 2006
Day 61 (week 13): Another bluff

Any thoughts about whether TheBoss had a point were only reinforced when it came to Christmas Day itself. I mean, don't get me wrong, my mother and I have been used to Christmas by ourselves since my father left when I was eight and we were certainly doing our utmost to be cheerful.

'Look, BabyB,' she said, 'I've been saving a little something each week for this, so let's enjoy it. Just these two days. We'll live like royalty.'

But nothing was going to get rid of the elephant in the room and my mother's efforts only made the situation more heartbreaking. By the end of Boxing Day I was keen to get back to work and so was in early this morning. It was eerily quiet with only two clerks and three barristers in addition to myself and, of course – who could ever forget? – BusyBody. She and I went out for lunch in festive spirit and I have to admit that when she's not trying to organise everybody, she's actually quite nice. Still, it didn't stop me trying to wind her up a little.

'I've applied to be on two chambers committees, you know. Thought I might be able to lend a hand and all that.'

'You what? How? Which? When?'

'Oh, I was told about them the other day. Finance and marketing committees. Apparently they're even open to pupils.'

Of course, I haven't really applied for anything of the sort but it might encourage her spirit of busybodying still further. Not that she needs much encouraging, to be fair.

Thursday 28 December 2006
Day 62 (week 13): . . . And another

Had another lunch with BusyBody today. Almost felt like it was becoming a tradition. Winding her up, that is.

'What do you think of TheBoss?' I asked.

'Why do you ask that, BabyB?'

'Er, well, I was just wondering, that was all.'

'No. What do you know?'

'What do you mean? Nothing.'

'Well, it's just a strange question to ask out of the blue like that, that's all.'

'OK then. It's just that, well, I'll only tell you this if you absolutely promise to keep it to yourself?'

'Of course I will, BabyB. You know that. We're all barristers now.'

'Well . . . Look, you absolutely mustn't tell him that I said this, OK?'

'Spit it out BabyB. What is it?'

'It's just that in a drunken moment at the chambers party he told me that he really fancies you, that's all.'

Well, the reaction I got was far more than I had expected. She positively blushed and after that was asking questions about him for the rest of lunch.

What I had told her was, of course, not true.

Friday 29 December 2006
Day 63 (week 13): Disinformation

Three lunches in three days. It might even get people talking. True to the spirit of any disinformation campaign, today I told BusyBody something that was not only true but also highly unlikely. Not only will this bolster my other claims when she realises its truth, but it will also serve its primary purpose of completely winding her up. I simply told her what HeadofChambers had said to Worrier about her sex discrimination claim.

I also told her that Worrier had taped the conversation, just to really get her going.

CHAPTER 4
JANUARY: YOUTUBE

Rapidity is the essence of war: take advantage of the
enemy's unreadiness, make your way by unexpected
routes, and attack unguarded spots.
                                   Sun Tzu, *The Art of War*

Tuesday 2 January 2007
Day 64 (week 14): Divorce

It's a new year and only nine months to go in the battle for tenancy. TheBoss was in work today even though he wasn't due back until next Monday. Seems his wife kicked him off the holiday. Wants a divorce. More importantly for TheBoss she wants half the assets and maintenance for their two children. This was all I managed to pick up. I can only speculate that he's been having an affair. Whatever the reason, he's back at work earning the cash in fear of the amount he'll be taken for.

All of which put him in a foul mood, and he's ready to take it out on whatever or whoever is at hand. Today, unfortunately, that was me. I kept out of his way as much as possible and took particular care over his coffee. But if there was a sanctuary for battered pupils run by the likes of the RSPCA, I would definitely have been knocking at their door.

Wednesday 3 January 2007
Day 65 (week 14): Mold

If ever there was a thankless task it was being sent to Mold in North Wales to photocopy documents for TheBoss. Not just for the length of the journey but also for the sheer grottiness of the town. A while back I learnt the word 'onomatopoeia', where the word sounds like its meaning. 'Splash', 'snooze', or, even better, 'plop' spring to mind. Mold is definitely one of those and though I've never been there, I imagine Grimsby comes into the same category. It was cold, miserable and thoroughly run down, with only the briefest respite coming from the town's wit who had scrawled the letter 'y' on a number of signs. Hence 'Moldy Industrial Estate', 'Moldy Social Club', etc.

As if all of this wasn't enough, I also had to put up with another baby barrister from London who I'll call Pashmina. What a liability. Made the characters in *Withnail and I* look positively provincial.

'Look at the prices on the menu, BabyB. Would you believe it? You could probably get a row of houses here for the cost of a decent meal in London.' . . . 'Hmm, prawn cocktail. Quite the height of sophistication.' . . . 'At least it's authentic. You've got to give it that.' . . . 'Do you think they talk so slowly due to learning difficulties?'

In the end I asked one of the solicitors on whom she'd cast aspersions as to inbreeding if he'd play along as I told her that he was my elder brother and that I'd been born and brought up in the town. It was of course, a lie, but it certainly served to shut her up for the rest of the afternoon.

Thursday 4 January 2007
Day 66 (week 14): Real clients

We had our first chambers training session today in preparation for our start in court in April. Time to get all the lovely pupils together in one room in chambers taking each other on like baby Jedi. Well actually, not exactly. Worrier was the first to crack.

'I'm not sure I'll be ready by April. It's just too soon.'

'Oh don't worry,' said OldSmoothie, who was leading the session, despite the complaint which had been made against him. 'You're expected to make mistakes for at least the first few years.'

'But it's such a responsibility having your own clients and absolute responsibility for their cases and what if they complain?'

'Look. It'll almost certainly be the only time for most of them that they'll ever see the back of a real-life courtroom. They won't know whether you're good or bad, even when you lose it for them.'

'Yeah, they're just pupil practice fodder,' said TopFirst.

'I'm not sure they'd quite like to be called that,' said OldSmoothie, 'but it isn't far from the truth.'

'But how do you control the nerves?' asked Worrier.

'Believe me, they'll be more nervous than you. They just won't notice,' replied OldSmoothie.

'Well, I'm looking forward to my first day,' said TopFirst in a kind of 'Well, I'll have a Babycham' type of voice. 'Great chance to prove yourself.'

'Oh, me too,' said BusyBody, following the leader. 'I've booked myself on a private advocacy course for a month beforehand so I'll be raring to go by that point.'

Everyone looked at her like she was mad. Where does she get the time, what with her committees and other stuff on top of all the pupillage work? Is she a machine?

'But what do we do,' Worrier was off again, 'if we want to object to something?'

'Stand up, walk up to the bench and shout "Objection!" in a thick American accent,' TopFirst said sarcastically.

'Stop teasing her. You can tell she's worried.' It was BusyBody. 'You just raise your voice and interrupt as best you can.'

Something at which BusyBody is particularly skilled.

Monday 8 January 2007
Day 68 (week 15): BusyBody bites

BusyBody came over for a chat in the library this afternoon. Having already heard from me about the existence of the tape the other day, it was almost as if she felt she had to report in to me today on her progress. She told me that she'd asked Worrier if she could listen to the tape. Worrier had apparently been reluctant but BusyBody had persisted, saying that this was something with which she wanted to help 'as a woman'. Being the trusting soul that she is, Worrier eventually dug the tape out of her desk and lent it to her for the afternoon along with the recorder. BusyBody said that she had it in her bag and wondered if I wanted to hear it. I replied that I was in a rush but would be very interested to hear what she thought about it later.

The most interesting piece of information from that conversation was that Worrier kept the tape in her desk.

Tuesday 9 January 2007
Day 69 (week 15): My recording

This evening after work I visited Worrier's room, which was empty. Found the tape in the recorder having been returned to its place by BusyBody. With the help of my trusty mobile phone I made my own recording of the conversation.

Wednesday 10 January 2007
Day 70 (week 15): Steps of the High Court

OldRuin was in this morning. All dressed up in his best tweed suit. Hair unusually combed down and looking almost coy. Like a schoolboy who had prematurely aged fifty years. It seems that it would have been his wedding anniversary today. He was married in Temple Church and he had proposed exactly a year before on bended knee on the steps of the High Court. Some thirty-five years later, his wife contracted cancer. When she was told that it was terminal, she told him that wherever she was taken in the afterlife (something in which they both believed), she would always ensure that at midday on their wedding anniversary she would be sitting on the steps of the High Court in exactly the same place that the two of them had sat after their engagement. Therefore, just in case she was not able to trace where he was, they could always ensure they would be together on that particular day.

It was 11 a.m. and OldRuin was ready for his love.

Thursday 11 January 2007
Day 71 (week 15): The set-up

A fact that I had found out from BusyBody during the Christmas break was that she had no access to her emails at home and therefore most evenings after work she spent twenty minutes in a

76

nearby internet café doing her personal emails (something which is disapproved of by chambers if it's on their time). It's a pretty big place and although it was a slightly risky move, I got changed after work into a so-called 'hoody' and jeans and went off there. Sure enough, BusyBody was beavering away in the corner.

I duly uploaded the recording of HeadofChambers onto YouTube. I didn't state what it was and am confident that no one would stumble on it accidentally as I didn't add any keywords which could have brought it up in a search. I then set up a fake Hotmail account and emailed HeadofChambers the link, thus putting various cats among various pigeons.

If any of it ever gets traced back to this internet café, the video footage should show very clearly that the only person related to chambers who was in here was BusyBody. My hood kept me completely and utterly anonymous.

Monday 15 January 2007
Day 73 (week 16): Worrier confesses

Went for coffee with Worrier this morning. She told me that HeadofChambers had come to see her on Friday and accused her of taping the conversation he had with her. She, of course, broke down immediately and told him everything. Given that there is nothing more sincere than Worrier under pressure (I have to admit she'll be a dreadful barrister) it must have been clear to HeadofChambers that she was also telling the truth when she denied putting the recording on YouTube. The inevitable question after that was who had had access to the tape? The only person as far as Worrier knew was BusyBody, to whom she had lent the tape last Monday. With forty years' experience of seeking justice and defending the rights of the accused, HeadofChambers put two and two together and came up with BusyBody as the only possible culprit. After all, it couldn't possibly be any of the tenants. They were as good as family. So if BusyBody was the only one of the pupils with access, then obviously it was her. All the more obvious given their little incident in chambers tea a while back.

Tuesday 16 January 2007
Day 74 (week 16): BusyBody panics

BusyBody came to see me in a panic today. HeadofChambers has asked to see her first thing tomorrow morning. Apparently he said the following: 'I'm sure you know what this is about. What on earth you were thinking with YouTube I cannot imagine but you should know that this is being taken extremely seriously.'

She had absolutely no idea what he was talking about and wondered if I could provide any insight. Obviously, I pleaded complete ignorance.

'Sounds like he's lost the plot,' was all I could offer.

Wednesday 17 January 2007
Day 75 (week 16): BusyBody convicted

I have now heard the full story from BusyBody and she appears to have been completely banged to rights. HeadofChambers called her in at 9.30 a.m. and asked for an explanation. Obviously, she pleaded ignorance. This just made him even more angry. He told her about the recording, the post on YouTube and the anonymous email he had received. She repeated her protestations. Again they didn't wash. He told her that over the weekend he had had a high-ranking police friend of his do a search on the source of the uploading of the recording and of the anonymous email and both had been traced to an IP address for a particular internet café not far from chambers at between 6.15 and 6.30 p.m. last Thursday. On Monday, that same friend had asked a local police officer to visit the café and obtain copies of the security videos covering those times. He had then played the video, fast forwarding to the time when BusyBody had entered the café and then to when she left. He also pointed out that there was no one else from chambers to be seen there. This had floored BusyBody. Though she continued to plead her innocence, she was bright enough to see that she was well and truly scuppered. HeadofChambers had then gone on to tell her that whilst the police had been involved it had been on an informal basis and he did not want them to press charges for the theft of the recording. Furthermore, whilst he considered this to be an extremely serious matter, it was one which he thought should be dealt with internally by chambers. He had already made a threatening request to YouTube via his police friend and the recording had now been taken down. As for BusyBody, she simply needed to know at this stage that she could not have made a worse start to pupillage. Her pupilmaster had been informed and in due course the tenancy committee would be given a summary of the events. At the very least, she would be well advised to consider applying to other sets of chambers for a 'third six', just in case. This is basically a continuation of the nightmare which is pupillage for another six months for those who fail to get taken on in their original chambers. At this stage, I can't think of anything worse.

Despite the fact that it was all down to me, I still felt pretty bad as I listened to her recount the full horrifying details, and my first thought was that I would never be able to tell Claire about this. As for BusyBody, all I could do was to offer her my sympathy.

Thursday 18 January 2007
Day 76 (week 16): Worrier again

Worrier was round today.

'I just don't understand, BabyB. I mean how could BusyBody do such a thing? It simply doesn't add up,' she mumbled.

'I know,' I answered.

'But why on earth?'

'People are strange creatures and life's mysteries are such that we cannot even hope to solve them all.'

Friday 19 January 2007
Day 77 (week 16): Bombshell

Today TheBoss received a bombshell in the form of another letter from the senior partner of the firm of solicitors in the shipping case. It stated that examination of chambers' hard disk by an expert showed that an amendment was made to the records at 7 a.m. on 4 November 2006. Specifically, an entry had been added stating that the papers in the case had been sent back in July along with an advice and a fee note. This was contrary to TheBoss's account and suggested that he had fraudulently doctored (or, the letter alleged, 'caused to be doctored') the records in order to avoid involvement in any professional negligence action. The letter stated that in the circumstances the firm had no option but to make a formal complaint to the Bar Standards Board. Furthermore, if the client brought an action for professional negligence, the solicitors would be blaming TheBoss and he was therefore advised to report this to his insurers.

It might be said that things are not looking good for TheBoss.

Monday 22 January 2007
Day 78 (week 17): Extraordinary meeting

Apparently an extraordinary chambers meeting has been called to decide whether TheBoss should be suspended from chambers pending the Bar Standards hearing, which could be several months away. Usually innocence is assumed until guilt is proven, apparently. However, the word on the street is that this won't apply to TheBoss due to the fact that the allegation involves the fiddling of chambers' own books and, furthermore, to the fact that TheBoss is yet to come up with any defence, never mind an arguable one. The meeting is to be held next Monday.

Tuesday 23 January 2007
Day 79 (week 17): FiveAmp

Understandably TheBoss has been out of chambers yesterday and today and I've been left to watch other members of chambers actually fighting cases. Today I had the pleasure once again of watching TheCreep. Quite a big trial with both parties and their witnesses all ready for a fight. The only problem was the judge. Not great when you know his nickname's FiveAmp due to his short fuse, but even worse when you discover he wants to adjourn the case to get off home early for some reason. First he tried suggesting he had a conflict of interest, which didn't get anywhere with either side. Then he pointed out that several of the witness statements had been served late. Both counsel immediately made clear that neither objected to this delay.

'Well, rules are rules, you know,' he said. 'I'm minded to adjourn this and to call the solicitors here personally to explain their breach.'

'With respect, Sir,' came a voice from the front of the court. It was TheCreep as he jumped up from his seat. 'Today is probably costing more than £10,000. We're ready for trial and to adjourn, Sir, would be contrary to the interests of justice.'

That would have been just the right submission. Yet he seemed oblivious to this and continued with the following:

'In fact, Sir, it is just the sort of case that if the Court of Appeal were to examine it, they would absolutely insist that it should have gone ahead today.'

Ouch. You could almost see a slow-motion scene of the words leaving his mouth and TheCreep desperately trying to grasp them back. Never said it. No. Never. Just your imagination. Except he just did.

'Are you threatening me?'

'No, Sir. Please, Sir, if that's what you imagine I mean by those words, I retract them wholeheartedly.'

'Which bit do you retract? The threat?'

'Yes. No. I mean . . .'

'Mr Creep. I've been in this game for a lot longer than I care to remember and I do not take kindly to being lectured on what the Court of Appeal might or might not think of my local justice.'

'No, Sir.'

'I care even less for direct threats made at my office. If you want to appeal me, by all means. But never, I repeat, never, threaten me. Do you understand?'

'Yes, Sir. I'm very . . .'

'Because if you threaten me, I will not only send you over to the cells at the magistrates court for contempt, I will also pass the case over to your brand new sparkling Standards Board.'

'Yes, Sir. Sorry, Sir.'

'Now. I am minded to adjourn this case unless I hear any objection to the contrary from either of you.'

There was silence.

Wednesday 24 January 2007
Day 80 (week 17): Multiple problems

TheBoss came in today and at midday suggested we go off to Inner Temple Hall for lunch. Seems that I'm the only one in whom he feels he can confide at this stage. I've noticed that when he's stressed he likes to eat, a lot, and today was no exception, as he plumped for the roast lamb with all the trimmings. As we sat down laden with huge platefuls of food, he started to tell me about his divorce.

'You know the reason why she's asking for a divorce?'

'No.'

'Pretty clichéd really, but I've been seeing one of my solicitors.'

'Ah.'

'It gets worse. Now her firm has reported it to chambers. Not that it's any of their business, but I've no doubt at the chambers meeting on Monday they'll start suggesting it raises some sort of conflict of interest.'

'Well, not necessarily.' I tried to be positive.

'The problem is, BabyB, that when you've been in chambers as long as I have, you've had the chance to annoy pretty much everyone at one time or another. Now it's their time to get me back. Put the boot in. You know, I really think they're simply going to kick me out.'

'But they're lawyers, first and foremost. Surely they'll allow you a fair hearing? Time to get all the facts out?'

'Well, now you're thinking like I'm thinking, BabyB. At least all that legal training will come in useful for something. You see, it's all governed by the chambers constitution which was written at a time when a place in chambers was a place for life. It makes it pretty hard to do anything drastic.'

'So how many votes do they need?'

'Seventy-five per cent of the whole of chambers has to vote in favour of suspension. If enough people fail to turn up then it'll have to be near unanimous to go against me.'

'Where does OldRuin stand on all this?'

'Bless him. He's never been one to cause a fuss, but he has already discreetly indicated that he is away shooting on the day of the hearing and therefore unfortunately will be unable to attend.'

Thursday 25 January 2007
Day 81 (week 17): Other pupils

Worrier has perked up in the last few days. Apparently she's been visiting a life coach who's set her the challenge of turning it all around. Some challenge.

BusyBody on the other hand has not been busying anybody recently. So much so that I'm concerned. And that's saying something. Suggested we had lunch today but I was politely but firmly rebuffed. I've had no vibes of suspicion. Simply those of abject defeat.

As for TopFirst, whatever he touches continues to turn to gold. It is somewhat perturbing, to say the least. Poisoning remains my last resort. I am joking. Honestly.

Monday 29 January 2007
Day 83 (week 18): Blinking tactics

Today was the extraordinary chambers meeting. Quite a social gathering, to say the least. All I saw were the comings and the goings. No pupils were allowed anywhere near. I'd considered leaving my phone in there to record proceedings but thought better of it given the present circumstances. Instead, I went off to a particular bar which I knew was frequented by at least half a dozen members of chambers and where I was therefore likely to pick up the outcome later on.

Claire had agreed to back me up on this mission to gain valuable information. Whilst we were waiting and after a couple of drinks she said, 'Hey, I've got a new theory for succeeding at the Bar.'

'Oh, yes, and what might that be, then?'

'Blinking.'

'Blinking what?'

'No. Blinking.' She scrunched up her eyes theatrically and opened them again.

'Right,' I said sceptically. 'You'll just blink people to death, will you?'

'Actually, you'll not blink them to death. Stare them out. I mean, if you're going to argue or negotiate well, you just can't afford to blink after a big bluff. You know, like Kennedy beat Khrushchev in the sixties because he didn't blink. Just the same at court. It's all Bay of Pigs.'

So we spent the next hour having blinking competitions, which raised a few odd looks when the various members of chambers finally arrived for a post-match drink or six. They were all very open about the outcome, on the basis that I was bound to find out sooner or later. Seems there were insufficient people in attendance to be able to suspend constitutionally and so they'd gone through the motions of having a debate on the issue (i.e. a good old-fashioned gossip), before concluding that in the circumstances it would be more seemly simply to withdraw the motion. A moral high ground could then be taken of innocence until guilt was proven. TheBoss therefore wasn't called upon to explain himself and was left outside during the whole meeting. Which is kind of lucky, as I'm not sure what explanation he would have come up with if he had been called.

So, TheBoss can continue earning his top dollar for at least a few more months until the Standards Board hearing. In the meantime, he'd better start working on his defence. So I continue to be shackled to the chambers pariah, though in many ways I am finding this is helpful from the expressions of sympathy it seems to be generating.

Tuesday 30 January 2007
Day 84 (week 18): Losing it

TheBoss was in early today and seemed almost chipper. Not sure if he's been seeing Worrier's life coach, but he was peculiarly positive about everything. Even started lecturing me about how pupillage isn't that bad, really. I think he's losing the plot on many different levels.

Wednesday 31 January 2007
Day 85 (week 18): An honourable profession

Dear, old-fashioned, well-mannered, loveable OldRuin. Who couldn't like him? He's seen scandals come and go but has himself spent most of his life playing by the rules. Rules which are as much a part of him as the weave of his tweed. Yet he's not the self-righteous sort and has a genuine sympathy for those who get themselves into difficulty, no matter how stupid they may have been. That is how he feels towards TheBoss. Not quite the prodigal son, but even so, a wayward child in one form or another. This all became clear when he took me out for lunch at Simpson's on the Strand today. The place very much suited OldRuin himself with its airs of great times gone before and with a very English manner about the whole thing. Today, for some reason, the smell of mothballs had gone from OldRuin and had been replaced by a very faint smell which reminded me of boiled cabbage from childhood.

'You must not take these difficulties to heart,' he said. 'It's sometimes hard to see the bigger picture when you feel you're being dragged down by events. It's a great and honourable profession which you are entering, BabyB. Of course, there'll always be bad eggs, but in my experience they generally come a cropper of their own making. But don't forget that they are far outnumbered by the honest, decent chaps (and chapesses may I say) who rarely come to anyone's attention.'

'I sometimes wonder which side of the line I actually fall,' I replied.

'And that's what'll save you, BabyB. Keep hold of that doubt.' Then he added enigmatically, 'There's many of us have suffered crises of conscience at one time or another.'

I didn't want to pry and replied simply, 'Thanks, OldRuin. It's good to take a step back.'

His kindly look shone through as he said, 'You'll weather this storm, BabyB.' He paused before adding, 'And be the stronger for it.'

CHAPTER 5

FEBRUARY: UPSTAIRS, DOWNSTAIRS

The difficulty of tactical manoeuvring consists in
turning the devious into the direct, and misfortune
into gain.

Sun Tzu, *The Art of War*

Friday 2 February 2007
Day 87 (week 18): Embarrassment

Less than two months to go until I get on my feet in court and I
have to admit that I'm starting to feel a little nervous. In order to
try and get an edge on the other pupils, and taking a tip out of
Busybody's book, I've hired a public-speaking coach who gets me
to recite Shakespeare and do breathing exercises.

All very well in itself. But it backfired today when I was caught
by the barrister I was following around at court doing one of these
exercises. Thought there was no one around in the robing room and
so started reciting one of the more soppy of the sonnets interspersed
with deep breathing (i.e. moaning) in between each line. You can
imagine my horror when the barrister emerged from the loo next
door with a smirk which told me he had overheard it all.

Monday 5 February 2007
Day 88 (week 19): Vexatious

Today TheBoss was against a litigant in person who I shall call
Vexatious. One of those people who was not represented by a
lawyer, not for lack of funds, but because he'd sacked all those
who had tried to help. He was a funny-looking man in his

mid-fifties who reminded me of Mr Burns from *The Simpsons,* with slightly mad, staring, shifty eyes and a head bald save for wisps of browny-grey hair sprouting out the back. But unlike the devious Mr Burns, Vexatious looked paranoid, worn down and above all sad. Melancholy, tired and probably depressed, which may well have explained the heavy dark patches under his eyes. He also smelt slightly of alcohol, which at eleven in the morning didn't bode well.

TheBoss had had some experience of such litigants and told me that it was wise to say as little as possible to them beforehand. Otherwise, he said, you risk finding whatever you say being twisted into a professional conduct complaint. He said this with such conviction that it made me wonder whether he was speaking from personal experience. So, after brief unpleasantries between Vexatious and TheBoss, we all marched into court.

Vexatious was suing the council for harassment and although the sad thing was that there may well have been some foundation for complaint at the start, it seems that he'd taken things just a little too far over the years. Reams of handwritten correspondence packed full of underlinings, exclamation marks and capital letters, as if he felt that the world wasn't listening. The judge had the measure of him from the start and when he started rambling through an introduction to his case, he was cut short with, 'I've read the papers, Mr Vexatious. At some length, if I may say. Do you have any witnesses?'

'Only myself.'

'In which case perhaps you would be kind enough as to direct yourself to the witness box.'

'Yes, My Lord.'

'Your Honour.'

'Yes, My Lord, very nice of you to say so.'

'No, you address me as Your Honour.'

'Sorry, Your Honour, My Lord.'

'Would you now like to take the oath?'

'No.'

'Why not?'

'Because I don't believe in this oppressive system of so-called justice and therefore I will not swear any oath of allegiance to it or anyone associated with it.'

'It's just an oath to tell the truth.'

'Oh.'

'Repeat the words on the card in front of you.'

So it went on all morning. It was what the Americans might call a 'slam dunk' for TheBoss. He just sat tight and didn't say a word. In fact he actually won the case without uttering a single word. The judge listened carefully to all that Vexatious had to say and when the rant was finished he summarised the case far more articulately and then said, 'Am I correct that that is your case?'

Somewhat dumbfounded, Vexatious said, 'Yes, Your Lord.'

The judge then turned to TheBoss and said, 'I don't need to hear from you,' with which he dismissed the claim. Tragically for Vexatious, his problems are now only made worse by the fact that he faces a costs bill of over £25,000.

Tuesday 6 February 2007
Day 89 (week 19): A kick while down

Poor old Boss. I am genuinely feeling sorry for him at this stage of his problems. No sooner has he been granted a reprieve by chambers than he is given a reminder of his difficulties with a double whammy today. One blow was the letter he had been expecting from the Bar Standards Board confirming that a complaint has been made against him. The other was from his professional insurers, the Bar Mutual, asking him to keep them posted about any further developments on the case. All this was then made worse by a phone call from his wife halfway through the afternoon in which it was clear that she was hassling him about the divorce and the financial arrangements which needed to be put in place. For all his lack of spine, the fact he is bearing up at all under all of this is a testament to a hitherto-invisible streak of mettle within.

Thursday 8 February 2007
Day 91 (week 19): Contingency plans

I am starting to wonder what TheBoss is taking. Perhaps I was wrong when I said he was bearing up well. He was hardly what you might call stable even when I started pupillage and he's certainly been through the mill since then. But in the last couple of days his behaviour has become even more erratic. Today he burst into the room around 11.30 a.m. and started walking around in a circle saying to himself, 'Who needs it anyway. I'll go and live on a desert island and become a writer. I'll motorbike around the world. I'll . . .'

He hesitated and stared at me during his pause.

'You know,' he continued, 'we start off in this job with so much potential. The world is our oyster and we can do anything we choose. We then spend years taking ourselves further and further away from the mainstream until we are so specialised that if we were to jump ship there would not even be a life-raft nearby. We are good only for being barristers. Otherwise it's straight back down to the bottom of the pile aged forty-four.'

Friday 9 February 2007
Day 92 (week 19): Two down . . .

That Friday feeling today. So far, I'm a third of the way through pupillage and I have, to say the least, neutralised two of my three opponents for tenancy. TheBoss and Sun Tzu would be proud of me. TopFirst remains a challenge but today I'm feeling optimistic. The opportunity will present itself, of that I have no doubt. In the meantime, I must prepare the ground. I think his arrogance and smugness could somehow end up helping me.

Tuesday 13 February 2007
Day 94 (week 20): Caught Room

TheBusker was on form today, hitting a con man in cross-examination from all angles. With his gentle style highlighting so many inconsistencies the claimant had no chance and it made me think that perhaps the name of the venue should be the 'Caught Room'. Which got me thinking about other such names. Maybe the venue for the corporate-type committee meetings might better be described as the 'Bored Room'. Then, a little more surreally, there's that great legal highway, Gray's Inn Road, surrounded by barristers' chambers and solicitors' firms. For some reason I always imagine it as 'Grazing Road', full of all those rich, fat lawyers grazing away on cold hard cash. Then of course, my thoughts come back to today and the claimant's own questioning of TheBusker's witnesses, which was done with such an irritated manner that it might almost have been described as 'cross' examination.

On the way back from court TheBusker mentioned in the most roundabout way TheBoss's reputation for settling his cases and said that I shouldn't assume that that was normal.

'We're paid to fight cases, and never forget that. Yes, sometimes cases may settle but remember, the solicitors will already have given it a pretty good go even before it gets anywhere near court. So, unless something changes, you get yourself right in there and fight.'

My guess is that there has been concern as to the influence which TheBoss may have been having on my training and development. They would be right to be worried.

Thursday 15 February 2007
Day 96 (week 20): Greed is good

SlipperySlope was in chambers to see TheBoss today and since he arrived early ended up spending about twenty minutes sitting in our room having coffee with me.

'What do you think of the Inns of Court?' he asked, making small talk. Then, before I got time to answer, he continued with, 'It's all a distraction, BabyB. The law's not about ivory towers or wigs and gowns. It's about one thing and that's costs. Not justice. Not rights. Not defending the innocent or prosecuting the guilty. It's cold, hard, stinking cash. Your time, literally, is money. You sign away your life, but for a price of which even Faust himself would be proud.'

'Oh.' I think I probably looked a little shocked at his outburst.

'Don't get taken in, BabyBarista. Get involved, make hay and you'll be all right. But you know what the biggest risk is for lawyers?'

'What?'

'Believing their own lies. You see, they live in the land of make-believe. They tell other people's lies and the very best of them even do it with the utmost sincerity. Deadly in court, but it'll send you mad if you're not careful.'

I think my mouth had probably fallen open at his outburst, but he hadn't finished.

'It's a fragile beast, that little neural network sitting on your shoulders, BabyBarista. So play the game. Play it hard. But never forget that it's just that and nothing more.'

Oh.

Friday 16 February 2007
Day 97 (week 20): SnakeEyes

Went off to court with TheBusker again today. With him, it's not always what he says but more the tone and sincerity with which it is said. The judge seemed in a particularly bad mood and appeared to have started off set against him. TheBusker's response? To smile at the judge and gently lift his spirits. It was almost as though he put on his snake eyes and somehow hypnotised the judge into looking favourably on his case. He started off talking about the weather and his journey to court and then went on to a bit of gossip from another court. Then he progressed to talking about his own client and a couple of quirks in his personality which had nothing to do with the case whatsoever. Eventually, he came round to mentioning the claim, but almost as an aside. His opponent just sat there getting more and more hot under the collar, as there was absolutely nothing he could do but watch TheBusker stroll slowly over the winning line. I mentioned this afterwards and he commented, 'It's not about the law, BabyB, and it's often not even about the facts. Most of the time it boils down to one question: does the judge like your client or not? Is he for him or agin?'

I wouldn't want to be against TheBusker.

Monday 19 February 2007
Day 98 (week 21): Cheaper to kill

Today we had a conference with the solicitor in a fatal accident case. Tragic accident at work when a builder was killed by machinery falling on top of him. TheBoss was representing the employer's insurers and commented pretty early on that the case was '. . . a lot cheaper by virtue of his having died. Could have been worth millions in loss of earnings if he'd lived.' As it is, the deceased was separated from his wife and had no kids and the claim is therefore worth hardly anything at all. Very strange law that makes it cheaper to kill than to maim.

In the meantime, BusyBody has gone from desolate moping to utterly hyper with no transition period in between. For her, it's all in the hair and it's definitely curlier when she's at her most interfering. At the moment she's a caricature even of her old self and the curls have taken on Medusa-like proportions. She's become an uber-BusyBody whose words are spewing out faster than ever. Mysteriously, her quite posh middle-England accent is occasionally dropping the odd vowel in favour of a south London drawl. I've also heard of sightings of her working in chambers as early as 6 a.m. and as late as midnight. All very strange. I have to admit to feeling some responsibility. Yet whenever I've asked how she is, all I've got back is a staccato 'All fine. Good. Excellent. Anyway. Very busy. Very. Lots of papers. Must get through them. Lots. Anyway. Thank you. Yes. All OK. Anyway. So. How are you?'

Wednesday 21 February 2007
Day 100 (week 21): BattleAxe

'What were you up to last night, BabyB?' It was Claire at lunch.

'Celebrating another settlement for TheBoss. He's cashing in as many cases as possible at the moment in case he gets struck off.'

'Hmm. Lucky you.'

'Well it wasn't so bad last night as I finally got to meet the mistress.'

'He's getting more reckless by the day.'

'Quite.'

'So what was she like?'

'Not at all what I expected. After everything I've heard about his high-maintenance wife, I thought she might be some meek, pouting solicitor pandering to his insecurities.'

'And was she?'

'Quite the opposite. Formidable would probably be the best word, and sturdy.'

'Doesn't sound like the type to be impressed by a Ferrari.'

'Exactly.'

'Why on earth does he even get the time of day from her? He's a walking disaster area,' said Claire.

'But the most interesting thing was that when she opened her mouth and the clipped vowels and overbearing opinions rolled forth, I suddenly realised that she was just an older version of BusyBody.'

Thursday 22 February 2007
Day 101 (week 21): TidySum

'Hey, BabyB, do you fancy earning a bit of extra money on the side devilling?' it was Worrier.

'Er, satanic cults? Not really my bag, Worrier.' I mean, I know she's been having a hard time, but really.

'Don't be silly. It's a Bar tradition. It involves working for other barristers.'

'But I thought we weren't allowed to be employed by other barristers.'

'True. But this is the loophole. Seems to slip by under the radar as "research".'

'Oh.'

Worrier went on to explain that there's a barrister who I'll call TidySum who's taken this to a new level with thirty little devils around the Bar all being paid a third of what he bills out. Out of curiosity I went along to his chambers in Gray's Inn which has the nickname 'Hell's Kitchen' for obvious reasons. The queue of pupils outside his room looked like that for a school tuck shop. I left with an advice to do by tomorrow which will apparently earn me £50, which will certainly come in handy.

As for BusyBody, I walked in on her today as she was lying on the ground with her noticeably thick ankles held aloft. I wondered whether she'd fallen over and simply couldn't right herself, though I thought it better not to ask.

'Hello, BabyB,' she said, without moving her legs. 'I've officially given up all hope of getting taken on in chambers and decided instead to achieve inner peace and harmony through yoga . . .'

'I see.'

'. . . and bagging a rich barrister to keep me.'

'Oh. You know TheBoss still holds a flame,' I lied.

'He's a loser. I'm not tagging on to that mess. No. I've got my eye on a bigger prize. Much richer and, for what it's worth, better looking. And with a wife and family at home, he's not likely to be too demanding on my time.'

I was to get no more details from her today, although OldSmoothie springs to mind as fitting her description.

Friday 23 February 2007
Day 102 (week 21): Scandal

There's nothing that makes a scandal more juicy than a bit of old-fashioned snobbery, and this had the snobs in a gossip frenzy this morning: BusyBody (allegedly) went home with one of chambers' clerks last night.

About twenty members of chambers had got together in a wine bar with a few friendly solicitors to launch a book written by a particularly boring member of chambers (and that's saying something). Not exactly the height of glamour for a so-called book launch, but nevertheless the champagne was flowing. The clerks had all been invited along as has been chambers policy now for the last two years. Before that, only HeadClerk was ever allowed out to social functions and even then only to marketing events. Last night the worries over the mixing of barristers and clerks came to fruition and BusyBody drunkenly stumbled into a taboo. So far, no one quite knows what happened but she and FanciesHimself, one of the junior clerks, were certainly seen canoodling on the street as they waited for a cab.

Poor BusyBody. Her head was bowed low today and she refused to talk to anybody. She's already ruined any chances of getting taken on and she's now gone and ruined her chances of bagging that rich barrister, too. Or at least one in these chambers.

Monday 26 February 2007
Day 103 (week 22): Hiring from below stairs

It's been like an episode of *Upstairs, Downstairs* today as the details of BusyBody's activities have emerged. It seems that FanciesHimself cracked under cross-examination and believed the assurance of complete confidence given by OldSmoothie. Which was foolish in the extreme. OldSmoothie immediately emailed about ten people in chambers with a word-for-word account of what FanciesHimself had told him. Obviously, this was then forwarded to the rest of chambers and is probably still rattling its way around cyberspace. Suffice it to say that BusyBody fell for FanciesHimself's not-too-subtle charms and for one beautiful evening they were a couple. As OldSmoothie's email quoted: 'You'll never believe it, OldSmoothie, she went wild. Like a switch had flipped in her head. Telling me she hated pompous barristers and that she just wanted the simple life . . . Then she started bossing me around. One instruction after another. Like an air hostess preparing you for take-off . . .'

Come the next morning, for once in his life, FanciesHimself was on the receiving end of the sort of rejection he was in the habit of inflicting on others. BusyBody apparently made it clear in no uncertain terms why things would be going no further. This has put FanciesHimself into unknown territory and it seems that he's actually claiming to be quite hurt. According to OldSmoothie, this meant that he had to go on 'a weekend bender' just to get his mind straight. Apparently HeadClerk has said that he's going to pretend it didn't even happen as to do otherwise would just be too much to contemplate. HeadofChambers is also officially turning a blind eye for similar reasons.

There was a flurry of emails around chambers following OldSmoothie's revelations. One sums up what many were saying: 'If you hire from below stairs, you can only expect below-stairs behaviour.' Reminded me of Alan Clark's wife, who once said, 'If you bed people of below-stairs class, they will go to the papers.' The email was basically a reference to BusyBody's working-class roots. Whilst a scholarship to a south London day school had led her to cover up her south London drawl, it has noticeably returned in recent weeks as she has become increasingly stressed. Some people had already started mimicking her accent and this has now turned into a full-on game show complete with clerk story to boot. So much for New Labour's New Britain.

I overheard TopFirst getting stuck in, too, to another member of chambers.

'You must have heard about BusyBody and FanciesHimself? . . . You haven't . . . Yes, it was after the party last week. Disastrous for her, really. Still, can't make a silk purse out of a pig's ear. Class will always out.'

Ouch. The cruelty not only surprised me but also left me relieved to discover that he has a weakness. Like a shark with the smell of a fellow pupil's blood in the water, his instincts took over and for the first time he showed a reckless streak.

All I have to do now is to work out how I can ultimately turn this against him.

CHAPTER 6
MARCH: THE BAIT

Hold out baits to entice the enemy.
Sun Tzu, *The Art of War*

Thursday 1 March 2007
Day 106 (week 22): Instincts

Spent some time with TheBoss today. He's been asked to write a summary of his defence for the Bar Standards Board. Hmm. The question in effect boiled down to, 'What do you have to say which can possibly mitigate your amending chambers' records and fraudulently deceiving your solicitors that it was them and not you who had missed the limitation deadline for issuing a case?' And the answer . . . 'Not a lot.' Poor Boss. If he's found guilty, he's extremely likely to get suspended for at least a year and maybe even permanently. It depends what he comes up with. My guess is that he'll plead guilty and go for stress brought on by a wicked wife who had driven him into the arms of one of his instructing solicitors. The pressure was all just too much. Yeah, right. Let's just hope there isn't a woman sitting on the tribunal, for his sake. He will also almost certainly get kicked out of chambers. But if he keeps his sentence down, he may walk back into a lesser chambers which is desperate for the rent. He's also likely to get the work back as solicitors are rarely aware of any barrister's professional misconduct history. He's even started to perk up, with the thought that a period of suspension would be a good time to sort out the divorce since any settlement would have to reflect his lack of earning capacity.

Meanwhile, BattleAxe, his sturdy instructing solicitor and mistress, has remained faithful both in her affection and, luckily for TheBoss, in the work that she continues to provide. In fact, such is the disdain of the clerks for TheBoss at the moment that she is almost his only source of work.

In the meantime, this week, TopFirst's been trying to chum up to me. The only reason I can think of is that, like me, he's realised that the other two are history and it's a straight fight between the two of us. Plus maybe he figures that in a showdown, he's not going to be second to draw. Not that I think he realises quite how the other two fell. But as OldRuin has often said, 'instinct can be a powerful thing'. 'Follow it, BabyB. It's worth a hundred times more than the limited amount of evidence which ever makes it into a courtroom.'

Friday 2 March 2007
Day 107 (week 22): Porridge

Today I was sent to jail. Only for an hour, but nonetheless . . .

It all happened when I was accompanying Teflon to Maidstone County Court, which also happens to adjoin the criminal courts and, significantly as it turned out, the cells. Halfway through the morning a mobile phone went off and Teflon immediately turned to me and glared, after which the whole courtroom did the same. I reacted by checking my mobile phone, realising it had not been me and putting it back in my pocket. Whilst everyone was staring at me, I noticed Teflon quickly take his mobile from his pocket and switch it off. All well and good, were it not for the fact that the judge continued staring at me rather than Teflon.

'Do you not know the rule against the use of mobile phones in this court?'

'Yes,' I answered. 'But . . .'

'But nothing, young man. It only makes it worse that you were aware of the rule.'

'But, it . . .'

'Young man, do not interrupt me when I am speaking. You are only making matters worse for yourself. Do I make myself clear?'

'Yes, Sir.'

'You are presumably also aware about how I deal with such an offence to the dignity of this court?'

'No, Sir.'

'Well you are about to find out. Please stand up.'

I stood.

'Young man, I hereby find you guilty of contempt of court and sentence you to one hour in the cell during which time you are to reflect on your lack of respect for the office of this court.'

He then telephoned for a security guard who immediately came to collect me and led me down to the cells, smirking as he did so. I wanted to shout out, 'It wasn't me', or as many clients call such a plea, after the song by that name, 'Taking the Shaggy'. But I was so utterly stunned by the speed of events and the scale of the escalation that I was silenced. I looked over to Teflon but he was staring at his notes. 'Save the Maidstone One!' I also wanted to shout. But again, nothing. Not even anything half witty. Do not pass go, do not collect £200. And then I was doing porridge. Time inside. No longer a free man. Not that I saw any evidence of oatmeal or gruel. I was put in a holding cell where I was able to catch up on the latest from Phillip Schofield and Fern Britton on *This Morning*.

I was collected by the security guard an hour later and led back to court and put behind Teflon. On the way, the guard told me that the judge had done this a few times. That I wasn't to worry. Just 'one of his foibles'. Some foible! When I arrived back, the judge made no further remarks. Worst of all, I never even got an apology from Teflon on the way back to chambers. Seems he'd decided to brave it out, figuring that I would decide that it wasn't in my interest to tell tales around chambers or to make any challenge to the judge's ruling. 'Strange thing for the judge to do . . . funny little incident . . .', was all that he said about it, before changing the subject. Well and truly stitched up. Though he was foolish. Even if I decide to let this one lie, he forgets quite how easy it is to cause trouble for barristers and their professional standing.

My real worry is whether I might be under an obligation to report this to the Bar Standards Board as we have to tell them of pretty much all crimes other than traffic offences. For the moment, I figured quid pro quo is that Teflon will also be wanting to keep it under his non-stick wig in case I am forced to defend myself at his expense. I have therefore decided it's better for me simply not to ask the Bar Standards Board than to risk what I might be told.

Monday 5 March 2007
Day 108 (week 23): Laughing stock

I was wrong about Teflon. He is stupider than I thought. Not only did he fail to keep quiet about the fact that I was sent to jail, he has deemed it fit to broadcast to chambers in a mass email entitled 'Pupillage just got tougher', in which he has taken the picture of me on the chambers website and added a wig along with a black-and-white-striped jailbird top and some fake prison bars. Cheap courtroom big lie tactic. If he hits me hard enough some of it will stick and any suggestion that fault lies elsewhere will fall on deaf ears. By now, he'll have deleted the records on his phone and without getting full details from his mobile company (no chance), there will be no way for me to prove it was him. So I'm left just to grin and bear it and hope the embarrassing episode passes by as quickly as possible. Needless to say it has led to many an amused look from members of chambers. Worst of all, I am the laughing stock of the library community of pupil skivers, who have been rattling their keys whenever I pass by their tables. Very funny, I must say. Forget the art of war, more like the art of making a complete prat of yourself. Something I seem to have mastered rather well.

Thankfully, at least HeadClerk called me in this afternoon and told me not to worry. He told me he'd once had to bail out one of his barristers from a local police station after a long and very boozy lunch which had ended in the barrister standing on the steps of the High Court in full court dress and suggesting an end to judicial tyranny and a call to revolution, before mooning for a TV camera which had been waiting for some big case or other to finish. OK, so they've got some perspective on the matter. Nevertheless, Teflon has damaged my chances of tenancy and he will pay. I haven't told anyone that he dropped me in it. That way, when I strike, no one will suspect other than (possibly) him, who will, of course, be unable to point the finger without at the same time incriminating himself. So far, I have set up Hotmail and Yahoo accounts in his name. I also have his home phone number, home address, date of birth and obviously his work address. Enough to be getting on with.

Identity fraud is so very easy.

Tuesday 6 March 2007
Day 109 (week 23): At what cost?

TopFirst came round to gloat today.

'So what was it like spending time in jail?' he asked with a smug grin.

'Oh, you know . . .'

'Must have been really cool. Did they give you a bowl of porridge?'

'Yeah, and black-and-white-stripey pyjamas as well. You'd just never believe it.'

'No, but seriously, did they take your fingerprints, add you to the national crime database and all that?'

'Only after they took me off the "most wanted" list, TopFirst.'

Once again, I only hope that he gets up other people's noses as much as he does mine. As I've noted before, he has a tendency to jump the gun when the smell of blood is in the air. That he becomes a gossip when it can damage a fellow pupil is not in the least unusual. That he becomes breathless with the exhilaration of it might be fatal. Vanity. Hubris, even. Enough for me for now. But planning will be essential – and, ultimately, a little luck.

After that, Worrier also came for a visit.

'Hi, BabyB. How do you like my new deadly weapon for my first day in court?'

'Sorry, I don't know what you mean.'

'My new glasses, silly.'

'Oh. But I didn't know you needed glasses,' I answered, looking at the thick-rimmed pair that now adorned her face.

'I don't,' she said in the tone of one of those dandruff ads.

'Oh.'

'Don't you get it? They're great. They're just filled with plain old glass.'

'But why?'

'Well, not only do they make me look more intelligent, kind of Lois Lane style, but they're also going to work a treat when I cross-examine and spin them around and about.' She took them off and gave me a lingering and slightly mad stare as she rabidly spun the glasses around in her left hand. I think I must have looked just a tiny bit sceptical.

'According to my life coach, taking off the glasses and spinning them around will not only intimidate the witness but also distract them from their story.'

Suddenly I had a vision of armies of Worriers entering the courts up and down the land wearing the same silly glasses and brandishing them at anyone who got in their way like a Worrier sword. But then it got worse.

'He's a genius, BabyB. I'd highly recommend him. Made me realise that my little difficulty with HeadofChambers is simply an opportunity for me to show my character by turning the situation on its head.'

Well she's certainly losing her head. Sounding more and more each day like a member of a cult. 'You know, I can now see that the reality is that pupillage is a gift,' she went on. 'I love it the way they challenge our patience. Despite first impressions, it's all a wonderful, life-enhancing experience.'

I needed to get out and I gave Claire a ring and arranged to meet her for a drink.

'I'm absolutely sick of this whole pupillage exercise,' I said after I'd told her about Worrier's latest episode.

'It's not good at all, BabyB. I think it's the time of year, you know, with court just around the corner and the pupillage game starting to hot up.'

'But it's no different to bear baiting or cock fighting. They plunge us into debt before we get here and then leave us to fight it out, Deathmatch style.'

I stopped, as I feared I had already said too much. I'd told Claire about BusyBody's YouTube episode but had stopped short of admitting my involvement. Don't get me wrong, I'd wanted to tell her more than anything. To confess. To seek forgiveness, even. Maybe also to plead in mitigation that I was driven to do it by my desperate home life and financial position. But shame had always prevented me, and even now its heavy burden held down the words I so wanted to say. She gave me a look of concern and then, somehow perhaps recognising my internal conflict, she let it go with, 'Maybe it's just a ruthlessly efficient way of working out who will make it at the Bar. After all, for all its airs and graces the courtroom is just as much of a low-down, dirty free-for-all as pupillage.'

At that moment I loved her for her patience, her gentle kindness as she held back the instincts pushing her to interrogate further. Then her look of concern returned and she added almost wistfully, 'But at what cost, BabyB? At what cost?'

Wednesday 7 March 2007
Day 110 (week 23): Revenge

Teflon was looking rather tired today. According to TopFirst, the pizza delivery company woke him up in the early hours of the last two mornings. Silly them. I hope he enjoyed his Margerita on Monday and his Hawaiian on Tuesday. Even better, I sent him an email yesterday under a false identity pretending to be a member of the public dangling a big personal injury case in front of him. I sought his preliminary advice on the merits of my case before approaching a solicitor. All I needed was a few lines telling me if I had a case or not. If he thought I did, then obviously the case would be his down the line. Maybe it was because he was tired, or maybe he's simply even more reckless than I thought, but he fell for it hook, line and sinker with the following reply:

'Dear Jane, Thank you very much for your email. Whilst strictly I am not meant to advise you directly without a solicitor, I have read what you have to say and can certainly tell you that you have a good case.'

Too right he's not allowed to advise without a solicitor. But greed can be good and it can be bad and for Teflon today, it sank him. I forwarded his email to the Bar Standards Board with the subject heading 'Professional Conduct Complaint'.

Thursday 8 March 2007
Day 111 (week 23): Introductions

I introduced Claire to my mother last night. Always a risky business as she does have a habit of embarrassing me in one way or another. Thankfully, though, there was nothing too disastrous this time round.

'I've tidied up the house, BabyB,' she said in a stage whisper loud enough for the next street to hear if they'd wanted.

'Oh, I hope you didn't do that on my behalf,' said Claire politely. 'It looks lovely, though,' she added, having more than a little nosy around our kitchen and then the living room.

'Well I hope you like cottage pie, Claire. I've been really looking forward to meeting you. BabyB's told me so much about you.'

'All good, I hope?'

'Definitely. In fact it's not just what he tells me. It's also what he doesn't tell me. You've been a good friend to him, Claire.'

'Gee, shucks. My little bit of charity for the year. Watch out for another long-suffering pupil.'

'I do worry for all you baby barristers,' replied my mother.

'I worry too,' Claire said. 'Particularly when I look at some of the older ones. Wouldn't want to turn out like them.'

'Yes, guard against that, I would. Though BabyB here doesn't seem to mind, the way he's been practising addressing the court in front of the mirror . . .'

'Yeah, thanks Mum, I don't think Claire wants to hear about . . .'

'Oh, but I do,' Claire smiled, in full-on tease mode now. 'Does he dress up for the practice sessions?'

It's often hard to tell with my mother if she's actually being funny or just literal, but this time she was smiling as she answered, which showed she already liked Claire. 'Oh, he'll come back and put on his wig and gown and start all "Yer Honouring" in front of the mirror. Very important he looks too.'

'It's what my public-speaking coach recommended,' I said, rising to the bait and blushing, despite the fact I knew they were only teasing.

'Bless his little horsehair wig,' said my mother, finishing me off completely.

'Thanks, Mum,' I commented with a wry smile.

'Well, can't have you getting above yourself, now can we? Just because you've been to Oxford and hang out with posh barristers and all that.'

'Oh, I don't think there's any risk of that,' said Claire. She smirked and added, 'Not when I can always remind him about doing his little stand-up routine in front of the mirror, anyway.'

Then she brought the conversation back to the race for tenancy. 'You're right though, it certainly isn't easy what we're having to go through.'

'I know. It's the uncertainty, I think, that's the worst. It just gnaws away at your soul,' my mother replied in a way which suggested that she understood that type of suffering more than she was letting on.

'Yes, we have to be careful that it doesn't drag us down.' Claire looked at me as she said this. Which made me wonder if she knew more than she was saying. I don't know what it was, but at that moment I suddenly experienced a feeling of supreme guilt as I sat listening to the two of them talking about me. What would they really think if they knew quite how far I was prepared to go to get that tenancy? But as soon as the thought came to me, I forced it from my mind. There was no way I could confess, since to do so would put each of them in a difficult position. Probably they would try to discourage me from going any further, but then how would that help our situation? As I was thinking this, my mother said, 'Sometimes I wish he was in touch with his father, you know, just so that he'd have him to talk to at times like these.'

'It must be hard.'

'Oh, we've got by. Just the two of us and I know it's out of loyalty to me that BabyB doesn't contact him.'

'Come on, Mum. I really don't think Claire wants to hear about the ins and outs of our family history.'

She smiled at Claire and said, 'There he goes again. Never wants to discuss it. Buries it away and hopes it will all disappear.'

But she was sensitive enough to move on and for the most part the evening seemed to go smoothly. That was until about ten thirty when my mother started moving into embarrassing mode, rushing around tidying before disappearing off to bed with a horribly unsubtle knowing look in my direction. 'Well, don't get up to anything I wouldn't,' she giggled as she left us sitting together on the sofa watching *Newsnight* on the television. I have to admit that there was an awkward moment at one point as Claire accidentally spilt her wine on the floor. Over the last few weeks we've got into the habit of playing the blinking game quite randomly, and it started up as we were both bent over clearing it up. She flicked a strand of hair back over her right ear as we both looked at each other, unblinking. I've always been aware that she was beautiful. Not just obvious beautiful like TheVamp, though in fact she is that too. Not even just intelligent beautiful though she has that in spades. She's beautiful in a way that is, above all, private. A dignified beauty that I think I've always tried to ignore in my own head so as not to be intimidated.

At that moment I found myself longing for the courage to reach over and kiss her. But the tiny distance between our heads as we continued to out-stare each other seemed like an abyss over which I dared not jump. Perhaps it was the fear of ruining a friendship with a thoughtless lunge or maybe it was just plain cowardice, but before I had time to reconsider the moment had passed. Perhaps she saw the doubt flash across my face, but no sooner had the thought been there than she broke off the stare with the words, 'You win, BabyB', and then she was on her way.

Friday 9 March 2007
Day 112 (week 23): Dr4Hire

Even in the most honourable of professions, there is the occasional bad egg, and Dr4Hire ticks all the boxes. He's a professional expert witness, an opinion for sale, and today he belonged to us. Well, to TheBoss, who had a conference with him. He's an orthopaedic surgeon whose CV boasts that he completes over 1,500 medico-legal reports each year. Which, at over £600 a pop, means he's bringing home almost £1 million a year just from this and that's on top of his two-days-a-week NHS practice. That's £600 for a copy-and-paste opinion after a ten-minute 'examination'. Luckily for him, most cases settle. Today was one of the few that slipped through the net. It was a case in which the other side were alleging that the claimant's injuries were caused not by the accident on which Dr4Hire had reported, but by a completely separate accident which happened later on. With the client not in attendance TheBoss and Dr4Hire could speak frankly. Here's how parts of the conference went:

'Why didn't you mention the second accident in your original report?'

'Because I didn't want to damage our case.'

'Yes ... I understand. Now, let's see if that can perhaps be phrased more . . . how shall I put it . . . objectively. Might it be that you considered it such a minor accident as to be irrelevant?'

'Yes, that might very well be. Quite.'

'And what do you have to say about the second accident?'

'Well ... what do you want me to say?' The top of his head was completely bald and, being offset by a little hair just below, gave the impression of a monk's tonsure. As he answered, despite the fact that the smile remained, his forehead showed a slight frown and he rubbed the top of his head, which I noticed for the first time was as shiny as I had ever seen a head to be.

'We've worked together many times, Dr4Hire. You know that I can't tell you what to say.'

'Absolutely.'

'However, it would be right to say that although he continued working after the first accident, it caused him enormous pain. I suppose you might want to comment on that.'

'Yes, that's a good idea. I suppose I might. In fact, I think that the fact that he soldiered on in such a way shows what an honest and reliable witness he is.'

'Quite so, Dr4Hire. Quite so.'

'Glad you agree. Would you like me to put that into a report?'

'Why not?'

And so it went on. Independent? Hardly. Hippocratic oath? Hypocritical oath, more like. Dr4Hire's only redeeming feature was a certain type of humour. This came out quite unexpectedly when I asked, 'What does that acronym "TUBE" stand for in the medical records?'

Dr4Hire and TheBoss looked up at each other and smirked.

'He's never been told?' asked Dr4Hire.

'Seems not,' replied TheBoss.

Dr4Hire turned to me and put on a rather amused lecturey-type expression and said, 'You know, BabyB, medical records are quite literally littered with coded acronyms. In-jokes for the medics who don't dream that those same records might one day end up in a court of law. The one you've asked about was very common in the past and stands for "Totally Unnecessary Breast Examination".'

'Oh.'

Dr4Hire warmed to his theme. 'Then there's "NFN" or "Normal For Norfolk" which refers, perhaps unfairly, to that particular county's reputation for inbreeding.' He was getting into his stride by this point, almost as if it was an issue of some academic importance. 'Curiously, the Scots apparently use Fife instead of Norfolk. Now, one that you'd hope not to see on the record of anyone you are fond of is "TF BUNDY" which means "Totally Effed But Unfortunately Not Dead Yet". Oh, and of course, there's "LOBNH" which is "Lights On But Nobody's Home".'

I can think of one for at least a couple of members of chambers with no work: 'MUPPET' or 'Mostly Unemployed Person Pretending Everything's Terrific'. But Dr4Hire hadn't finished. 'Then, of course, there's the question of how we describe the patient in medico-legal reports. If a doctor calls someone an "attractive lady" then you can guess what he was actually thinking. On the other hand "somewhat large" might be a polite way of telling the reader that she couldn't actually fit through the door.'

All of which caused me to revisit Dr4Hire's own report after the conference to see if I'd missed any of the nuances from this secret world of medical reporting. Sure enough, though I'd skipped over it previously, I realised that Dr4Hire had outdone himself. Under 'Marital status of the claimant' he had written: 'Single. Right-handed.'

Monday 12 March 2007
Day 113 (week 24): Prisoner's dilemma

TopFirst telephoned me over the weekend. Said he wanted to talk about pupillage. To keep the upper hand, I said I wasn't around but could meet on Monday. Today, therefore, we had lunch on Chancery Lane and he immediately started setting out his thoughts.

'Look, BabyB, we're all in competition for tenancy, but let's be realistic about this. Worrier and BusyBody are both now dead in the water and it's developed into a straight fight between you and me.'

'OK.' No prizes for that one, Mr Brainbox.

'Well, look, I've been thinking. You ever heard of the prisoner's dilemma?'

'Is it something to do with economics?'

'Yeah. Shows that cooperation's often better than fighting.'

'So why don't you just say so then?'

'Look, I'm getting to it, OK?'

'You're suggesting a truce. Fine by me,' I lied.

'Exactly so. Fight and we may both die. Cooperate and there's at least a small chance that maybe we'll convince them to take us both on.'

'Makes sense,' I lied again. 'You can count on me.'

This seemed to satisfy him and he went off in rather a cheery mood. What he failed to mention about his prisoner's dilemma is that if one prisoner betrays the pact he wins outright. Either he's trying to pull a fast one or, despite his intelligence, he's more naïve and foolish than even I give him credit for.

Whatever it is, there will be no cooperation.

Wednesday 14 March 2007
Day 115 (week 24): ElephantTrap

'I'm worried about BusyBody.' It was Worrier.

'You think she's having a breakdown?' I asked.

'No, I think she might be pregnant.'

'What? Why do you think that?'

'Well, I hate to say it but I heard her being sick in the women's loo the other day over at the library.'

'But that could be alcohol, food poisoning, anything . . .'

'Well, that and the fact that I spotted a pregnancy-test kit in her handbag when I went round to her room yesterday.'

'You were going through her handbag?'

'Not at all. I think I might have surprised her when I entered and it was sticking up from the bag for all to see.'

'Oh.'

'So, do you think it's after that night with FanciesHimself?'

'It could be.'

She fidgeted, obviously wanting to share further but looking uncomfortable about doing so.

'What is it?'

'I hate to be a gossip, BabyB, but I'm concerned for her and I guess I know this won't go any further.'

'Of course not,' I lied. 'What is it?'

'Well, I think she might have been seeing OldSmoothie around the same time. Just something she alluded to a few weeks ago and I didn't push it any further at the time.'

'So she might be pregnant and if she is then it could be by either FanciesHimself or OldSmoothie.'

'You can see why I'm worried for her.'

Golly.

But needs must, and with all the sympathy in the world for BusyBody, opportunities have to be grasped – and this was a prime one to set something of an elephant trap for TopFirst, who has fast become the chambers gossip. A lot of scope for him to put his foot in it if he is just fed *slightly* inaccurate information. So in our new spirit of cooperation I popped round to his room for coffee this afternoon when his pupilmaster was out.

'BusyBody's been sick the last couple of mornings, apparently.' Just to get the ball rolling.

'Heavy nights or something?'

'Don't think so, she's been off the booze for the last few weeks since . . .'

'Yes, don't blame her, the way it affects her. Couple of gins . . .'

'Yes, and she drops her briefs. You told me that one last week.'

'I mean, what was she doing with FanciesHimself of all people?'

'I know . . . Not as bad as TheBoss, though.'

'What do you mean? Her and TheBoss too? Surely not?'

'No, I'm sure you're right.'

But we'll let it ferment a little. As he's prone to do when his mind is whirring (you can almost hear it), TopFirst cleaned his glasses with his tie and straightened them up on his face. He'd be a dreadful poker player and he's definitely going to have to get rid of some of these nervous tics if he ever wants to bluff in court.

'You don't suppose she's pregnant, do you?' he mused.

'No.'

'She might be, you know.'

'Couldn't be.'

'Would explain the sickness. And I did see her looking pretty stressed today.'

'No . . . doesn't bear thinking about.'

'It could be really bad for her. Maybe she doesn't even know whether it belongs to FanciesHimself or TheBoss.'

'Wouldn't be good.'

'I'll say.'

And then . . . I'm afraid I couldn't resist, 'Old Smoothie was the one who mentioned TheBoss and BusyBody. He always knows what's going on.'

Just enough, I hope, to set TopFirst on the path to asking OldSmoothie whether BusyBody is pregnant by a barrister in chambers. Not only might OldSmoothie actually be that barrister, but he's also on the tenancy committee.

Thursday 15 March 2007
Day 116 (week 24): FoodFights

Poor Worrier. Like me she's more than a little strapped for cash this year and she was round my room today complaining. 'It's just getting too much, BabyB, even with the devilling. I tried eBay using chambers' free postage, but I ran out of things to sell within a couple of weeks. So I had to come up with something else and I heard one of my friends mentioning that they'd got food vouchers from one of the supermarkets when they'd complained about one of the products.'

'I've heard that.'

'So I tried it out myself. Drafted a letter mentioning the Supply of Goods Act just to get a little bit legal and I got a £20 voucher back by return of post. Since then I've got my letter into a standard form and I'm doing two of them each evening when I get back from chambers. First I went through the big shops and now I'm on to the manufacturers. On my calculations I've already almost got enough to feed me through the second six.'

Having sent over the first little bomb to TopFirst earlier in the week, I decided this evening that it was perhaps the right time to throw over a second. Let me put this in as nice a way as I can. TopFirst is a very clever and sometimes even witty individual (in a catty kind of way). But his academic abilities are not reflected in his dealings with the fairer sex. First, despite the fact he's engaged, he always seems to be off flirting with someone else, albeit unsuccessfully. Worse, though, are his fisherman-like tales about the ones that got away. The intellectual arrogance passes over into other spheres, it's just the results don't follow.

If I'm going to get anywhere with TopFirst I need to draw him out from where he's on safe ground. So. It was time for me to set up an email account for a new imaginary friend. Miss Virginia Haddocks-Brown, who chooses to go by the address ginnyandtonic@hotmail.co.uk. Of course she does. With this done, I then sent the following email:

From: ginnyandtonic@hotmail.co.uk
To: TopFirst
Date: 16 March 2007, 20.43

Dear TopFirst,

I am the daughter of a close friend of OldRuin, one of your colleagues in chambers. My father, Charles Haddocks-Brown, was at Oxford with him. I thought I would drop you a line after I heard mention of you in conversation the other day when OldRuin came for dinner. Basically, I am just coming to the end of my final year at university and I am trying to decide whether to change to law at the end of my degree. I know it might seem a bit presumptuous of me to write out of the blue, but the way OldRuin described you I felt sure that you wouldn't mind. I do hope that I am right. Please don't tell OldRuin, though, as I haven't yet told my parents that I'm thinking of giving up my dream of being an actress. I know that most parents would heartily approve of a career in law, but not mine.

Anyway, sorry to go on. I was wondering if you might possibly be able to spare me some time in the future to talk to me about your life at the Bar and to give some advice as to where I might go from here? I'm very occasionally down in London as I do a little bit of part-time modelling, just to make ends meet. Extremely boring but better than taking out a student loan, I guess. I can imagine how terribly busy you are with your cases and so forth but it really would be a help.

I look forward to hearing from you.

With best wishes,

Ginny Haddocks-Brown

The bait is in place and the line now fully cast.

Let's see if he bites.

Monday 19 March 2007
Day 118 (week 25): Hooked

First bite on the email arrived today from TopFirst. I don't think he will have been playing it cool by leaving it a few days. Instead, given how fastidious and generally obsessive he is, I'm sure he must have written innumerable drafts of his reply over the weekend. In the end, he settled for this one:

From: TopFirst
To: ginnyandtonic@hotmail.co.uk
Date: 19 March 2007, 10.41

Dear Ginny,

I would be very happy to give you advice and you can be assured of my utmost discretion. Consider me bound by professional confidentiality! What subject are you currently studying and at what educational establishment?

Yours sincerely,

TopFirst

BA (Hons) (Cantab), Barrister

The pompous little twerp seems to have been hooked. Now I need to reel him in. But first, I'll let him stew for a couple of days.

Meanwhile, TheBoss was in all sorts of trouble today. Around 9.30 a.m. his wife stormed into his room in chambers. If she were to have a name other than MrsBoss, it would definitely be HighMaintenance. In every way. Financially, I can now see why TheBoss is so money-obsessed as she was dripping designer from head to foot. Emotionally, she looked like someone who would never be happy with her lot. I'd certainly be pretty scared if I found myself married to her. But then again, there's none much worse than TheBoss so maybe it's better that they stick together and don't spoil two houses.

Not that there's much chance of that. From the moment she arrived today she was almost hysterical with anger. She took one look at me as she came in but rather than asking for a bit of privacy she simply ignored me and started straight on TheBoss. 'I've brought Harriet into chambers for you to look after. See how you like it.'

Harriet is their youngest child, just three years old. TheBoss looked shocked.

'What do you mean? Where is she?'

'One of the clerks is looking after her in the waiting room at the moment. It's about time you started taking responsibility.'

'But I've got a conference with a client in half an hour. How on earth do you expect me to look after her in chambers?'

'Just deal with it, you greedy, fat, philandering, lying scum.'

Well, I have to say that I couldn't have put it better myself and with those parting words she was gone. TheBoss was in all sorts of difficulties, eventually being forced to cancel his conference and take Harriet back to his house for the day.

Tuesday 20 March 2007
Day 119 (week 25): StrikeOne

A wonderful spectacle in chambers tea today. TopFirst was gossiping with OldSmoothie (they are as bad as each other) and he finally got around to whispering that BusyBody might be pregnant by a barrister in chambers and wondered if OldSmoothie had heard anything. Needless to say, OldSmoothie took this as a direct insult to himself as he was in fact that barrister, unbeknown to TopFirst. 'I will not put up with such impudence from anyone, TopFirst, never mind from a pupil. Whatever you achieved at Cambridge, never

ever forget that you are soundly at the bottom of the tree here in chambers. The very bottom as it happens.'

And with that he stormed off and a hush descended on the gathering. TopFirst didn't just look crestfallen. He looked truly mortified and skulked away after a few more minutes of awkward small talk. I followed him out, for appearance's sake wanting to offer a sympathetic ear.

'What was that about?' I asked.

'I have absolutely no idea whatsoever,' he replied.

'But what did you say to prompt such an outburst?'

'I simply mentioned BusyBody's predicament . . . Maybe he already knows and feels protective of TheBoss? Though that would be a turnaround from his recent attitude.'

'Maybe he'd just had a bad day in court.'

'Maybe. But he seemed to take it very personally . . . You don't think he's been with BusyBody too, do you?'

'No way! I mean, how could she find the time?'

'Well it would explain his reaction.'

'I guess so.'

'So that's my tenancy chances finished, anyway.'

'I hardly think so. It would be almost actionable if he held that against you. How were you possibly to know? And anyway, it's his fault, not yours.'

'You may be right, but it doesn't feel like that at the moment.'

'Remember our pact. All for one and all that. It'll turn out OK.'

'I hope so.'

Not that I meant it. He has just received a blow that will certainly wound him although in itself is unlikely to be fatal. The real significance is that it stops his momentum in chambers.

. . . And undermines his self-confidence, which is where good old Ginny comes in.

Wednesday 21 March 2007
Day 120 (week 25): Hiring a professional

Here is my rather breathless reply to TopFirst's email on Monday:

From: ginnyandtonic@hotmail.co.uk
To: TopFirst
Date: 19 March 2007, 15.28

Dear TopFirst,

I'm so grateful and pleased that you found the time to reply. You asked me what university I attend. I am at Hatfield College in Durham. Mummy didn't want me going to Oxford even though I had an offer. You might say my parents are somewhat alternative generally. Hippies who never really grew up, I guess, after Oxford in the sixties. As for my subject, I am studying English literature. I have to admit that I got a third in my first year, due mainly I think to just a teeny-weeny bit too much partying as well as travelling down to see my (now ex-) boyfriend in Cambridge. But to my own surprise I managed to pull it back last year when I got a first. Where did you go to university? What do you think of being a barrister? Sounds very grown up. Do you have to go off to court and represent murderers?

Best wishes,
Ginny

Should press a few of TopFirst's buttons . . . which is a little weird to say the least. But hey, it doesn't count if it's anonymous . . . right? Now I need to start thinking about how I'm going to get someone to play Ginny on her visit. It strikes me that it might be worth every penny to hire a professional. There could be so much scope for trouble if he falls for someone who turns out to be a prostitute, particularly if this became public knowledge. The real difficulty will be affording it. I will have to approach my bank for an extension to my professional studies loan. I'm sure they'll understand if I explain that it will help me in getting a tenancy.

Thursday 22 March 2007
Day 121 (week 25): Nobody's perfect

Today TheBoss was 'off' once again and I was left under the gentle supervision of OldRuin.

'You must be starting out on your feet next month,' he observed with an understanding smile.

'Yes, that's right.' I answered a little sheepishly, despite myself.

'Bound to be nervous, but remember that whatever happens, you'll get through. Life at the Bar is a very long journey and your first teetering steps will have very little influence on your ultimate destination. Easy to get it out of perspective.'

With that he left me to mull over his words as he returned to his papers and dictated an advice into his ancient tape recorder. It's true that it's a pretty scary prospect, particularly given that I've had less than a dozen outings at speaking in public and that includes the speech I was forced to make at my eighth birthday party. I just hope the clients don't realise that for the first few months we'll all be playing target practice with their lives and sometimes even their liberty. All the baby barristers let out into the big playground which is the court system. Running around, fighting, falling over, grazing their legs and generally misbehaving.

Later in the day, OldRuin turned to me again and mused, 'I remember my own first day in court. Vividly. Bright sunshine outside. Cherry blossom just showing. I had been married a year and Valerie desperately wanted to come and see my big day. Cheer me on, as it were. A magical time. No money, of course, but we had a glorious flat in Hammersmith which had been lent to us by my uncle whilst I got myself established. All back in the early fifties. Long time now.'

He disappeared into a world of his own before continuing. 'Yes. Bow Street Magistrates. Pickpocket, you know. Full trial. Made a hash of it really but Valerie was kind. She always was. Chap went down for two years. Guilty as sin but I should have got him off. The identification evidence was inadmissible and I let it in. Anyway, all worked out in the end. My Head of Chambers appealed the verdict and got him released. I was very ashamed that I had missed such an important point. I think my Head of Chambers must have realised that. "We're none of us perfect, OldRuin. Not even barristers." Not even barristers indeed. Not that you would believe it the way some members of this profession go on. He's long dead now, BabyB. Great man.'

After OldRuin had left for the day, I opened the drawer of my desk and took out TheBoss's magic book and looked at it a little ruefully. It fell open at the following quote: 'He who wishes to fight must first count the cost.'

There's something about being a barrister that changes the way many of them speak. Over the years the voice travels further back into the throat until by the time they're a QC like OldSmoothie it's sometimes impossible to believe that their families hadn't been Suffolk gentry since time began. Today I was following TheBusker and his opponent was one such person, though his accent was still in a state of transition. Which was a bit like his voice was breaking all over again with 'sarf Landon' occasionally breaking into his otherwise cut-glass west-London submissions. As if the accent was jumping in to expose and maybe cock a snook at pretentiousness.

It really started to go wrong for him whilst he was cross-examining a witness who was obviously proud of his south-London roots. The more the witness talked the more the accent rubbed off, popping out in a sort of yodel as posh flew south a few words at a time. This was exacerbated by contrast with TheBusker who couldn't be more down to earth with a manner which is so laid back you'd think he'd just strolled off the beach. Then there was the judge herself who today was the glamorous JudgeJewellery. As the accent started to slip more frequently backwards and forwards she suddenly turned away and started to stare intently out of the window. Then she started looking even more intently at her notebook. Her face was a kind of constipated agony and however unbelievable it was to witness, I think it was fairly obvious to us all that the expression was not one of judicial rumination or gnashing of legal teeth. No, it was nothing more than a suppression of the giggles. A fully fledged, colourfully robed bearer of high office with the judicial giggles. Or maybe the jiggles?

Meanwhile, the emails between Ginny and TopFirst are now becoming more regular. The only problem is that they're also starting to get just a little flirty, which is definitely not my bag, I can tell you. In fact let's just not go there. But this is war, and in a conflict there are different rules. Well, no rules, truth be told.

I've got an appointment with the bank next week.

Monday 26 March 2007
Day 123 (week 26): ThirdSix

Today was possibly the worst start to the week imaginable. Just as I'm making some progress in my battle with TopFirst, we are all told that for the second six months of pupillage we will be joined by a 'third six pupil'. This is basically a barrister who failed to get taken on in his own chambers and is giving it another go elsewhere. 'Git orrrf ma land' was the pretty universal reaction to the news as we got together to discuss it in the wine bar around the corner after work. However much the four of us are in competition (and don't imagine for a minute that it's only me being sneaky), there remains a kind of honour among thieves. Whatever we get up to, we're all in it together.

'I mean, it's one thing for Big Brother to bring someone new in to spice up the mix,' said BusyBody, 'but for a barristers' chambers to do it in pupillage . . . well . . .'

'It's just not cricket,' I said.

'And have you seen his CV?' said Worrier. 'It even puts TopFirst and BusyBody into the shade with his Oxford first and then his scholarship to Harvard.'

You could tell that she regretted saying it as soon as the words left her mouth and she immediately blushed and looked down at the table. 'Not that I'm trying to say that you all aren't clever. I mean. You are. Oh, you know what I mean.' She clammed up and carried on staring downwards.

Then TopFirst stepped in, trying to take control.

'Well I think we should all make sure that we watch out for each other first and foremost. It's just not fair him trying to muscle in now when he hasn't had to go through half the pupillage. Don't you all agree?'

No one really knew what to say. That's the only good thing, I guess: that it further destabilises TopFirst.

But even so, it's just not cricket at all.

Tuesday 27 March 2007
Day 124 (week 26): Hail fellow, well met

After having been warned about ThirdSix yesterday, we were all gathered together this morning and were formally introduced to him by HeadofChambers as we slowly moved from one awkward silence to another. To be fair (not something I like to make a habit of), he didn't seem as awful on first impressions as we'd all have liked to imagine. Not the geeky swot I'd been expecting. Instead, he's very much a 'hail fellow, well met' kind of hearty, rugby-playing type. Clubbable (though in mentioning that word a baseball bat springs to mind) and extremely normal. Kind of a Clark Kent-type look without the glasses, his dark hair combed very neatly and his suit perfectly fitted as if trying to take the attention away from the fact that he looks the part of a sportsman rather than a barrister. All of which makes it worse. BusyBody and Worrier only added to the problem as they stood there salivating at this attractive new addition to the pupillage game. It was as if 'ThirdSix' now referred to their scores for presentation in some ridiculous 'Pupillage on Ice' routine. Scorecards held aloft and showing all the sixes in rapturous approval. With all this charm on top of his ridiculous qualifications, I can't understand why he wasn't taken on in his previous chambers. Which is a question I need to be investigating a little more closely.

As for TopFirst, he asked Ginny for a photo of herself today which means that I need to find someone to play her, fast. The problem is, from where? I hardly want to go round ringing those numbers you see posted in phone boxes.

Wednesday 28 March 2007
Day 125 (week 26): Up to your neck

Had a meeting with TheBoss today. He's decided to go on the counter-offensive against his firm of solicitors.

'You're in up to your neck in this, you realise,' he told me. 'If I go down, you go with me.'

This was the last thing I needed to hear.

'I don't think so. All I did was to keep quiet about seeing that set of papers.'

'That may be so, BabyB, but it looks far worse than that now, and you know it. You knew everything about the plan itself and then even worse for you is that you've since officially denied knowing anything about it. You'd better start realising that soon.'

'So what do you want from me? Why would you want to implicate your pupil?'

'Well, since you're asking . . .'

He then went on to explain that he'd heard rumours about the firm of solicitors that is attacking him. He said that there's been some suggestion that they're involved in a fake claims scam but he knows nothing more. He wants me to investigate. 'You'll be my spy, BabyB.'

'I'll think about it,' was all I could reply.

Afterwards I told Claire about my predicament.

'The problem is, the more I try to get out of trouble, the worse it gets. The loan company, tampering with chambers' computer records and now this.'

'But if you do nothing, BabyB, then I've got no doubt that he'll carry out his threat, just to spite you.'

'So what do you think I should do?'

'It's not good, BabyB, but I think you're going to have to try and get something on the solicitors. I mean it's not such a bad thing to do if they really are involved in fraud. You know the other thing you need to do? Help him to fight his case more effectively.'

'How?'

'Well you could start by telling him to get his own computer expert to examine the original hard disk and challenge the other side's evidence.'

Thursday 29 March 2007
Day 126 (week 26): Cab Rank Rule

My first case in court is on Monday and the papers arrived today. It's a plea in mitigation and all I have is the charge sheet and a few lines of instructions from the solicitor, which read as follows:

Instructing Solicitors apologise for the scant nature of the paperwork. Suffice to say that the client is no average scumbag or petty thief caught with his hands in the till, though this is what he is being charged with. Counsel will see what Instructing Solicitors mean when he meets the client at court. He is hereby instructed to enter whatever plea in mitigation he sees fit.

Sounds cryptic and not a little peculiar. Out of curiosity, I Googled my client's name. The instructions then started to make a little more sense. Seems he's not only a tealeaf but a notorious football hooligan with the Chelsea Headhunters. Worse than that though was a story I stumbled across in which he had been convicted for beating up his own lawyer. Just what I needed on my first day in court. I wondered if there was any way to get out of the case on the basis of this past form.

I phoned the Bar Council anonymously to seek their guidance. No way out, they said. Cab Rank Rule. Like a black cab, if your light is on and you're available for work then you're not allowed to pick and choose between the jobs you take. Even so, why do I have to be the one doing it? And on my first day, too?

In my irritation I decided to check out this so-called Cab Rank Rule and hailed a black cab.

'Can you take me to the top of Chancery Lane, please?' I asked in my best barrister voice.

'But that's only fifty yards away, mate. Just over there. You don't need a cab.'

'Yes, but I'd like to travel in a cab.'

'Just not worth the hassle, mate. Have you seen the traffic jam I'd get caught in over there?'

'What about the Cab Rank Rule? Don't you have to take me wherever I want?'

'Oh. I get it. You're another of those barristers. I hate 'em. Always reminding me of that stupid rule. Well forget it, mate. Taking the mickey. Report me if you like.'

And with that he drove off.

Friday 30 March 2007
Day 127 (week 26): MoneyMatters

At lunch today I overheard OldSmoothie asking Worrier what area of law she wants to do when she grows up.

'Criminal defence,' the answer came back.

'Oh, that'll change,' replied OldSmoothie. 'You'll struggle to push it above two hundred doing that.'

'Two hundred pounds a day doesn't sound so bad,' replied Worrier.

'Such a lot to learn, young lady. Two hundred grand and that's in a year. It's the absolute bare minimum if you're going to maintain any sort of middle-class life in this town. And that's assuming your kids get scholarships and that you can put up with living in some grotty terrace in south London.'

Whilst we're on the subject of finance, I've returned to TheBoss and agreed to investigate the firm of solicitors. Let's call them FakeClaims&Co. I also gave him Claire's suggestion of obtaining his own computer expert evidence and he seemed genuinely grateful. With all this goodwill going my way I realised that there may have been an opportunity for assistance in funding my Ginny project against TopFirst. I therefore asked him how much he was going to pay me. He didn't flinch. '£1,500 to start investigating and £1,500 for any evidence which will implicate them,' he replied.

Should be enough to be getting on with.

CHAPTER 7
APRIL: FIRST DAYS IN COURT

To secure ourselves against defeat lies in our own
hands, but the opportunity of defeating the enemy is
provided by the enemy himself.

Sun Tzu, *The Art of War*

Monday 2 April 2007
Day 128 (week 27): BullDog

I seriously considered calling in sick over the weekend after someone whispered that this was one way of getting around the Cab Rank Rule and avoiding having to represent the less enticing of clients. The problem was, no one would have believed me and the damage I'd have done my tenancy chances would be just too much. So I trotted off to the salubrious surroundings of Brent Magistrates' Court where I met my first ever client, a short, bald, very fat man in his late forties whom I shall politely call BullDog.

'So you're my brief are ya?'

'That's right.'

He then looked at me a little more closely and came out with one of the two questions I had been dreading most.

'How old are ya, mate?'

'Twenty-seven,' I lied, my voice rising an octave in the process and my prepared spiel going out the window. This was followed by the only other question I had been fearing:

'And how long you bin practisin'?'

'Three years.' My voice going two octaves deeper as I made a fresh attempt to assert even the tiniest bit of authority. Great. My first words on my first day with my first client and they're all unadulterated big fat porky pies.

'No way, mate! You must be one of them new 'uns. It's April ain't it? My brief once told me about you lot. Look, there's another one over there.'

And so there was, all fresh-faced, shoes polished, new suit and wide-eyed earnestness. A replica of myself, in fact. I admitted my inexperience.

'So, mate. You've just lied to your client, have you? Guess you'd better get me a good result today then. Or I might just have to think about reporting you.'

Just what I needed. A client who knew his rights and who now held my professional future in his grubby, fat hands. It doesn't come much more serious than lying to clients.

'So, mate. This is the way I see it. I might have been a bad boy in the past but I ain't bin caught doin' nuffin' for two years. Goin' straight, you can say. Tell 'em about me daughter and 'ow I've been workin' the doors to look after 'er. Might've skimmed a bit off the takings that night but never done it before. Know what I mean, mate? So you tell 'em I bin lookin' after me daughter and that if they sends me inside she'd be back in care.'

When we eventually got into court, the bench was chaired by a stern-looking lady who resembled an older version of TheBoss's mistress BattleAxe.

'I see Mr BullDog has a long list of previous convictions. How does he expect to avoid a custodial sentence in these circumstances?'

I explained BullDog's sorry tale and was met with an unflinching glare from the bench.

'Anything more?' I was asked at the end of my submissions.

'Er, no, I don't think so,' I wavered, not sure if they were suggesting that I had missed something.

'Good.'

They then disappeared for a few minutes and came back and sentenced BullDog to six months in prison. Before he was taken away, he asked for a word with me, which was granted.

'Shame about that, mate. 'Fraid I'm gonna have to report you now. Real shame that. Just when you done all that work an' all to qualify.'

'I'm very sorry, Mr BullDog. I honestly did my best in there. Honestly. And I'm also really sorry I didn't tell you that I was new.'

'Too late mate. Although . . . it might be useful to have another brief on me books. Get quite a lot of me staff up on drugs charges, if ya know what I mean?'

'Well, if I can help with their defences . . .'

'Might take you up on that mate. S'pose I could 'old off on that complaint . . .' he said as he was led away. Then he turned round and gave me his best chubby little smile, '. . . for now, anyway.'

So, one appearance in court and already I'm in debt to a hard-core gangster.

On balance, not a good day.

Tuesday 3 April 2007
Day 129 (week 27): Up and coming

In my search for someone to play the fictional Ginny, TopFirst's new pen pal, I contacted one of those 'Test Your Boyfriend' agencies you see mentioned in the newspapers and went to visit them in my lunch hour. Easier, in the end, to hire someone who can later simply claim to be a prostitute than the real McCoy. As I embark upon my biggest act of war so far, I take some consolation in the fact that he professes to be happily engaged and the reality is that my plan will fail if he remains faithful.

I found this agency in an extremely seedy office in King's Cross. Whatever the estate agents say, the only thing that is 'up and coming' in that hole of a grottsville area is the kerb crawlers. I explained the email correspondence by saying that I was the brother of TopFirst's fiancée and was concerned about his fidelity. It was a tall order, but Ginny had to be posh, bright and beautiful. They said that they had a couple of star students on their books who only occasionally worked for them to pay off their student debts at the end of each academic year. I looked at their profiles and one in particular stood out due to a particularly haughty look which I think TopFirst might go for. They said they'd get back to me as to when she'd be available. I then returned to chambers and emailed TopFirst from Ginny's account with the photo of Ginny the HoneyTrap, my virtual creation, who is suddenly becoming very real.

'The car came from the offside.'

'No, the nearside.'

'Offside.' It was my first small claims hearing and I was getting my nearside and offside thoroughly mixed up. So much so that the witness was also becoming confused since he couldn't believe that a barrister could get it so wrong.

'Er, OK, maybe the offside. I don't know.'

Not the most dignified way to win the case but I'll take it any way it comes, particularly when the client saw my mistake as some sort of inspired tactical manoeuvre . . .

In the meantime, Worrier was round again reporting on BusyBody's progress.

'This is top secret, BabyB.' She had started to sound like the secret agent from *'Allo 'Allo*.

'Of course.'

'It's just I think you should probably know as she's going to need supporting through this.'

'So what have you heard?'

'I asked her outright yesterday morning. She denied it outright and went off in a storm. But then today she came round to visit and told me that I was right.'

'She's pregnant.'

'Yes. But you can't tell a soul.'

'Because of the father issue or because it'd ruin her career?'

'Both, but probably more the career thing actually. She figures no one will take her on if there's any suggestion she'll be a part-timer.'

'Sad, but possibly true.'

'Equality for all. Except barristers.'

'So what's she going to do?' I asked.

'Sit tight for the moment, though she's realistic enough to realise that it's probably not going to be long before someone guesses.'

'Is she going to continue with pupillage?'

'I think so. Kind of got a nothing-to-lose attitude now which might actually be quite healthy.'

Hmm.

'So how was your first case?' I asked, trying to change the subject.

'I'd rather forget it if I could.'

'That bad?' I asked.

'Oh BabyB, the difficulty was that I just couldn't simplify it all down. You know, sort out the wood from the trees.'

Oh, now that's one to put in my back pocket if ever there was one. Out of the mouths of babes. Poor Worrier had put her finger on the problem she had with life, not merely court hearings. Except it's not wood from trees. Worrier will show you the whole forest. There are just too many details in WorrierLand. Couldn't be more clear than that.

'The judge said I was "wittering" at one point, BabyB, and then later told me to "spit it out".'

'That sounds a bit rude to be saying in a court of law,' I said, trying to make light of it all.

'Oh BabyB, you are awful.' She perked up slightly, smiled and put on her best comedy voice. 'But I like you.'

Thursday 5 April 2007
Day 131 (week 27): FaceOff

I spent the day at court with my new pupilmistress, UpTights. Quite a contrast to TheBoss who would generally sidle up to opponents and suggest something like, 'Don't suppose we can get rid of this and be back in chambers for lunch can we?' UpTights on the other hand hardly ever settles a case at court, on the basis that 'we're paid to fight, not settle', and therefore she said to her opponent today, 'There's no point talking if you're not prepared to look at this case sensibly.'

'Well, quite,' said the other side's barrister, who today just happened to be OldSmoothie. He clearly knows her well enough to have decided the best strategy was to wind her up. He leaned in a little too close for her liking, given her 'personal space' issues, and continued, 'Though I'm sure you'll take your client's instructions if I do make an offer.'

UpTights moved away from OldSmoothie. 'A little space please . . . Of course I'd take instructions, not that that's any of your business. But I really don't think there's any point talking further.'

After this, OldSmoothie needled her further by getting a mini-pupil who was following him to come over and make an offer to UpTights.

'Can't he be bothered to come over here and tell me himself?'

'No, he can't,' the mini-pupil answered, obviously having been briefed what to say. The offer itself was ridiculously low and only served to irritate UpTights further. The mini-pupil didn't make it any better when he followed up with, 'OldSmoothie says that if you don't accept by the start of the hearing, it will be withdrawn.'

'Well, you can tell OldSmoothie . . .'

'. . . and he also said to tell you that he looks forward to hearing what your client has to say about the offer.' After which the mini-pupil turned on his heels.

It only got worse when we went into court. OldSmoothie started calling UpTights 'Mrs' rather than 'Ms' which, though she didn't correct him, clearly grated, particularly when he also started mispronouncing her name. He also took two extremely weak points at the start of the hearing which left UpTights even more jumpy and impatient than usual. It only took a couple of hours of this before UpTights finally snapped at the judge in response to a question he had asked.

'With respect, Your Honour, if you read the witness statement of the claimant you will see . . .'

'Are you suggesting that I haven't read the witness statements?'

'Of course not, Your Honour . . .'

UpTights by this point couldn't help herself and during OldSmoothie's provocative submissions she started shaking her head and muttering, 'No, no, no.' OldSmoothie stopped mid-flow and said to the judge, 'I'm sorry, Your Honour, but it seems my learned friend Mrs UpTights wishes to address you early.' At which point he sat down.

'Yes, Ms UpTights. Your opponent is right. I, too, find your constant interrupting and muttering extremely irritating and would be grateful if you would refrain from it in future.'

UpTights was speechless and simply nodded angrily at the judge before OldSmoothie stood up, smiled over at her and continued.

By which point we were done for.

Tuesday 10 April 2007
Day 132 (week 28): Horsehair and HoneyTraps

TopFirst has really done it now. I went off to court today and, relying on his advice, didn't take my wig and gown. 'You don't need them for fast-track trials these days,' he said. 'Only multi-track ones.'

That made sense to me as fast-track trials are often not much bigger than small claims hearings and you definitely don't need your robes for those. I say that because without a second thought I trotted off to court, happy not to be lumbered with the cumbersome paraphernalia that comes with this job. Two hours' travel and I was at Swindon, chatting with my clients and all ready for our hearing. Just as we were about to go into court, my opponent arrived in the waiting room all dolled up in his robes.

'You're robed, I see,' I commented, trying to sound nonchalant.

'I know. It's in fast track, so no option.'

I tried not to look too stupid in front of my client and decided that the only hope was to try and brazen it out with the judge. In we went. We all rose as the judge entered in full court dress. He nodded and we sat down.

'Mr BabyBarista. Please stand up.'

'Yes, Sir.' I rose.

'I'm afraid I can't hear you.'

'Is this better, Sir?' I spoke a little more loudly.

'No. I said I can't hear you.'

'How about this, Sir?' Just less than a shout.

'No, you don't understand. I can't hear you.'

'I'm sorry, Sir,' I shouted. 'Would it be better if I approached nearer to the bench?'

'Mr BabyBarista. You are in enough trouble without adding insolence to your problems. You seem determined not to understand what I am telling you. Without your wig and gown, I am unable to hear from you.'

'Oh. Sorry, Sir. Er . . . might you be able to hear me as to why I don't have them?' That seemed to get him and he paused and had a think. We were now definitely in Alice in Wonderland territory.

'After all,' I added, 'it would cause great injustice to my client if you were unable to hear the case today.'

'So. What is your excuse, then?'

'I'm afraid, Sir, that they were stolen on the train this morning,' I lied. Not clever, I know, but hey.

'Oh . . . well . . . that puts a different complexion on things. Please continue.'

After which no more mention was made of the issue. Now, I realise how serious it is to lie to a judge and normally I wouldn't defend it but it felt like the world had gone mad and no one seemed to be even questioning it. I was furious with TopFirst by the time I arrived back into chambers. A smug 'Oh, sorry, didn't realise' was all I got from him. Makes me more determined to implement my plan. Got on the phone to Ginny's agency and booked her for next Monday. I then emailed TopFirst from Ginny's account suggesting a meeting in a bar in Covent Garden. Within half an hour, TopFirst had emailed back saying, 'Great. Very much look forward finally to meeting you. By the way, liked your photo. Here's one to help identify me on Monday ;-)'

Well, I had to laugh. TopFirst may be many things, but a lager-drinking sportsman he is not. In fact this couldn't be further from what he is. Yet, there he was, with probably the only pint of lager he's ever sipped in his life held aloft with one hand, whilst the other clutched a rugby ball. And to cap it, a huge pair of shades, Blues Brothers style. What he was thinking by sending that photo I just don't know. It was neither cool nor in any way recognisable as him. It'll be interesting to see what he turns up wearing on Monday.

Meanwhile, Worrier was back in my room whispering about BusyBody. 'She's been spending quite some time with ThirdSix, who's a very good listener, apparently. Can't think of a more attractive shoulder to cry on, I'd say.' By her look you could tell that Worrier also has something of a soft spot for him.

'How very gallant,' I replied.

'Well, quite,' said Worrier, not picking up the sarcasm of my last comment.

Wednesday 11 April 2007
Day 133 (week 28): UpTights's briefs

One thing I miss about TheBoss now that I'm forced to hang around with UpTights and her lofty attitude is that he may be a low-down, snivelling coward, but at least he is honest in one significant respect. He accepts he is driven by greed. Plain and simple. UpTights, on the other hand, can mention Atticus Finch with no sense of irony as she settles into defending an insurance company against a father of four who's lost both legs. At least she does seem to be softening, anyway. Mid-afternoon yesterday and she blessed me with the first smile of my pupillage when I mentioned the story of my mum coming into chambers and embarrassing me with a cake. There might even be a human being lurking beneath that stretched exterior.

Meanwhile, TopFirst is looking smugger than ever. He's made it known around chambers that I went to court without my robes and he knows full well that I won't drop him in it as it would look even worse that I had relied on the word of a fellow pupil rather than finding out for myself. Even the clerks have been teasing me with 'Don't forget your suit for court tomorrow, Sir.' I hope at least that TopFirst's hubris will only make him more blind when it comes to meeting Ginny on Monday.

Thursday 12 April 2007
Day 134 (week 28): Phone manner

On returning from court today, I had the pleasure of overhearing UpTights deal with a call centre operative. I'm sure you can imagine. It was a call to her telephone-banking service which she had on loudspeaker, presumably so that she could successfully 'multitask', as she likes to call it. She'd obviously been on the phone for a while by the time I arrived.

'Yes, I realise it's late but all I want you to do is to transfer some money for me from one account to another.'

'Well you can do that with internet banking these days, madam.'

'Look, young man, if I had wanted to use the internet, I would have used the internet. Now please take my account number.'

'Actually madam, I am not authorised to deal with financial transactions.'

'Well are you a bank or a bunch of jokers?'

'I am neither, madam. I am simply doing my job. I will put you through to someone in our problem resolution division.'

'I am not a problem. All I want to do is to transfer some money. It is you who is the problem.'

'And because you have a problem with me I am obliged to put you through to that department. Please hold.'

If she were a cartoon character (which in many ways she sometimes seems to be), steam would by now have been coming out of her ears, her hair would have been standing completely on end and she would be looking more Cruella De Vil than ever before.

'No. No. I don't want to be . . .'

'Hello, I am sorry for the delay . . .'

'Ah good. So am I. Now listen to me, young lady . . .'

'. . . My name is Andrea, the automated telephone system for problem resolution and I will be taking you through the next procedure . . .'

'No. No. No. I want a human being. Bring me back a human being.'

'. . . Press one if you have a problem with internet banking . . . Press two if you have a problem with one of our operatives . . .'

By this point UpTights had hold of the phone and was pressing almost all of the buttons furiously. Eventually it elicited a result and we heard the following, '. . . Please hold whilst you are transferred to an operator . . .' followed by some annoying music and then, '. . . We apologise for the delay. We very much appreciate your custom and are very sorry for any inconvenience . . .'

Then after about another thirty seconds of UpTights winding herself up even more tightly than might be thought humanly possible, a female voice came out of the ether, 'Hello madam. Sorry for the delay. How can I help?'

'Ah, finally. I want to transfer some money.'

She had started to sound like the guy who sings that song 'Two Pints of Lager and a Packet of Crisps', where he starts screaming, 'I've got all the right money and everything' and continues 'Why won't somebody serve me?!'

'Well, madam. We are the problem resolution department. You need money transfers for that. What has the problem been, exactly?'

As if to show her exactly what the problem had been she answered, 'Look. I've had enough of this nonsense. Just put me through to someone with an ounce of authority.'

'Certainly, madam. Please hold while I . . .'

'No. Don't cut me off. Just give me the direct number I can call.'

'Certainly, madam. Please hold while I transfer you to the person who . . .'

'No! Look. Please just pass the phone over to your manager.'

'Please hold, madam . . .'

'What on earth is this world coming to, BabyB? You can't even pass wind without getting put on hold by some dozy little worker who's too busy polishing her nails to actually do any work.'

'Hello, madam, I've been told that you want to transfer some money from one account to another?'

'Finally,' she screeched. 'Finally, I have found the one sane person in the whole organisation. Yes, that is exactly what I want to do. Immediately.'

'Well madam, I am sorry to tell you that our computers are down and you will have to call back later, I am afraid.'

It was at this point that she completely lost it and threw the phone across the room and stormed out, screaming, 'I need a drink.'

Which for a strict teetotaller was an interesting reaction.

Friday 13 April 2007
Day 135 (week 28): FakeClaims&Co

Claire and I did some research into FakeClaims&Co last night. Found a bit written about them in a number of comments on an anonymous blog. It appeared to be written by a disgruntled employee. The suggestion is that FakeClaims were in some way connected to an accident management firm which fabricates personal injury cases in the south-east. It seems they get their 'clients' to drive in front of another car and then stop suddenly. Rear-end shunts are near impossible to defend and it means that insurers often have little option but to pay up for the whiplash claims that follow. Claims not only for the driver but generally for three or four 'phantom' passengers who suddenly appear when a claim is entered. I left a message on the blog from an anonymous email account saying that I was a journalist investigating car scams and would be very interested to chat. With a bit more evidence, it might even be enough to encourage FakeClaims to withdraw their complaint against TheBoss.

Monday 16 April 2007
Day 136 (week 29): Not a penny more

As I write this, TopFirst is on his way to meet Ginny for a drink in Covent Garden. All going to plan as it stands and I shall report tomorrow on the outcome. As for today, Old Smoothie popped round to UpTights's room. If it doesn't rain, it pours, and it appears that they have yet another case listed against each other next week and he wanted to try and settle it early. OldSmoothie is representing a mother who was knocked over by a drunk driver and seriously injured.

'The clerks tell me that I will be having the pleasure of your company once again next week,' said OldSmoothie.

'So it seems,' she replied curtly.

'Yes, well. As you might imagine, my client's not in a good way and I'm keen to settle this if we can and avoid her having to go through the ordeal of a court hearing.'

'I'm sure you are, OldSmoothie. On a no-win, no-fee, by any chance?'

'Still your old charming self, UpTights, I see. Anyway, my instructions said you might have an offer for me. No point playing games with each other at our age. What's your bottom line?'

'Touché, OldSmoothie. At least you'll always be the elder.'

'So what can you come up with? We've already said we'd go away for £200,000.'

'Fair enough, OldSmoothie. You're right. Cutting to the chase, the very maximum we'll go up to is £120,000 and not a penny more. No games, remember, so that's the absolute tops. Not a single penny more. Understood? Not a penny.'

'Understood. Not a penny. I'll go and take instructions.'

OldSmoothie left and then returned about an hour later.

'Well, UpTights. I've taken instructions on your offer and it is rejected. However, we do have a counter-offer of £120,000 and . . .' he paused, for effect, '. . . one penny.' He smirked directly at her.

'I hope you're joking. I don't believe that's what your client would have said.'

'Funny sense of humour, my client.'

'As if. Completely out of order. What if I say no and your client loses the offer?'

'But you won't, UpTights. I know you too well. You wouldn't want to lose face with your beloved cash cow of an insurance company over one penny. Now, off you go and take instructions if you really need to. You might want to get back by 3 p.m. as my solicitors will start preparing the trial bundle and incurring even more costs after that. Cheerio!'

As he waltzed out, UpTights was fuming, as you might imagine. She didn't say a word to me even though she was walking round the room at a hundred miles an hour, fists clenched and muttering curses under her breath which would have had her burned as a witch in days gone by.

At one minute to three, she dialled the number and fired into the phone, 'Agreed, OldSmoothie. Never, ever do that to me again,' before slamming it back down.

Tuesday 17 April 2007
Day 137 (week 29): First meeting

Last night TopFirst finally met Ginny the HoneyTrap. All recorded on digital video camera discreetly placed in her handbag. Her instructions were to play it quite cool but at the same time hint that she is available and even that she might find him attractive. Not that Ginny needed any help with these matters.

Today she uploaded the video onto a secure site and I've just had a chance to watch it. Not great quality, to be honest, but it shows that she certainly did the job. Though it seems from what I saw that the job had pretty much been done even before she arrived, as he was flirting from the off. Pretty swanky bar they were at too. I shudder to think what the bill would have been for the evening but hey, not me paying, so who cares? The video starts with Ginny introducing the place to the camera and then hiding it away. You don't actually see TopFirst walk through the door but you hear him arrive and there's an awkward, 'Ginny?'

'Yes. TopFirst?'

'Definitely. Nice to meet you, babe.'

Babe? What planet is he on? Babe is possibly the very last word that would usually come from TopFirst's lips, which showed that he was already feeling awkward, I guess.

'And you too.'

'You look as stunning as I imagined you would.'

'Thank you very much. You look very casual for a barrister.'

As he sat down you could see on the video that he was wearing chinos and a Ralph Lauren polo shirt with a pair of Ray-Bans perched on top of his head.

'Yeah. You know how it is. They let me get away with it, basically. Kind of nice that they give me extra little privileges.'

'Why's that?'

'Oh. Who knows. They're probably pretty keen to take me on so maybe they give me a little extra leeway.'

I mean. Come on. What a pathetic thing to lie about.

'Anyway, let's get some champagne.' He clicked his fingers at a waiter.

'Sounds lovely.'

Two bottles later and they were staggering around as they moved on to a swanky restaurant nearby. 'They know me there and so we'll get a little peace and quiet.'

Which didn't turn out to be quite true. They arrived only to discover that not only was he not known, but they didn't even have a record of his booking. Then the cool façade came tumbling down and he ended up begging.

'But I came here a couple of months ago with my parents. You said that I should give you a ring if I ever needed to book a table.'

'I'm sure I did, Sir, but that does not make us friends and simply leaving a phone message for me is not the way that you go about making a booking, I'm afraid.'

'But, but . . .'

He was obviously at a loss and tailed off with, '. . . but, please. I'm on a date and well, you know. Please . . .'

'I am sorry, Sir, but we are fully booked for the next month. I suggest you try the local pasta place around the corner.'

Which eventually they did, but not before TopFirst had turned nasty.

'Do you know who I am?'

'Yes, I do. You've already told me that you are TopFirst and a barrister. I am very pleased for you.'

'Well let me speak to the manager.'

'I am the manager.'

'Well let me speak to your boss.'

'My boss lives in the Bahamas. I really don't think he wants to be disturbed by you.'

'Well . . . well . . . I will complain, I promise.'

'I am sure you will, Mr TopFirst. I look forward to it. Goodbye now.'

When they finally settled into the next restaurant, Ginny led TopFirst into a bit of FiancéeDenial.

'So, how come a clever, handsome guy like you doesn't have a girlfriend?' (Nice leading question – might even make a good barrister.)

'Ah . . . you know how it is. Still waiting for the right girl to come along and all that.'

No action other than a bit of hand holding across the table but it's all still damning enough. There's also plenty of time for round two and in that respect Ginny did me proud, leaving him salivating on the street as she hopped into a cab.

'Wonderful to meet you Ginny. Would be great to see you next time you're in London.'

I'll keep him on the boil through email over the next few weeks and then hit him with the big one on the next occasion.

Wednesday 18 April 2007
Day 138 (week 29): Obsessions

One of the clerks brought a big box up to UpTights's room today and she became unusually animated. As she started opening it she even went about explaining to me what it was. 'Pomegranate tea, BabyB! Antioxidants! They're the answer to everything. Absolutely everything!'

I decided this was a good moment to say I needed to do some research in the library. Which was where I bumped into BusyBody telling Worrier all about her advocacy coach.

'Hi, BabyB,' said Worrier. 'BusyBody is telling me how she's being taught to be more assertive.'

Hmm, that sounds a bit like teaching Hannibal Lecter to cook. BusyBody then asserted herself. 'Yes, it's definitely working, BabyB. You've got to stand up to the judge. Tell him what you think. You know, they can smell weakness, so you've got to be in there and answering back before they get a chance to pin you down. Why not try it in your next case and see how it goes.'

Not that I've been submissive so far, but maybe I will try upping the ante. Just to see. Come the afternoon, my mind was on to other things after I saw a curious little incident: BusyBody and ThirdSix emerging from the usually deserted storeroom on the top floor of chambers.

Thursday 19 April 2007
Day 139 (week 29): The system

Off to court in Reading today and I thought I'd put BusyBody's advice to the test.

'Mr BabyBarista. I've had a look at the papers and am struggling to understand your case.'

'Well, Sir, that may indeed be so.'

'Yes, Mr BabyBarista, it is so. Would you like to enlighten me as to what you intend to argue?'

'All in good time, Sir, all in good time.'

'No, Mr BabyBarista, you will do so now or not at all.'

'No I won't.'

'Yes you will.'

'No I won't.'

'Mr BabyBarista. Despite all appearances this is not a pantomime. Either you will tell me your case now or I will strike it out and commit you for contempt.'

Which brought to an abrupt end my career in assertiveness. 'Er, yes, Sir. Of course, Sir,' I said, my voice slightly raised and I am ashamed to say, my cheeks feeling flushed. I had started to sound like the Kevin and Perry sketch where they speak to each other's parents and suddenly put their best goody-goody voice on, despite themselves. My opponent looked particularly smug as I backed down and I just hope he doesn't send sniping remarks back to chambers.

Once back from court, I bumped into ThirdSix outside the clerks' room. He was looking slightly dishevelled.

'How's it going in court, BabyB?' He's a big guy and can therefore carry off the odd crease a little more easily, but my guess is that he had been out on a big one after rugby practice last night.

'Oh, not bad for a beginner.'

'Pretty nerve-racking, isn't it? I know I've already been on my feet for six months but I still get nervous, I have to say.'

The admission was disarming in its honesty.

'It's certainly not easy trying to keep it all together.'

'Then there's the whole pupillage thing on top. I'm sorry to have added to your woes by increasing the numbers. Last thing I wanted, actually, but there you go. That was the problem at my last set of chambers. Too many people for too few places and I just got pushed aside in the stampede.'

Well, despite the fact I'd like to see a repeat of that performance this time around, I'm afraid to say that all in all I found him extremely charming and likeable. Which is annoying. But, hey. No one said pupillage was going to be easy and anything I do . . . well, it's just not personal, that's all. I mean, it never is in war and if the system encourages a fight, that's what it'll get. So don't blame me if anyone gets hurt. That's all I say. Change that system, reward cooperation and I'm an all-round nice guy. On the team. All for one and all that.

Until then, it's a fight.

Monday 23 April 2007
Day 141 (week 30): Gleaning

'It wasn't stealing, Madam.' It was TheBusker during his closing speech at Minehead Magistrates' Court. He had been hired at great expense by a local solicitor to come down to the West Country to get his son off a charge of scrumping apples. TheBusker had suggested I tag along as I might find it interesting.

'What do you mean it wasn't stealing? This boy stole twenty-five apples out of Mrs Frobisher's orchard. If that's not stealing, what is?'

'Madam, when *Peter Rabbit* was read to you as a child, were you on the side of Peter as he took the carrots from the field or that of Mr McGregor?'

'Yes but he was a fictional character, it's hardly the same.'

'But it's the same as those times you have been blackberrying with your family and strayed off a public footpath and into a farmer's field or watched as your child ran across that field and delighted in collecting mushrooms for the evening meal.'

'Mr Busker, however sympathetic you make your case sound, how can you say that climbing into an orchard and running off with all those apples isn't stealing?'

'Madam, it's because when you take something that it's customary for everyone to take at one time or another it isn't stealing as you don't have the necessary dishonest intent.'

'So what is it then, Mr Busker? Enlighten me.'

'Madam, the correct word is gleaning. Peter gleaned the carrots, you gleaned the blackberries, your children gleaned the mushrooms and yes, my client gleaned the apples. Without the element of dishonesty, none of these people, Madam, are thieves and thankfully the common law of England does not yet recognise a crime of gleaning.'

With which the magistrate dismissed the charges and the solicitor's son walked free.

Tuesday 24 April 2007
Day 142 (week 30): Cloak and dagger

I went to see a mole from FakeClaims&Co today. I'd found this whistle-blower in the blogosphere and we'd corresponded by email last week. Eventually we set up lunch for today in Canary Wharf. Claire had agreed to come along and support me by secretly taking video footage from nearby. We arrived separately about five minutes early. Claire took a seat in a café and I walked around trying not to look too suspicious, which was a little difficult given that I had donned my best disguise of jeans, baseball cap and shades for the day. OK, it might have looked odd but the last thing I want is him recognising me if I'm dragged into TheBoss's disciplinary hearing in the future. We'd both agreed to be carrying something yellow, which proved to have been a particularly silly idea since the café we were to meet in was right next door to a fruit stall selling copious amounts of bananas to passers-by. We eventually found each other owing to the fact that our mutual efforts to blend in had failed so abysmally as to turn us into a very obvious odd couple. He was trying to dress as a foreign student with brightly coloured trousers and T-shirt. This was in addition to a ridiculously large pair of 1970s style shades and a gaudy yellow rucksack. Hardly John le Carré, but the future of the world wasn't exactly at stake either.

'Hello, you must be John,' I said and went to shake his hand.

'Oh, thank goodness. I thought it must be you,' he replied. 'Yes, I am he, and you must be Harold.'

'That's right.'

I handed him the forged identification for a national newspaper journalist which Claire had downloaded off the internet for £25. He examined it as though it were some kind of fake currency, rubbing it between his forefinger and thumb, holding it up to the light and then going so far as to smell it. I was starting to get a little worried, particularly as there was no watermark and definitely no smell.

'That all appears satisfactory to me,' he eventually said, somewhat pompously. 'By the way, is that how you usually dress for work?' He pointed at my cap and shades.

'Only when I'm undercover. You never know who's around. After all these years I have so many different groups that I've brought down wanting my scalp that I just can't be too careful.'

'That makes sense,' he replied in a way which suggested that he knew about these sorts of things. Which he obviously didn't. Actually, it would have been pretty obvious to anyone else that neither of us did.

'So what do you have for me?'

He had visibly relaxed after checking the ID and now he got down to business. 'Well, I've put it all on this USB memory stick. Have a look through and then tell me what you think. Should be enough to sink 'em, I'd say.'

I decided that it was probably better at this stage to say very little and so I simply thanked him very much, after which he left me with it and sloped off saying, 'If you have any questions about it, just email me. All I want is to see 'em go down and for justice to be done. Oh, and a bit of bad press against them wouldn't do my claim for unfair dismissal any harm either.' You just can't get away from litigation.

Well, as you might imagine, I was quite enjoying the role of undercover reporter and Claire seemed quite animated after her role as undercover camerawoman. We sloped off to a different café and opened my laptop to check through the material I'd been given. Unfortunately, it wasn't quite the bombshell he'd suggested – and certainly not enough to nail FakeClaims. Thankfully, though, it has provided me with a couple of leads which I'll be able to follow up in the next few weeks. Best of all is the name and address of the accident management company that it is alleged FakeClaims are in bed with.

'Maybe you'll just have to go and try a fake claim for yourself,' said Claire mischievously.

Wednesday 25 April 2007
Day 143 (week 30): Flirtometer

Today I was against TheVamp whom I've continued to admire from a distance since our tryst just before Christmas. Her flirtometer was on high for today's hearing. Her highlighted blonde hair was down on her shoulders and perfectly ruffled, her jacket was what one might describe as well-fitted and her skirt came just above the knee. Those details in themselves would not perhaps have drawn any attention, but coupled with the look she had in her eye, oh and the top two buttons of her shirt lying open, there was more than enough to distract me from the job at hand.

'So, BabyB, how have your first few days in court been? I bet you've been socking it to your opponents.'

'Er, they've been OK. Yeah.' I admit that I actually felt slightly tongue-tied. This only got worse as she moved closer. No personal space issues on her part.

'Oh, come on, BabyB. I've seen you charming people around chambers. I bet you've been doing just the same at court. Masterful, I imagine.' She leaned in. 'Let's take a look at your,' she paused, 'draft directions.'

'Er. Well. Here's the ones prepared by my solicitors. What do you, er, think?' I mumbled and blushed at the same time.

'They look fine to me,' she said. 'Although I'd say your application for an extension was a little, er, premature if you ask me. But, hey, if that's how you want it, then I'm happy to oblige. The only thing I'd suggest is that we use my draft. Pretty much says the same thing, but written more clearly, if you know what I mean.' She smiled knowingly and I tried to reciprocate as if I did know what she meant, which I didn't. 'It's barristers who should always draft the directions, BabyB. Always much clearer that way.'

Well, I couldn't see anything wrong with my solicitors' directions at all, but I didn't have a problem using TheVamp's either, particularly in the flustered state she'd now put me. 'OK. Er. Cool. I'll have a read.' Which I did and then went back to her. 'Er. Just a couple of small things. Hope you don't, er, mind.'

'Why would I mind, BabyB? You just say what you're thinking.' She again leaned in close, making it impossible to do as she was suggesting, given that my thoughts had strayed somewhat from the directions.

'Er. Well.' I tried to regain a little composure. 'Er. Well. I was just thinking. Er . . .' There it was again, my thoughts straying. 'Er.' Must concentrate. 'Er, anyway, you seem to be wanting to call two new witnesses and, er, the trial is only a few weeks away.'

'Oh. You know how it is, BabyB. Only just tracked them down. Judges always let them in anyway.'

Well my instructions were to do what I thought best on the day and I wasn't in any fit state to be trying to argue small points in front of the judge, so I relented. My only worry is how I'm going to get through the trial if she continues to put the pressure on next time round. Again, it's just not cricket. That's what I say. Not cricket at all.

When I arrived back into chambers, I bumped into TheBoss just near the clerks' room. He looked in a terrible state and I guessed that the pressure from both home and work was getting to him.

'How are you?' I asked politely.

'Not good, BabyB, to be honest. The wife's decided she wants to try and stop access to my kids altogether now.'

'But she can't do that.'

'She knows and I know that she can't do that. But she can certainly pick a fight over it for the next six months and make life even more difficult than it already is.'

'I'm sorry to hear that.'

I actually meant it, though for the children's sake, not his. It's the only time I haven't seen him positively glowering with arrogance and he actually looked like he was grateful for the sympathy in a strange sort of way. Which makes me worry about him more than ever as he is not merely in some difficulties but at risk of losing it completely. Certainly not someone you'd choose to tie your fate to.

Thursday 26 April 2007
Day 144 (week 30): SetUp

After court today, I called chambers and asked to speak to FanciesHimself. I told him I wanted to meet him out of chambers and suggested a nearby café, explaining only that, 'It's about BusyBody'. Given that he's been raging in the last few weeks about how he was tossed aside by her, I thought he might be interested to hear what I had discovered about the chambers storeroom.

When he arrived at the café, he looked a little nervous. He's got a likely look with his slim-fitting suit, shortish hair topped with a quiff and sideburns, and I saw that he was just putting a cigarette out in the street before he entered the café.

'Look,' I said, 'I really don't want to interfere but I've been told something by Worrier that I thought you should know. However, I want you to promise me that my involvement will go no further.'

'You and me, BabyBarista. We're straightforward people. That sounds fair enough as far as I'm concerned. What is it you want to tell me?'

'Well, apparently there's something going on between ThirdSix and Busybody.'

His mouth dropped. 'There's just no end to it, is there?' he said.

'It's worse than that, I'm afraid.'

'How?'

'They're doing it in chambers itself. Kind of rubbing your nose in it, I'd say.'

'What do you mean "in chambers", exactly?'

'The old storeroom at the top of chambers.'

'Oh.' His look turned from upset to angry. 'The storeroom? I was the one who introduced her to that room. Of all the places. She certainly has a cheek.'

'Well, I just thought you should know, that's all.'

'But what do you think I can do about it?'

Well, it's funny he should ask. I'd been waiting for that question.

'Oh, I don't know, really. Up to you. Probably not much.'

'But it's so offensive to be at it so blatantly.'

I smiled at him and said in a completely jokey tone, 'Well I guess you could broadcast it to chambers tea.'

'What do you mean?'

'No, I'm joking.'

'How would you do that?'

'It was a joke. No, you wouldn't want to do that. Though I admit it would be funny. The phone in there is always on loudspeaker.'

'You don't suppose I could get ThirdSix's phone to dial that number do you?'

'No. Terrible idea. It'd cause all sorts of trouble.'

'Well, thanks for the information, BabyB. I owe you one.'

Oh, my pleasure indeed.

Friday 27 April 2007
Day 145 (week 30): Golf day

Today was golf day. Nothing else to call it. Glorious sunshine and absolutely no wind and the golfers were twitching. First I overheard my opponent on the train on the way to court on the telephone to one of his friends.

'I know, mate, perfect conditions. Tell me about it. Look, I've got a case at the moment but definitely count me in. I'm gonna have a chat with my opponent and see if I can't get rid of it at the door of court . . . Yeah, Yeah, I know. Another "golf settlement". Good thing no one's done a graph comparing my settlement days to golfing conditions.'

Now you'd think that this would give me the upper hand in court and in normal circumstances it would. Were it not for the fact that the judge called us into his chambers as soon as we arrived.

'Gentlemen. I've been looking at the papers in this case and I am extremely unhappy that this has come anywhere near a courtroom. It should have settled years ago, a car case like this, one side saying one thing, the other side saying another. Looks like a straightforward fifty-fifty case to me. But whatever your own views, let me tell you now that unless this case settles, I shall seriously be considering wasted costs orders against the lawyers after this case has finished for encouraging litigation where none was needed.'

Now if ever there was a code red to kick lawyers into doing what the judge wanted it would be the threat of wasted costs against them personally. Threaten the clients and the amount of damages and it was water off a duck's back. By tomorrow they'd be on to the next one. Like some croupier in a big casino, all they were doing was administering other people's bets. Judges know this better than anyone and so when they really want something they threaten to hit the lawyers where it hurts, which is one place and one place only. Their own pockets.

'And don't start getting into arguing about which side I might blame for this litigation. In my view you're both as bad as each other. In fact, I'm even minded to send these papers off to be reviewed by the disciplinary committees of the Law Society and the Bar Council,' he added just for good measure.

Actually, there's another hole in a lawyer's thick hide and that's the fear of being hauled in front of his professional body. This judge had hit a double whammy with his first two blows. He wanted to get rid of this case, and fast. After we left the court, I went to my client and explained that the judge was encouraging us to settle at fifty-fifty. Actually, this would be an excellent result for us as I'd been expecting to lose the case outright on the evidence.

'But I've been fighting this for over four years now and they've never made any offers in the past. Why would they do so now?'

I could hardly tell him that it was because my opponent was desperate to get to the golf course and the judge was in a bad mood. It doesn't exactly inspire faith in the system of justice.

'Well, being at court often focuses people's minds on the potential weaknesses in their own cases, I guess. Let's see what they come back with.' We both then looked over at my opponent on the other side of the room, who was having a heated discussion with his own client, who looked very unhappy. At one point the client stormed off in a rage only for my opponent to follow him and continue the conversation. Eventually, I saw the client nodding reluctantly and then my opponent came over and asked if he could have a word with me. 'Been a bit of a difficult one as you can imagine but I've eventually brought him around. Told him that he could be going home with nothing and a horrendous costs order against him personally if he wasn't careful.'

Which just wasn't true, but, hey, not my business.

'So, I eventually convinced him of the merits of the judge's suggestion. I think we can settle on fifty-fifty.'

Now this was an absolute gift for my client and I really should have grabbed the offer immediately. However, I felt that his desire to play golf might squeeze just a little bit more.

'Look, I know you've got the stronger case but my client's here after four years of worry and he's ready to have his day in court. I've talked to him about settlement but the most that he'll come down to is sixty-forty in his favour.'

'BabyBarista, are you mad?' He appeared quite angry at my response, no doubt due to the fact that he could see his golf game receding into the distance.

'Sorry. Sixty-forty or we have a day in front of the judge.'

He looked at me for a while, weighing up whether I was bluffing or not. I suddenly realised that after weeks of refining my staring skills with Claire, this was my moment for putting them to work. After I'd said my bit, I looked him straight in the eye and held my gaze . . . and held it still. Not a blink to be seen, although my eyes were starting to water. Eventually he cracked and blinked first. 'I'll take instructions,' he said and went back to his client.

Ten minutes later and a sixty-forty settlement was ours and my opponent whisked us back in front of the judge.

'Excellent, gentlemen. What an eminently sensible course of action, if I may say so.' He then took a look at his watch. 'And conveniently enough, should be just enough time to make the first tee after lunch.'

It was only at that point that I suddenly took in the various memorabilia which were spread around his room. Not for him the pictures of old judges. Instead, it was old cartoons of golfers and the odd photo and trophy. Suddenly it all became clear.

CHAPTER 8

MAY: FAKECLAIM

Spies cannot be usefully employed without a certain intuitive sagacity.

Sun Tzu, *The Art of War*

Tuesday 1 May 2007
Day 147 (week 31): Fatal flaws

TopFirst tried to play it cool with Ginny last week by only emailing every other day. This week he's become a little more needy and I've had to put him in his place in the replies I've been writing in her name. I've told him she'll be back in London in a few weeks and that in the meantime she has her head down studying for her exams. This is all driving TopFirst mad as he wants to see her again as soon as possible. In itself this is good as it's distracting him from pupillage. It's just that I don't want to push it too far as it may end up backfiring. For example, he threatened to come and visit Ginny in Durham the other day. Obviously I scotched that thought pretty fast, but nevertheless . . .

In the meantime, ThirdSix seems to be going from strength to strength. I even overheard UpTights singing his praises the other day. My own pupilmistress. Bit too close to home there. I still have no idea how I'm going to do anything about it either. He has no obvious character flaws that I can exploit. Worrier's insecurity was clear even to TheBoss. As for BusyBody, it was easy to get people to believe that she'd been an over-exuberant, well, busybody. Even TopFirst has two chinks in his armour: vanity and women. But as for ThirdSix, he's almost too perfect a pupil to be real. The only thing I can think of so far is that he knows it. Over-confidence.

How I use even this limited insight for the moment escapes me.

Wednesday 2 May 2007
Day 148 (week 31): Bovvered

I was against TheCreep today who decided that he'd have a go
at bullying me into submission before we even got into court. He
didn't just badger me or go on a little bit. He positively harangued
me about the strength of my case throughout the whole journey
to Ipswich, which proved to be a long one. 'Your case is obviously
hopeless. Can't even understand why your instructing solicitor has
brought it.'

Eventually I decided to go for a Busker-type response. Except
it didn't quite come out right. 'Er . . .' I paused, trying to think of
what TheBusker might say. It didn't come and all that eventually
escaped from my lips was a very unbecoming, '. . . bovvered,' . . .
which was more Catherine Tate than TheBusker. But it had the
unintended merit of getting up TheCreep's nose.

'If that's all you can say you're obviously no better than
your instructing solicitor. Haven't you even read our witness
statement?'

Well, when a strategy appears to be working, why change
course?

'Bovvered.' I was starting to enjoy myself.

'Can you even explain why you didn't accept our offer? Seems
ridiculous that we're here. I have far more important matters to be
getting on with.'

Oh, I was waiting for that. The self-important excuse for being
seen in the small claims court. Yeah, right. I took a deep breath. I
was beginning to get into my stride. 'Er . . .' I paused for dramatic
effect, '. . . bovvered.'

'Are you sure you're best representing your client's interests?'

Eventually I put it to him straight:

'Liability. Quantum. Generals. Specials. Interest . . .' I paused for
more dramatic effect. 'Bovvered.'

He flushed with anger. 'If that's what you think.' He stuttered
as he tried to decide what to say. 'If that's how seriously you take
your cases . . .'

We travelled the rest of the way in silence after I interrupted with
a final, 'Bovvered.' The nice thing was that his anger only served to
irritate the judge. Which I have to admit got me going once more

and when the judge wasn't looking I held up a piece of paper to TheCreep upon which was written a single word . . .

You guessed it once again.

In case you're wondering, he lost.

Back in chambers and there were even more high jinks. FanciesHimself had put together a plan. Earlier, whilst ThirdSix was out of his room, he'd snuck in, taken his mobile which was lying on his desk and dialled the direct number for the room where chambers tea is held. He then replaced the phone, making sure it was unlocked, onto the desk. The hope was that he would pocket it before going off for his little tête-à-tête, as you might say, with BusyBody. ThirdSix disappeared from his room just before 4.30 p.m., the same time that everyone else was going to chambers tea. FanciesHimself tipped me off with a quick phone call and I dashed along to tea to see exactly what would happen. However, nothing prepared me for what then followed.

'Good day in court?' HeadofChambers asked OldSmoothie.

'Not bad, yes. We were in . . .'

He was interrupted by the phone ringing.

'Who on earth can that be?' said HeadofChambers irritably. 'Must be the clerks.' He pressed the answer button and the loudspeaker of the phone sprung into action. Everybody turned in surprise as they heard rustling noises and then giggling at full volume.

'What on earth is that,' said HeadofChambers.

'Shh,' said OldSmoothie.

The whole room craned to hear as best they could as BusyBody's voice suddenly came through on the little loudspeaker.

'You're a very very naughty pupil, ThirdSix. Very naughty indeed.'

'Yes, My Lady. I apologise unreservedly, My Lady.' It was ThirdSix providing the answers in this little game.

'Now I've been looking over your application this afternoon and have to admit that I find many of its features to be extremely attractive. But I'm afraid I shall still need a little more convincing before I decide to grant your request for relief.'

'My Lady I stand here erect before the court of the great storeroom and lay my case out in all its naked glory . . .'

OldSmoothie's jaw was the first to drop as it dawned on the whole room what was actually going on. 'The storeroom? Of all the places. The cheek of it.'

BusyBody had obviously shared its charms with him as well as with FanciesHimself. Eventually and almost reluctantly, HeadofChambers interrupted the broadcast and switched it off, saying, 'I really don't think we should be listening to this.'

There was a general answer of 'No' by which everyone meant, 'Well actually we're still being highly amused by it but we wouldn't want to admit it.' HeadofChambers then telephoned down to HeadClerk and said, 'Please could you ask one of the clerks to go and interrupt BusyBody and ThirdSix from their . . . er . . . proceedings, in the top floor storeroom.'

As we left chambers tea, we passed the two of them being led downstairs by FanciesHimself in the direction of HeadofChambers's room.

Friday 4 May 2007
Day 150 (week 31): Pigs might fly

'You know, BabyB, it's never easy doing pupillage and I know that sometimes I can be difficult. That's why I thought we'd have lunch and get to know each other a little better.'

This was yesterday and UpTights was for once in a good mood, having just settled a case which was due to start on Monday and in the process gained a brief fee of over £30,000 and a week off. She'd spent the previous week getting more and more stressed, and though she's not usually a settler, the relief was evident yesterday morning as she packed up the twenty lever arch files to send back to her solicitors.

Before we went off for lunch, I bumped into OldSmoothie in the clerks' room and when I told him what I was up to he responded with, 'I'd treasure that one, BabyB. Kind gestures from the wicked witch are as rare as rocking horse . . .' he paused, and then realising he had an audience who might be offended by his swearing, he smiled and added slowly, 'manure'. Then, just as he'd said this, UpTights herself came around the corner smiling and offering greetings to each of the assembled barristers and clerks.

'There's a Gloucester Old Spot at ten thousand feet,' said OldSmoothie.

'Life is grand, OldSmoothie, wouldn't you agree?' said UpTights, ignoring his dig.

As I left, trailing behind in her wake, I overheard HeadClerk whispering 'UpTights in a good mood. Pigs have indeed flown, OldSmoothie.'

'Obviously just upped her dose,' replied OldSmoothie.

So there we were, eating lunch in a posh restaurant at 12 noon. But more than that. She was ordering a bottle of champagne.

'Well, BabyB. We all have to let our hair down sometimes.'

Thoroughly confused as I was, I was certainly not averse to being wined and dined on a Friday afternoon . . . and into the early evening. I started off promising myself that I wouldn't have more than two glasses. But what was I meant to do when UpTights (of all people) was saying, 'Oh, come on, BabyB. Don't be such a prude.' In which case, you betcha. I'll have another. And another. So long as it's one fewer than the (usually) teetotal facelift opposite.

All of which meant that I stumbled upon all sorts of chambers gossip, though the problem is that I'm struggling to remember much of what she said. 'Well, of course, everybody knew about OldSmoothie and TheVamp after they were caught *in flagrante*, so to speak, in the Temple Gardens after some big dinner or other. Can't have been a pretty sight for the poor porter to stumble upon . . . Don't believe everything you might hear about HeadofChambers and me. Despite the fact it only lasted about a month during my pupillage, I've never heard the end of it since. You can never be too careful, BabyB.'

After she came out with this particular gem I was suddenly concerned that there may even have been a glint in her eye, although I chose to ignore it if there was. I have to say though, that despite her many neuroses and bouts of hysteria, she can at times be extremely charming. The difficulty is trying to predict precisely what person she's going to be on that particular day. The only thing I've managed to work out so far is that the best signs of her madness coming on are an increase in make-up and added bouffant to the hair.

I managed to garner some interesting information about TopFirst, thanks to UpTights's drunken indiscretion . . . 'You know, BabyB, that TopFirst's dad was a founder member of this chambers? We never realised until TopFirst had already arrived, despite the fact they share the same surname. Left in disgrace, you see, after he stole a judge's wife. Everyone's having to be terribly careful not to hold all this against him.'

Yeah, and the fact that he's arrogant and smug and already strolls around chambers as though he owns it. I nodded politely. Not really sure whether this will ultimately count for or against him, or if there is any other way I may use it.

But there's no doubt that it's always better to be one step ahead.

Tuesday 8 May 2007
Day 151 (week 32): Get-out-of-jail-free card

Followed UpTights to a client conference today. It all concerned a car accident in which our man drove into an old lady on a zebra crossing. The client's concerned as he's being prosecuted for dangerous driving and risks losing his licence. The insurer is even more concerned about the civil claim which might follow. The client's come up with the ingenious wheeze of getting himself off by saying that he blacked out at the wheel. I don't think any of us believed him, particularly after he mentioned that 'a friend of a friend got off in the same way' and chuckled that he was playing his 'get-out-of-jail-free card'. Not that this seemed to bother UpTights, who simply said, 'Well, if that's what you say happened then we ought to raise the defence of automatism.'

The insurer went further and suggested that we instruct his 'tame neurologist' who apparently 'always backs up an automatism claim'. UpTights turned a blind eye whilst her instructing solicitor nodded his assent, keen to ensure the old lady wouldn't receive a penny.

After the conference I asked UpTights if she had believed the client.

'Not for me to say, BabyB. That's the judge's job.'

'But what if it's completely obvious?'

'Come on, BabyB. You should know this by now. If we only represented clients we thought were telling the truth we wouldn't be working.'

'But aren't you misleading the court?'

'Not unless he actually tells me he's lying.'

'But he'd never do that.'

'There you are, BabyB. You're starting to get it.'

I also had a chat with TheBoss's old solicitor SlipperySlope today. I've been given five cases by him in my first month on my feet and I told him how much I appreciated the work. He replied with, 'BabyB, it's my pleasure. Always happy to put bread on the table of the junior Bar.' Then, without even skipping a beat, he continued, 'Of course, I'm even happier when I can chat over those cases at Stamford Bridge?'

Well, what can you say? It didn't even qualify as a hint. More a blatant request for Chelsea tickets in return for regular work. Now, I've checked this before with the Bar Standards Board guidance and it seems that the best way of deciding if behaviour is appropriate or not is what they call the 'blush test'. If it's something that would make you blush then it's probably inappropriate. Since I am conveniently blushing at very little these days, I ordered the tickets.

Speaking of blushes, Worrier filled me in on BusyBody's progress today.

'He's dumped her, BabyB.'

'Who? What?'

'ThirdSix. BusyBody. After the chambers tea episode HeadofChambers threw the rule book at them.'

'So what was the outcome?'

'They both got official warnings. No more naked court proceedings for them and it's apparently given ThirdSix pupillage paranoia. Says they can't carry on.'

'How do you know all this?'

'BusyBody's been confiding.' She looked guilty and continued, 'I know I shouldn't even be telling you, but after all we've gone through already and, well, I just have to share it with someone.'

'I understand.'

'She thinks OldSmoothie set them up with the telephone thing. Apparently HeadofChambers thinks so too and that's why he's not holding an investigation as to who might have done it.'

Of course. All makes sense.

Thursday 10 May 2007
Day 153 (week 32): AmbulanceChaserLtd

I've been doing some online research into the accident management company which works with FakeClaims&Co. Let's call them AmbulanceChaserLtd, as I found out that much of their work comes from hanging around accident-and-emergency departments at various London hospitals. I visited one last night with Claire once again playing camerawoman. I went in complaining of a stiff neck from having tripped over a hole in a pavement. After waiting a couple of hours I was finally seen by a doctor who prescribed me some painkillers and gave me a neck collar to wear. Sure enough, as I emerged from A&E I was approached in the car park by a man wearing a suit and tie. His swagger was a confident one, with kind of a cheap-salesman feel to it, but his look was something a little more dodgy, almost seedy. When he opened his mouth he sounded like an estate agent. Respectable patter, clearly scripted. When he asked me if I'd had an accident, I told him about the paving stone and he then made his pitch.

'You can definitely get compensation for that.'

'Oh really?'

'Easy.'

'And how much would I get?'

'Probably about £1,500 for your injury and a couple of weeks' loss of earnings.'

'But I haven't lost any earnings.'

'Don't worry about that. We do all the documentation.'

'And how much will it cost me?'

'Absolutely nothing. Totally guaranteed.'

I gave him my (false) details along with a number for a pay-as-you-go mobile that I bought over the weekend. Today I got a call and booked myself in to go and see them next week.

Monday 14 May 2007
Day 155 (week 33): Attention deficit disorder

'We're in front of Bart today?' It was my opponent.

'You mean the judge who plays online bridge . . .'

'. . . during the hearings. The same, and who also, er, what's the word?'

'Aromes, perhaps?' I suggested.

'Quite.'

We smiled at the reference to the judge's well-known problem with flatulence. But his nickname isn't just slang for that, since it also refers directly to Bart Simpson and his infamous attention deficit disorder. For the judge this is manifested in the handling of his cases. My opponent seemed particularly animated about this.

'Someone in chambers has given me the judge's online-gaming name and I'm going to take him on during the hearing on my phone.'

'Without him realising.'

'Precisely. Except you'll have to cover me if he gets suspicious.'

When the hearing started the judge was carefully guarding his computer screen so that no one could see it. My opponent had his phone under the desk, and whilst I was cross-examining his client, he passed me a note saying that his online challenge to the judge had been accepted. You'd think that with both judge and opponent otherwise occupied it should have been a shoe-in, but it was quite the opposite as no one was properly listening to anything anyone said. At one point my opponent had to put forward a legal point.

'That case on causation. Wotsit's name?'

'Oh, wotsit called?' the judge said as he continued to stare at the screen in front of him.

'Wotsit's name?' said my opponent again, scratching his head.

'Oh. Wotsit . . . wotsit . . . wotsit?' the judge echoed.

At which point, just because I couldn't resist, I added a 'wotsit?' myself. Just for fun. In the end it seemed the only way for me to bring the judge's attention back to the case and the points I was making was to add, and particularly emphasise, the word 'bridge' ('building a *bridge* between the two versions of events', '*bridging* the gaps in the evidence') and other related words ('the *trick* to understanding the defendant's evidence', 'in his *bid* to win the case'). After it had caused the judge to jump back into judicial action a few times he was eventually forced to resign his game and start paying attention.

Which made my opponent smile on two fronts since he not only won money from the judge online but he was also handed victory in court.

Tuesday 15 May 2007
Day 156 (week 33): Fake claim

Court finished at 11.30 a.m. though I didn't phone the clerks until 4 p.m. to tell them so. Which gave me the time to visit AmbulanceChaserLtd. I arrived at around 2 p.m. and was put straight onto their conveyor belt. Around 2.15 p.m. I was taken around the corner to see a doctor who asked me two questions about the accident and then said, 'So, would it be right to say that you have an aching neck?'

'Er, I did have for a day or two.'

He then got up and briefly felt it.

'And is it continuing at all? Perhaps there's a little pain when you wake up?'

'Well . . . maybe. Just a little.'

'Excellent. Now, if you just bear with me I will finish my report.'

He spent about two minutes typing and then printed off a ten-page medical report on my injuries. Almost all of it was generic save for my name, date of birth and one paragraph about the accident. As I'd guessed, the prognosis was that I would be better within six months of the accident. That'd fetch around £1,500 and might just slip below the insurers' fraud radar. By 2.30 p.m. I returned to the office and was asked to sign a witness statement along with a form which gave them the right to take off a £500 'administration charge' from my damages. Apparently my case will now get handed over to FakeClaims&Co.

Which might give me a little more insight into their practice.

Wednesday 16 May 2007
Day 157 (week 33): Email frolics

As part of the ongoing correspondence between TopFirst and the fictional Ginny, I prompted him into commenting about members of chambers the other day. In his usual arrogant way, the email I got back included the following little nuggets:

I don't think you'd like our head of chambers. He's pompous, sexist and, you might be surprised to hear, not the brightest cookie in the jar. Shows how far you could get in the past just on being the son of a QC.

Chambers is a hotbed of gossip at the moment. One of my fellow pupils has slept with two or three barristers and a clerk in only the last few months and I've heard that she might even be pregnant by one of them.

As for the other pupils, I don't see that much competition, to be honest. One's like a frightened mouse who'd struggle to address an envelope, never mind a court, another one still lives with his mother and then there's a new one who might well score points on the rugby field but I doubt very much his brawn will come in handy elsewhere. Cream, as they say, always rises to the top.

For a little while now TopFirst has been using his Hotmail account rather than his work one for obvious reasons. But after I pressed 'reply', I added another email address which amounted to his surname and then @ followed by chambers' domain name. This address belongs to another member of chambers with the same surname as TopFirst. Oops! I then prefaced my reply, which sought spurious advice over summer jobs with, 'I'm copying in your work email as I'd be keen to get your advice as soon as possible.'

Obviously, I'm taking a risk, as TopFirst may now guess he's being stitched up. But I'm fortified by the fact that he has met Ginny in the flesh and, further, that he is somewhat blinded by lust.

Thursday 17 May 2007
Day 158 (week 33): Back on track

It seems that TopFirst didn't check his email until last night, when he fired back a reply:

Ginny! What were you thinking? That's not even my work email address. It belongs to someone else with the same surname in my chambers. I really don't know what to say but you might just have ruined my chances of tenancy with that single mistake.

Oh, please. Spoilt brat throwing his toys out of the pram. But I had to get him back onside, so I replied this morning:

That's just terrible. I'm so very, very sorry. Please accept my most sincere apologies. I've been worrying about it constantly since receiving your email and couldn't sleep a wink last night. Is there any way I can make it up to you? I promise that I'll try in whatever way I can. Maybe I could email the barrister and explain the mistake? Do tell me how I can help. Please. I very much hope we don't fall out over this as I've so enjoyed our emails and meeting you and was really looking forward to seeing you again. As you might imagine, I don't exactly get the same stimulation from my fellow students here in Durham, who have neither your brains nor your experience.

TopFirst replied almost immediately with:

No! Please don't send any more emails at all to chambers. Ginny, there's no question that we'll fall out. I'm still totally looking forward to seeing you soon in London, I promise.

All back on track and one more body blow to TopFirst. As for the email, I have no doubt that it has now done the rounds in chambers. The person who shares TopFirst's surname is almost as much of a gossip as his namesake.

Friday 18 May 2007
Day 159 (week 33): You're nicked

News on JudgeJewellery – she with the penchant for cheap jewellery from CheapnNasty. Well, gossip, anyway. Apparently a couple of days ago she was actually caught in the act of stealing the said jewellery, as we already knew was her wont. A security guard first spotted her acting suspiciously and asked to look in her handbag. She then got all high and mighty and 'do you know who I am' about it. Which, of course, just made the security guard more suspicious and they descended into a bit of a set-to which ended up with the security guard physically grabbing her by the arm and pulling her into one of the side rooms. When she still refused to open her handbag, the guard eventually called the police, a little concerned about forcing a judge, of all people, any further. Anyway, eventually earrings were found and she was nicked. Taken down the station, charged and then sent on her way. I know all this because UpTights has been instructed to defend her. What a pair!

Monday 21 May 2007
Day 160 (week 34): Karma

Today I was doodling over UpTights's picture using MS Paint. I'd added a witch's hat and a broomstick along with a few warts and was about to send it off to Claire when an email from the stretched one pinged into my inbox and I read it quickly. Now, you might now be guessing what happened next, but for my part, in that split second, I was innocent as to what was about to happen . . . Yes, I pressed 'send', thinking my email was going to Claire when somehow UpTights's email address had inveigled its way into the address bar, presumably through the post I'd just received.

Now, after what I did to TopFirst last week, you would be right to point out that this was simply a good dose of karma winging its way back and hitting me full in the face. Be that as it may, the question which arose was, what to do next? Having sent her email, UpTights had popped out and her computer terminal was therefore vacant. Did I rush in and try and delete the offending email before her return or did I instead 'fess up as soon as she got back and make the best of it? Or there was the very English 'more tea, vicar?' option of simply pretending it didn't happen and hoping for the best. Needless to say, I took the first option and sat down quickly at her computer and started trying to find my email. Didn't take long and within a few seconds it was deleted.

At which point UpTights re-entered the room and exploded. Well, not literally, you understand, though with all that stretching you figure there's always a risk. 'What are you doing at my computer?'

Similar options faced me once again, but this time with the stakes having been raised somewhat. I was well aware that the email would continue to be visible in the 'deleted items' folder. 'Er . . . well . . . er . . .' Oh, I forgot to mention the prevarication option. 'Er . . . well . . . you see . . .'

'What do I see, BabyB? What?'

'Well . . . the thing is . . . I . . . er . . .'

To lie at this stage would risk the whole caboodle but at least give me a small chance of getting off. To tell the truth carried the same risk but with no upside as far as I could see. What was it OldRuin had once said? 'Instincts, BabyB. Follow your instincts.' My instincts at that moment were simply to sprint out of the room as fast as I could and never return. Instead I blurted an enormous kind of a sentence in one breath.

'I drew an unkind picture of you and sent it to your email by mistake and I was trying to delete it before you came back and I'm really, really sorry . . . so sorry, maybe I should resign my pupillage . . . so very sorry . . .' I was actually starting to feel slightly ashamed and I think this probably showed.

'So let's see it then, BabyB. Let's see it. Come on. Let's see it.'

I turned to the computer and went to the 'deleted items' folder and eventually brought up the email and with it my masterpiece. UpTights stared at it. Then stared at me. Then back at the picture. Then back at me. She then leant back as if she was winding up her body to deliver an almighty thump to my head. And then she started laughing. Not a chuckle. Not a giggle. Far from it. An almighty roar that made me think only of the tragically demented Mrs Rochester. And she continued to roar. Then, as quickly as the storm had erupted, it ceased. 'BabyB, you've made my week with that one.' After which she pointed me back to my desk and silently got on with her work.

Nowt, as they say, so queer as folk.

Tuesday 22 May 2007
Day 161 (week 34): Divas

Apparently there was an opera singer dining on High Table in Gray's Inn Hall last night. The diva was surrounded by some of the country's most distinguished barristers and judges.

'Doesn't open her mouth for less than £20,000 apparently,' HeadOfChambers reported at tea this afternoon.

'She was in good company then,' said OldSmoothie.

Wednesday 23 May 2007
Day 162 (week 34): Don't mess with me

Went to see TheBoss today and told him how I've been getting on with FakeClaims&Co. He's not looking good at the moment. Put on even more weight and struggling to maintain eye contact. Also getting more aggressive: I do wonder sometimes what he's taking.

'Not bad, BabyB. Keep it coming. And don't forget, our interests coincide. If I go down, you're coming with me. Important point to bear in mind when you're scratching around doing your Sherlock Holmes routine.'

It was time for the worm to have a go at turning.

'Don't forget that I could sink you.'

'But you wouldn't do that, BabyB. Sink me and you sink yourself. Don't start trying to get tricky with me, BabyB, when I'm the one who taught you how.'

He is, of course, right – and my fortunes are undeniably linked to this con man of a barrister. However well I succeed against the other pupils, there remains TheBoss, like the fabled sword, hanging over my chances of tenancy.

Thursday 24 May 2007
Day 163 (week 34): Quality of mercy

There's something about the Temple and its inhabitants which seems to defy the onward march of time. As if Old Father Time himself had just popped in a few hundred years ago and decided to perch here for a rest. 'Here you are my friend. Have a seat next to the fountain. Put your feet up. A cigar maybe? Then perhaps a stroll around the garden? Won't keep you long.' And after all, there'd be no rush if you were Old Father Time.

'Oh, go on then. Maybe just one dinner in Hall. And my, this is rather fine wine, I must say, and not bad conversation either. Maybe I'll stay just a little longer ...'

It's certainly what sprung to mind today as I accompanied OldRuin on an early-morning stroll there before going off to court. As we walked through Pump Court, once the home of the infamous Judge Jeffreys, he pointed to the sundial and quoted the inscription: 'Shadows we are and like shadows we depart, BabyB.' After our little tour of the Temple, we travelled to court where OldRuin was representing a fourteen-year-old boy accused of theft. As the case progressed I realised how refreshing it was to spend time with OldRuin. It wasn't just that his fee or the time spent at court were irrelevant to him. It was the care he took with the case and the reassurance he was able to provide. Despite the fact that the client was found guilty, it was clear OldRuin was intent on making some difference through his plea in mitigation and it was all going extremely well until he mentioned the word 'mercy'. The district judge immediately jumped in and said, 'Mercy? This young tearaway doesn't deserve our mercy.'

'Sir,' OldRuin replied with a gentle smile. 'When Napoleon said that to the mother of a condemned man, she replied, "But sire, would it be mercy if he deserved it?" '

Yet though these were fine words, it was the look of compassion which accompanied them which I think won the day. A look which went from OldRuin's client to the client's mother and then to the judge. As I now sit at my tiny little desk and write this post, I wonder whether things may well have been different on all fronts if OldRuin had been my pupilmaster instead of TheBoss.

But he wasn't.

And they're not.

Friday 25 May 2007
Day 164 (week 34): Rookie error

Yesterday I was in Southend, the day before, Bournemouth, and today it was Brighton, which sounds more like the itinerary of a stand-up comedian than a baby barrister. Though come to think of it, the wages are probably as paltry and the audience as humourless.

Today my opponent was another pupil. She opened with the line, 'Sir, my client is a very old lady of . . .' Wait for it, '. . . fifty-seven.'

The cracking sound of the point of the judge's pencil breaking reverberated around the courtroom long after judgement had been given against her client.

Monday 28 May 2007
Day 165 (week 35): Squaring up

There was a chambers party this evening to celebrate OldSmoothie being made a bencher. The pupils were all invited along to serve the booze. At one point we were in the small kitchen and for once there was a real sense of camaraderie, due partly to the demob-happy Friday feeling and partly to the fact that the room took us away from the constant glare of attention that pupillage brings with it. Worrier had already started giggling nervously and TopFirst was kicking back looking particularly smug as he poured himself a small glass of champagne.

With everyone together, I came up with the wheeze of a couple of little drinking games which ended up in most of us having to down a few glasses of wine in one. Worrier and BusyBody soon exempted themselves and TopFirst mysteriously disappeared after the first couple, claiming that he had to finish a piece of work, which was a pretty lame excuse for a Friday, even for him. ThirdSix, on the other hand, was a veritable drinking machine. Perhaps it's his rugby background or perhaps he was trying to win a point against me. Or even just maybe (shock horror) he was simply trying to make friends. Either way, my ears pricked up when I heard that he'd never been beaten at downing a pint.

'Never been beaten? Never ever? That's a bit much, isn't it? Surely there must have been once?'

ThirdSix looked pensive.

'Well, no, actually.'

For some reason, probably the couple of glasses she'd been forced to down, Worrier looked impressed.

'Well, I'd have you any day,' I jousted.

'Yeah, right.'

There were a few exchanges of 'yeah' and 'yeah, right' until I said, 'Come on then, let's have a go. Red wine, pint glass. I challenge you. Now.'

I think it might have been the word 'challenge' which made him step up to the mark, although I'm sure his intake up to that moment also had something to do with it. Whatever it was, ThirdSix said, 'OK then, BabyB. You're on.' And so we squared up. I'd like to say it was like Clint Eastwood and Lee Van Cleef, each weighing up the odds and staring death in the face, or at the very least a reckless bout of pistols at dawn. But it was far from either. A sloppy and rather quick pouring of the drinks in the kitchen followed by a 'go' from a worried-looking Worrier and we were off. Except I wasn't quite as off as ThirdSix. To say the least. Within a few seconds he'd downed the pint, as might have been predicted, whilst I had finished, hmm, very little of mine, in fact.

'Lightweight, BabyB. Nice try.'

Aw, shucks. I shrugged and extended my hand in congratulation.

'You were right. Long live the king!'

So that was all going on behind the scenes whilst the rest of chambers continued their discreet little drinks party. That was until ThirdSix burst through the door and sidled up to TheVamp. 'More champagne?' he grunted, and put his arm around her waist. TheVamp immediately registered his state and palmed him off. After which he moved on to UpTights, who was slightly more forthcoming. 'Hello, kind sir. Well, if you insist.' She pawed at his chest and then asked, 'So, how are you enjoying your third six?'

They became engrossed in conversation, if you can call it that on his part. UpTights didn't seem to mind in the least, and was last seen with her arm around him walking down Chancery Lane.

Tuesday 29 May 2007
Day 166 (week 35): Hangovers

UpTights, I have to say, was far from living up to her nickname today. And that's putting it mildly. She breezed in at 11 a.m. rather than her usual 8.30 with a very cheery, 'Good morning, BabyB.' Top of the morning to you too, I'm sure. I was suspicious. Maybe my plan to get ThirdSix drunk had backfired and somehow worked in his favour. I kept my head down. No doubt I'd hear soon enough.

It didn't take long. OldSmoothie took ThirdSix out for lunch and threatened him with cancelling his pupillage unless he gave him all the details. Well, turns out there were none. Or very few, anyway. He'd made a lunge at UpTights, who had slapped him in the face and then proceeded to drag him home. Well, to his home actually. Except that he passed out in the cab and woke up in his front garden several hours later.

Can't work out whether it works for or against him, but at least we've started to get some sort of action. Gives me something to work on.

Thursday 31 May 2007
Day 168 (week 35): First offer

I got a call from FakeClaims&Co out of the blue today. They said that they'd had an offer of £1,500 for my injury and loss of earnings and advised that I accept it. This was all happening a little quickly. I needed to get a meeting and I didn't actually want any money but they were adamant that there was no need to visit. I asked if I could ring them back and gave Claire a quick call.

'Why don't you exaggerate the size of the claim? That way they'll need to get more evidence and to interview you.'

'But again that'll just get me in deeper.'

'Which is the point. If you're going to slay the dragon, you've first got to enter its lair.'

She was right, though I also think she is starting to like the intrigue a little. I phoned them back.

'My injuries have actually been getting worse recently and I've not been able to work this last week.'

'Oh. Well then. That's different. I think perhaps you should come in.'

CHAPTER 9
JUNE: HONEYTRAPPED

To subdue the enemy without fighting is the supreme
excellence.

Sun Tzu, *The Art of War*

Monday 4 June 2007
Day 170 (week 36): Attrition

After ThirdSix's drinking episode, I thought it was time to start adding a little more pressure in this war of attrition that is pupillage. This time I aimed at TopFirst. Simple enough, this one. Looked up his solicitor for tomorrow's case and set up a Hotmail account in her name. Then sent him an email this morning from her stating:

> Dear TopFirst,
>   Please could you check the attached and confirm that it is all correct?
>   Many thanks.

Just enough to look personalised and yet general enough to be regarded on closer inspection and with the benefit of hindsight as spam. And yes, you guessed it. I attached a virus to the email attachment which I'd found within a few Google searches online. Not one which would kill the whole network, mind. Just one which would mean that it'd need fixing. Sure enough, this afternoon we all received a reminder email from HeadofChambers:

> Not that I thought I needed to remind people but in the light of an incident this morning, it seems that I do. You are therefore all

reminded that you must not open any email attachments unless you are expecting them.

Tut-tut.

Tuesday 5 June 2007
Day 171 (week 36): What's it all about?

'What on earth's it really all about?'

It was UpTights musing aloud as I've noticed she's prone to do from time to time. It's as if she's spent so many years working in a job she despises that her little thought bubbles of resentment sometimes rise to the surface and gently slip out into speech without her even being able to stop them. As if the walls of her mind have slowly eroded away through years of making compromises. Today she was working on the case where the client was spuriously claiming he had blacked out. Seems the 'tame neurologist's' report has come back saying that in his opinion this is the most likely explanation for the accident, which may well mean no money for the old lady.

'Why do we dedicate our lives to this, BabyB? Why?'

'Search me, UpTights. I kind of figure that you work to pay for the plastic surgery and health spas that you think will reduce the visible effects of your stressful job. You work to be able to afford to look like you don't work. You climb on board your treadmill until it's going so fast that you can't jump off. You tell me, UpTights. Am I right?'

That's what I'd like to have said. What actually came out was, 'We search for the truth, UpTights. A noble endeavour.'

'There are no heroes here, BabyB. We're all just shadows. Dim reflections of the real world. Sitting around packaging it all into neat and tidy little issues.' She got up and strutted. 'I can't stand it, BabyB. The law. The whole thing. It sucks the poetry from our souls. Boils it all down to cynical platitudes.' She looked out the window. 'You know. If it wasn't for the money . . .'

She tailed off, returned to her desk and didn't say another thing to me all day.

Wednesday 6 June 2007
Day 172 (week 36): Going backwards

Last week Claire was extolling her new theory for successful litigation.

'Forget blinking. That's just child's play. If you're going to really step up to the mark then playing Rewind's where it's really at.'

'What's that?'

'Just get the witness to tell their story backwards. Start with the incident and work back from there. Screws their brains up.'

So for the last week, inevitably, we've been practising it whenever we've chatted, particularly down the pub. Always finishes with me saying, 'And then I woke up in the morning,' and Claire adding, 'And then I was born.'

Today was the first chance I had to put all this hard work into practice. My client was a thief and the witness I was wanting to trip up had identified him leaving the scene of the crime. What I kind of figured was that asking even an honest witness to tell his story backwards might cause some difficulties. What I hadn't counted on was the assistance of a certain eccentric district judge.

'Perhaps,' I asked, 'you might just take us through your story backwards.'

'What do you mean, backwards?'

'Just what I say. No more, no less.'

'Literally?'

'Quite so.'

He went to his witness statement and very slowly he started reading. '2007, 14th April. Williams John. Belief and knowledge my of best the to true are statement this of contents the believe I.'

He was reading it word for word . . . backwards, as he said, literally, and was obviously confused about what I'd been asking. The magistrate wasn't having any of it.

'Why on earth are you doing that?'

'Because I was asked to.'

'No you weren't.'

'Yes I was.'

My client and I at this point became the audience to a very peculiar stand-off. The witness eventually got angry, the judge even more annoyed and despite my own efforts a miscarriage of justice was achieved. My client got off.

Thursday 7 June 2007
Day 173 (week 36): BigFatTramp

The trial against The Vamp is coming up next week and already she's been around looking for offers. Of settlement, that is, though it's true to say that her flirting has gone to level 'trial minus one week and counting'. The temperature's definitely increasing. Yesterday she offered to buy me a drink after work, but I was already booked, which is a shame since she's been looking particularly attractive of late. Although the case is not particularly big, I've worked out that the reason it is so important is that this solicitor provides some of the juiciest cases at the Bar. How far she'll go to secure a result remains to be seen. In the meantime, I made the mistake of mentioning the case to Claire after a couple of beers this evening.

'What, against The Tramp? That same woman you got off with a few months ago?'

Being a simple-minded soul I didn't spot this commenty-type question for what it was: a huge gaping ManTrap ready to strike. I was soon to find out after I replied in full ManBlindness mode with, 'I don't think that's particularly relevant, although come to think of it I think she might be making hints and I guess I am trying to decide what I'd do . . .'

At which point the ManTrap closed around me and I spent the next hour or so trying to escape its barbs in the form of sarcastic remarks about myself, men in general, their egos and now and again, their lack of scruples. This was only tempered when, with her usual impeccably bad timing, TheBigFatTramp (as Claire was by this time calling her) nonchalantly strolled into the bar and spotted the two of us sitting at a table.

'BabyB. How lovely to see you. Oh, and with your little pupillage friend. What's her name?' She hadn't actually looked at Claire yet.

'It's Claire.'

'Oh, that's right. "JustGoodFriendsClaire".' Finally she turned to her and added, 'How sweet.'

Not that Claire was going to take it lying down, so to speak.

'Have you run out of tenants and solicitors or something? Only the pupils left, is it?'

'Ooh. She's terribly big for her little pupil boots, our Claire, isn't she?'

'Or maybe it's just your own version of the Cab Rank Rule. Wouldn't be right to turn down passing trade, would it? Except you don't drop your wig for every guy in town now, do you? Only for whom exactly? Fellow members of chambers and solicitors with big fat juicy briefs to give you?'

'Oh, perrrleeeease. Says who? Sanctimonious little MissPrissy over here? Hardly. Next you'll be telling me that your intentions with your best friend here are wholly platonic.'

Then Claire was at her from another angle. 'I see you've been on the sunbed again. Did you get bonus hours or something? Looks great.' A dramatic pause and then the right hook: 'For buffalo hide.'

Went on for about twenty minutes and all I can say is that from the off I wasn't just a little out of my depth. I was well and truly in the deep end and floundering. Silence wasn't a choice. It simply happened as I watched the whole gruesome scene unfold. I have to say though that despite TheVamp's reputation for the killer put-downs, it was Claire who won this particular showdown, albeit on points. Eventually TheVamp started to feel the strain of fighting away from home and sidled off with a parting crack.

'I've heard about going out with protection, BabyB.' She looked at Claire. 'But I do wonder whether you've perhaps gone a little too far with this guard dog. Anyway, I look forward to seeing you in court next week. Without her around I'm sure we'll be able to come to some sort of mutually beneficial arrangement.'

She was back to flirtation mode and sidled off to see her next victim. I just hope Claire and TheVamp are never against each other in court.

Friday 8 June 2007
Day 174 (week 36): HoneyTrap countdown

Been organising the final showdown between TopFirst and Ginny the HoneyTrap. Emailed him from Ginny's account saying that she would be visiting London in a couple of weeks and asking whether he was free to meet up one evening. Would he be free? Or would he have a last-minute pang of conscience for his beloved? Not TopFirst. He replied in a flash telling Ginny to name the day and he'd be there. So I went to check his diary on the chambers network and suggested a day when he was booked in on a case in Manchester. It'll be interesting to see what he comes up with to get out of the case. To his credit, TopFirst didn't let on about his difficulties when he replied saying that he looked forward to it. Oh, but silly me. It completely slipped my mind to tell him that Ginny won't actually be available that evening. Guess I'll leave it a little while until I do. Wouldn't like to make things too easy. He might get suspicious.

Monday 11 June 2007
Day 175 (week 37): DataMining

There's a squat in Camden which I heard about from a friend whilst I was at Bar School who used it whenever he was having an affair. Bunch of hippies running a nice little business allowing 'their' house to be used as a postal address for people who want to give false details but still receive the mail. Apparently they have a strictly no-drugs policy which keeps the police off their backs. The reason I mention this is that I visited it this evening as FakeClaims&Co are now insisting on a postal address from me.

'Yeah, what do you want?' It was a tall, doped-out hippy in T-shirt and jeans who answered the door with a matching hippy chick under his arm. I mentioned the name of my friend from Bar School and they relaxed a little, which didn't surprise me given the amount he'd used their services.

'So how can we help?' He was about as businesslike as a real hippy can get.

'I just need a postal address.'

'So why did you come dressed in that ridiculous tie-dye outfit? We don't demand fancy dress, you know.'

It was a fair comment, really. I'd spent ages trying to work out what disguise to wear and tie-dye old-school nineties traveller-hippy was my best effort. Unfortunately, with my short hair and clean-shaven face I looked like a cross between Gordon Gecko and Swampy the anti-road campaigner.

'Er, that's a fair cop, I guess.' I smiled and then he beamed back.

'Don't worry about it. Look, come in and let me get you a cup of tea.'

'So what's the deal with this forwarding service?' I asked as we sat down around the table.

'Well, it's ten pounds a letter.'

'That sounds like pretty good value. How many letters do you do a day?'

'About two hundred at present,' he replied and he looked at his girlfriend. They caught me doing the sums in my head.

'Yeah, dude, I know what you're thinking. How can a bunch of anti-capitalist hippies be bringing in half a mill a year. Go on, say it.'

'Well, I was . . .' I trailed off.

'Look. It's what you do with the money that matters.'

I didn't ask any further but since we were chatting and they were being so businesslike about everything, it also occurred to me that I might be able to use the address for another bit of mischief on the side.

'Do you also allow us to sign up with a false name as well as this address?' In fact this would mean two false names for me.

'Whatever you like, man. So long as you're not dealing or money laundering or anything like that we ask no questions. Kind of like a Swiss bank, really.' He looked pleased with that one. 'Yeah, I think I might even use that one in our marketing.'

Actually, it couldn't have been further from what they were, but I understood what he was saying.

'Sounds good. I'll have two please, one with a made-up name.'

'What name do you want? No Disney characters please. Just not cool.'

'I'll have, er, let's think. Yes, I'll have "ThirdSix", please.'

On my return home I then rattled off a letter in ThirdSix's name addressed to his old chambers in which I made a Data Protection Act request for all information they held on him. I mentioned that they must not contact him in chambers for obvious reasons and that they should simply send him the information to his home address (i.e. the hippy dead drop). Very little to lose, and depending upon what they have, if the chambers simply replies without checking the address there may be a lot to gain.

Wednesday 13 June 2007
Day 177 (week 37): An uplifting offer

Yesterday was the big day for my case against TheVamp. First thing I got a call from my instructing solicitor telling me that our client had rung up to say that he wouldn't be turning up. Not just today. Not ever. Given that he was our only witness in defending the claim, my instructions were clear: settle. All of which The Vamp was unaware of when she arrived at court. Just to reinforce this information gap, as I came out of my conference room to talk to her, I popped my head back in the room and shouted into the emptiness, loud enough to be heard outside, 'You just read your witness statement and we'll have a chat later.'

Desperate as I knew she was to settle, The Vamp came over and with a kind of self-mocking pout and flick of the hair said, 'Come on, BabyB, how about just a teeny-weeny little offer? Just for me. Promise to vote for you in tenancy.'

Which was a nice opening gambit and made me wonder how far she was prepared to go. The skirt, I noticed, had risen since the last hearing making me wonder if it was giving away more than merely a glimpse of her legs. Perhaps her bargaining position had weakened. Or maybe it simply reflected the fact that today was the one that mattered.

'Believe me,' I replied, 'I'd love to settle, but I'm going to need more even than your sweet words to convince me to tell my solicitor to cave in at this late stage. Sorry, no deal.'

'Look, BabyB. We're not going to solve the world's problems with that kind of approach. Maybe we should agree to put aside our differences for now and we can talk about them later over dinner at mine this evening? How does that sound?'

'And what will be on the menu?' I asked.

'Oh, BabyB, you should know me well enough by now. I may have been accused of many things, but being a tease is not one of them.'

'Well, dinner might be a good time to put the world to rights. Maybe I could just give my solicitor that call. After all, if we can't agree on something as easy as this, what hope is there for the world?'

'Quite, BabyB. Very constructive, if I may say so.'

And so we settled, subject to costs which we went in front of the judge to argue.

'And what do you say about my uplift, BabyB?' The Vamp purred her question to me in front of the judge and made a point of bending over her papers as she said it. What could I say? Barbara Windsor couldn't have delivered the line better. The lady might be a tramp but she had a certain something. Even the (male) judge got the innuendo and, obviously demob happy from getting a free day due to the settlement, added, 'Yes, Mr BabyBarista. What do you say about your opponent's, er, uplift?'

'Sir, it is the finest uplift in all the Bar,' is what I might have replied. Instead I went for, 'On careful reflection, Sir, and considering it from all angles, I have no objection whatsoever to my learned friend's, er, uplift. None. At all. The uplift is, might I say, just right.'

'My thoughts entirely,' the judge responded. 'I shall make an award for your uplift . . .' He peered over his glasses at TheVamp and paused for a long moment, before continuing, 'in full.'

As for what happened later, I shall only go so far as to report that I eventually arrived home from court at seven in the morning. Maybe after TheVamp's voted for me at the tenancy meeting I might just tell her that there had been no need for such generosity on her part, given that I didn't even have a client.

As I struggled home in the morning with a hangover, I have to admit that the person at the forefront of my mind was Claire. Not that there's anything going on between the two of us, it's just that I know she'd be disappointed.

Thursday 14 June 2007
Day 178 (week 37): Private and confidential

Almost by return of post, the hippy house received an A4 brown envelope today from ThirdSix's old chambers. It contained photocopies of a bunch of documents accompanied by a covering letter addressed to ThirdSix. It gave rise to much interesting reading. Seems he had an affair with a client who then complained to chambers about him after he finished it. When the internal investigation (read: 'kangaroo court') got under way, he denied the affair entirely, only to be forced into an embarrassing climb-down when the ex-client presented as evidence a pair of his underpants which had tags emblazoned with his name and Oxford college carefully sewn into the hem. Bless. It was agreed by all concerned that the client would receive an apology and that ThirdSix would leave chambers. As part of the compromise, it was also agreed that nothing more would be mentioned about the matter around the Bar.

Until now, that is. I neatly packed the papers into another brown envelope addressed to ThirdSix and marked it 'Private and confidential: highly sensitive and personal information'. I then put it in TopFirst's pigeon-hole, which is right next to that of ThirdSix. We'll see if TopFirst bites.

Friday 15 June 2007
Day 179 (week 37): Announcement

Today BusyBody announced publicly that she's pregnant. Very publicly in fact. In chambers tea.

'Excuse me, everybody, but I'd like to make a little announcement. Some of you might already have heard but I would just like to say that I'm going to be having a baby. I will finish my pupillage and then take a few months out before returning to the Bar. Thank you.'

Stunned silence and a few open mouths from those who had no idea. Others simply nodded as if they knew already, which probably explains BusyBody's direct approach. Obviously no mention of the identity of the father and according to Worrier there's no prospect of her trying to find this out either. In the meantime, FanciesHimself (who knows nothing of the possibility of OldSmoothie being the father) got wind of this announcement and quietly took BusyBody to one side and proposed to her in the photocopying room. She apparently thanked him very much but declined. Somehow I don't foresee OldSmoothie taking on the same level of responsibility. Since the announcement, he has disappeared from chambers and is apparently off next week 'at the dentist'.

Monday 18 June 2007
Day 180 (week 38): Ask BusyBody

It's all starting to kick off in chambers following the envelope I left in TopFirst's pigeon-hole about ThirdSix and his affair with a client. Predictably, TopFirst couldn't resist and got to work on the rumour mill pretty sharpish. By Friday lunchtime Worrier had come round to my room asking for advice.

'BabyB, have you heard about ThirdSix?'

'I have, yes. TopFirst did mention something in passing although I didn't really get the full details.'

'Well, it seems that he's not as squeaky clean as he first appeared.'

'Something about an affair at his last chambers, wasn't it?' I said vaguely.

'More than just any affair. It was with a client.'

'Golly, I hadn't realised that.'

'The problem is, BabyB, I've been fretting about what I should do.'

Oh, here we go. Worrier doing what she does best. 'How so?' I asked.

'Well, I know he's our competition and everything but it does feel pretty bad knowing that all this nasty stuff's being said behind his back and he knows nothing about it at all.'

'And what were you thinking?'

'Well the last thing I want to do is interfere. But at the same time it seems pretty unfair for TopFirst to be spreading these rumours without giving him any chance to answer them. I just don't know what to do actually. I was hoping you might be able to help.'

'Oh, I'm not really sure. I can certainly see the difficulties,' I said, trying to look as thoughtful and sensitive as possible. 'Sounds like the sort of thing that BusyBody might be able to help with, though.' A suggestion made knowing full well that BusyBody would live up to her name. Sure enough, by this morning BusyBody had had a long talk with ThirdSix, who had in turn had gone to Worrier and asked how TopFirst had got hold of this information. It won't take long for him to find out that a Data Protection Act request was made to his old chambers and TopFirst is going to have difficulties explaining how he came upon the information, given that he did in fact open a letter addressed to ThirdSix.

Tuesday 19 June 2007
Day 181 (week 38): Infighting

'So what do you think I should do, BabyB?'

'About what exactly, ThirdSix?'

'You know. The rumours started by TopFirst.'

Well, it seems they're all after my advice at the moment and aren't I the one who's only just too happy to dispense it with a smile? Of course, you might by now anticipate my answer. 'Oh, you know, I think if I were you I'd probably ask BusyBody. She's bound to know.'

Sure enough, by this afternoon, BusyBody had once again been my unwitting accomplice and over lunch had helped ThirdSix to decide that he needed to take action. So it was that at chambers tea, TopFirst and ThirdSix were starting to square up to each other.

'You made a data protection request to my chambers?'

'No I didn't.'

ThirdSix poked TopFirst in the chest with his finger in a very unbarristerish form of advocacy and you could see the blood rising to his cheeks. 'So how did you come across the information you've been spreading?'

'I don't know what you're talking about.'

'Yes you do.'

'No I don't.'

At this point I wanted to interrupt and start the rest of chambers tea up with a pantomime chorus of 'Oh yes he does' but I just managed to restrain myself as their tempers started to flare. The thing is TopFirst will never admit to his duplicity in reading the confidential letter and so ironically the buck will remain firmly with him. Eventually ThirdSix stormed off in a huff. It'll be interesting to see if and how ThirdSix takes his revenge.

So, as my two main competitors start to fight each other, I think I shall retire quietly into the background and put my feet up for a while. Not.

Wednesday 20 June 2007
Day 182 (week 38): Kick while down

Having weakened TopFirst with all the ThirdSix nonsense, today was the perfect day to arrange the final meeting with Ginny the HoneyTrap. Last week I'd already re-arranged it for this evening, but just to keep him on his toes I sent him an email from Ginny today rearranging it once again, this time for tomorrow evening. Despite this, he confirmed without any reservations, even though he'll have to get out of yet another case to be there. Last week he claimed he had a family funeral today. It'll be interesting to see what he comes up with for tomorrow.

Thursday 21 June 2007
Day 183 (week 38): Mystery illness

Well, I now know what TopFirst came up with as an excuse, since I was given his case after he phoned in this morning claiming to have gone down with the flu. HeadClerk's response to this as he handed me the papers one hour before the hearing was, 'There are only four other people in chambers who have missed cases more than once. Most of these have been because of so-called 'illnesses', which in fact involved either alcohol or young ladies, or both. I don't wish to know which of these is responsible for TopFirst's little 'flu bug' but I certainly hope it was something more attractive than that wine bar plonk of which he's so fond.'

Just to add further spice to the mix, I suggested a drink with ThirdSix this evening in the pub next door to the wine bar where TopFirst is meeting Ginny.

Friday 22 June 2007
Day 184 (week 38): Debrief

So last night was the big one for Ginny and TopFirst. Didn't go quite as I'd planned, but I'll take it as a result nonetheless. Ginny gave me a call this morning and gave me a debrief, so to speak. 'He's so sad, BabyB. He's completely full of himself on the surface and yet he simply can't hide his desperation.'

'So where did he take you?'

'Oh, it was non-stop. First there was a wine bar and then some posh restaurant or other in Covent Garden. Managed to get in this time as well. Then, after he was already pretty much blind drunk on champagne, he insisted on going on to some trendy bar around the corner for mojitos.'

'And what did he come out with?'

'So much, BabyB. I think you'll be pleased with the video. Had lots to say both about the pupils and about other people in chambers. Not very flattering about anyone. Certainly enough to embarrass him pretty badly.'

'Any lunges?'

'Far worse. Once we were at the final bar he started saying that he was falling in love with me and then followed it up with a "lunge", as you call it. Well, I managed to palm him off with an invitation back to mine and we left and got a cab. I told him I'd been lent the flat by an old schoolfriend who was away on holiday.'

'And . . .'

'Hold your horses. I'll get to it. It's worth the wait, I promise. Anyway, back at mine he kept on trying to grope me until eventually I just told him to get undressed whilst I popped downstairs for something. I went out of the flat and then there was nothing for it but to scream. Did a pretty good job as well.'

'I'm starting to see where this is going.'

'Spot on. My only worry was that TopFirst made it out to the rescue before one of the neighbours.'

'And?'

'Like clockwork. Out he comes, so to speak and there was me straight back in the flat and locking the door.'

'Well, that's certainly above and beyond the call of duty. What did he do after that?'

'Not much he could do. Lots of sad, pathetic mewing outside until he realised that he was done for and had to go onto the streets of Stratford in his birthday suit. Can't imagine how he got home since there aren't many cabs out at that sort of time.'

Somehow he must have made it home as I saw him today in chambers, although Ginny's story explains why he was looking rougher even than the apocryphal badger's rear end. All of this has apparently been caught on camera by Ginny. Certainly the stuff he said about chambers will help. But the fact he was trying it on with Ginny when his fiancée was sitting quietly at home is likely to worry him most. It's not helped by the fact that his fiancée is the daughter of an extremely well-known judge in the Court of Appeal.

Overall, should be enough to finish him for good. The problem is that Ginny can also see the value of the tape.

'The thing is, this job was far bigger than you ever explained it might be and the results I got couldn't be more helpful to you. I think you and I understand each other, BabyB, and I don't actually think you'll be surprised to hear that the price has gone up.'

'What? How much?'

'Five grand, BabyB. In cash. And then you get your video. Every last second of it.'

This is money I simply don't have available. Might be time to move things along with FakeClaims&Co and then speak to TheBoss about an advance.

Monday 25 June 2007
Day 185 (week 39): Quelle chance

One thing I didn't mention on Friday is the other part of the story of Thursday night, which might actually result in my not needing to use Ginny's tape. It starts back in the pub to which I'd casually invited ThirdSix.

'Isn't that our friend Mr Stab-You-In-The-Back TopFirst?' asked ThirdSix, as he pointed through the window to the tables outside the wine bar next door.

'So it is,' I remarked casually.

'And who's the stunning girl he's with? It's definitely not his fiancée. I've seen a picture of her on his desk.'

'No idea,' I said.

'He's holding her hand,' he continued.

'So he is,' I observed neutrally.

'He's playing away from home, BabyB. Could be perfect for getting him back. Maybe I can video him canoodling with her using my mobile?'

'I'd be careful if I were you,' I warned.

'Definitely. No worries there. I'll just keep a safe distance.'

'Your fight, I guess,' I rejoined, with which ThirdSix set about getting some dirt on TopFirst.

I certainly look forward to hearing how he got on. Either way, though, I still need to get that tape from Ginny, even if it ends up simply being an insurance option.

Tuesday 26 June 2007
Day 186 (week 39): Loose ends

Just to tie up the loose ends, as TheVamp might say, I sent the following email from Ginny's account to TopFirst today:

From: ginnyandtonic@hotmail.co.uk
To: TopFirst
Date: 26 June 2007, 13.15

Dear TopFirst,
   To a limited extent I guess I should apologise for my undignified behaviour the other evening. I hope that you might forgive this when you learn that earlier that day I had learned on the grapevine via OldRuin that you are, in fact, engaged to be married. I wish you both a long and happy marriage. Please do not contact me ever again.
   Ginny

Wednesday 27 June 2007
Day 187 (week 39): Sleeping dogs

Went out for coffee with ThirdSix today and got the low-down on his own results. Apparently he followed TopFirst and Ginny at a safe distance and then sat at a nearby table in the restaurant where he was able to take a video with his phone. Says that he got loads of comments about members of chambers and, most importantly, the romantic advances which were being made. He's mulling over what he should do with the video. By the level of his nervous energy, it was clear that he had already decided to use it in some way against TopFirst. With the knowledge that my advice would be ignored, I said, 'You know, if I were you, I'd just let sleeping dogs lie.'

Thursday 28 June 2007
Day 188 (week 39): UsherCraft

I won't say what court I was in today. To do so would probably trigger an investigation from the new Ministry of Justice. The reason is simple. One of the judges is having an affair with his usher and all the barristers know about it. But what's unusual about this, you might ask? The answer is the fact that the barristers also know that the usher actually insists on deciding all of the cases for the judge. This led to a feeding frenzy in the waiting room as barristers queued up to book in and try and slip in a few submissions in the process. I didn't realise this until afterwards, unfortunately, and was a little perplexed as to why my opponent spent so much time explaining what a hard journey he'd had and how his mother wasn't very well at the moment and how important this case was to his client. In hindsight, I can now see that the usher had been charmed. Following our submissions, the judge asked for five minutes to consider his judgement. The usher showed us out and then returned into court for the deliberations. Needless to say, I lost, though at least I will know better for next time. Just to make it worse, when we came out of court the client couldn't have been more grateful. It reminded me of something TheBoss once said, 'It's the losers that'll thank you, BabyB. The winners just assume it was down to them. The losers see you as fighting the good fight against the odds.'

Friday 29 June 2007
Day 189 (week 39): Cherish the gift

'How's the family, BabyB?'

OldRuin's sympathetic tone reaches parts of a BabyBarista's heart that his fellow members of the Bar fail to reach. Today he was again treating me to a catch-up lunch at Simpson's in the Strand. 'I'd have the roast beef, if I were you,' he followed up, softening his enquiry after I had paused.

'Good idea. It's very kind of you to treat me like this. Not something you get very often as a pupil.'

'Some things don't change, BabyB. Don't worry. It'll all turn out for the best.' He looked at me and then quietly asked, 'How's home life?'

Without even realising I was doing it, I slowly started to open up in a way I had only ever done with Claire before. 'It's OK, though it can be difficult at times.'

'It's just you and your mother, I believe?'

'That's right.'

'I sometimes think it's hard being young these days.'

'Oh, it's OK. Plenty of people in the same boat.'

'Forgive me for asking, but are there financial pressures?'

'You know, sometimes I don't even know how we've made it through this far. We're both absolutely laden to the hilt with debts and are just counting on my making it at some point at the Bar. That's a big worry. That it'll all have been for nothing. That I'll have inflicted all this on my mother and for no benefit whatsoever.'

'And how does your mother cope?'

'That's my biggest fear, OldRuin. She's extremely fragile. Struggled ever since my dad left and sometimes I do worry . . .'

'Fear, BabyB. It's a part of caring for someone. My wife was ill for five years before she finally passed away. Each day I kissed her goodbye in the morning, I prayed, literally prayed, that it would not be our last goodbye. Then one day, it was.'

I was silent.

'I'm sorry, BabyB. I think I'm doing no more than articulating your worst fears. It's not a bad thing to take them out and examine them once in a while. Makes it easier to put them away afterwards.'

I nodded and he smiled. I wanted to tell him about the loan company, about TheBoss blackmailing me to help him and even to confess about my scheming with the pupils. But the shame and the fear were simply too great. Perhaps he saw this cross my eyes as he continued, 'The Bar, BabyB, isn't about dusty law books. It's all about people and their problems. You'll be the stronger for it.'

'Thank you, OldRuin. I'm sorry to offload.'

'It's the dark ingredients of the soul which give us strength, BabyB. Cherish the gift, for it takes us closer to heaven than ever we'd realise . . .' He looked at me and paused wistfully before continuing, '. . . though it takes us closer to hell too.' Again he paused and added something in a tone which left me unsure whether he was providing encouragement or a warning, 'It's how we use that strength that matters.'

CHAPTER 10
JULY: FACEBOOKED

That general is skilful in attack whose opponent does
not know what to defend.

Sun Tzu, *The Art of War*

Monday 2 July 2007
Day 190 (week 40): Rear-end shunts

I went with Claire to see FakeClaims&Co this weekend. I was looking for something more than simply a bit of professional misconduct. I'd been told that they were involved with a fraud ring and yet had found nothing more than an association with an aggressive ambulance chaser and a dodgy doctor. Not great behaviour, but not enough either. We turned up on Saturday to find a person from the accident management company covering for them.

'Poor you having to work on a Saturday.'

It was Claire and she was all charm as she small-talked him for probably half an hour before giving him a big sob story about me having money problems and needing to get as much money as possible from my claim. Eventually, he turned to me and suggested, 'Of course, you could always have another accident.'

'What do you mean?' I asked.

'Do you have a car?'

'Well, if you could call it that. An old banger worth about ten pence.'

'Perfect. Then you're all set. All boils down to rear-end shunts, you know.'

'Is that rhyming slang?' I asked.

My lame attempt at lightening the conversation was lost even as the words entered the ether and he stared back at me deadpan. 'What?'

I went on to dig my hole a little deeper with, 'You know. Things with double meanings. Like "see you next Tuesday".'

'What? I can't do Tuesday.'

Our cross-purposes were getting crosser and I backtracked awkwardly to the job in hand and added the question, 'So how does it work exactly?'

'Er, we'll take you out and show you how. Let's see. How about Monday evening?'

'Should be OK. What will I get out of it?'

'Now, let's see. You'll obviously get some money for your new injuries. Then there's a new car. We should be able to get it written off and valued at, say, £3,000. After that we'll give you a share of the hire charges on a replacement car which obviously you'll be wanting to incur until the other side pay up. That might give you another £2,000. Oh, and then there's your four passengers. We'll give you £500 per passenger as well. How does that sound?'

Well, as I listen to it back on the tape that Claire made, it sounds good. Tonight we'll see how this little scam works.

Tuesday 3 July 2007
Day 191 (week 40): Dodgy claim

Busy evening last night. Claire and I went and met up with the dodgy claims man in a late-night greasy spoon in east London. Well, Claire was in disguise again and we both had a camera this time. Seems I was one of many appointments for that night. I had the 10.30 slot. I was introduced to my four passengers and then we went off to my car. What I had to do, apparently, was to drive to the dual carriageway and then pull in front of a slow-moving lorry and stop suddenly. We'd get a gentle shove and that would be it. No dispute on liability. I said I'd rather one of the other 'passengers' drove if they had insurance to do so. One of them eventually volunteered by saying that he was insured to drive any car and was happy to step in.

So off we went. Frighteningly simple. The lorry driver got out and apologised and said that he was sorry. Didn't even see us pull in front. He handed over his insurance details and that was that.

All on tape. Should be enough for TheBoss to nail FakeClaims&Co and get them to drop their complaint (as well as the fake claim itself). More importantly for me at the moment, it should be enough to convince TheBoss to give me some extra cash so that I can pay off Ginny and get the tape she made of TopFirst.

Wednesday 4 July 2007
Day 192 (week 40): Five grand

'Well done, BabyB. This is just what we needed.' TheBoss had watched the low-quality videos that Claire and I had covertly made of the various meetings with FakeClaims&Co and their associates. I took back the tape. He'd given me £1,500 when I started investigating and now was the time to seek the balance.

'Given the results, I was wondering if you might not increase my fee? I've got myself into a little financial difficulty and it really would make a difference.'

'How much are you talking, BabyB?'

'It's cash flow, I'm afraid. No one's paid me for my own cases yet and the pupillage award came to an end with my first six. Rock and a hard place, you know. No sympathy from the bank either.'

'How much, BabyB? Give me a figure.'

'Ten thousand on top of the original fifteen hundred. That'd cover my immediate problems.'

'No chance, BabyB.'

He pulled a wad of notes tied up with an elastic band from his pocket. He'd anticipated this conversation. 'Here's five grand. More than we agreed, but I figure you deserve it.'

Just enough to be buying that tape from Ginny.

Thursday 5 July 2007
Day 193 (week 40): Priceless

My client today was a young man of twenty. Quite likely and a bit of a know-all but nice enough as they go. His evidence was chugging along smoothly until the judge noticed that he was chewing gum in the witness box. He looked furious.

'Young man, there are many things that one has to put up with as a judge but one thing I simply will not tolerate is mastication in my court.'

My client's look was priceless. His mouth dropped as, probably, did mine. Clearly the judge was losing it. Seeing that this was having no effect, the judge turned to his clerk and told him to ask the witness to stop masticating. The clerk looked shocked but put on a serious po-faced look and said to the witness, 'The judge would like you to take your hands out of your pockets.'

Now the judge looked shocked and interrupted with, 'No, no, no. You have all misunderstood what I was saying. Young man, will you please refrain from the masticating of that dreadful gum. At once.'

In unison my client, the clerk and I all took on an 'Oh, now I see what you're getting at' look. My guess is that's not the first time the judge has pulled that gag.

Friday 6 July 2007
Day 194 (week 40): Making the trade

Met up with Ginny last night and handed over the cash in return for the tape. I think my favourite bit was the pleading from TopFirst as he banged on Ginny's door, completely starkers. Eventually he had become nasty and started threatening her both with unspecified trouble at university and with getting OldRuin to tell her family about her modelling in London.

'You'll regret this, Ginny. You wouldn't want me as your enemy, I can assure you.'

'Go home, TopFirst.'

'Let me in right now. If you don't I'll make sure you never get taken on anywhere at the Bar.'

'Go home, TopFirst.'

'Believe me, Ginny, there'll be trouble . . . please Ginny let me in . . . or just give me my clothes . . . I'll call the police . . . please . . . maybe just my boxer shorts?'

'Go home, TopFirst.'

There's also some great stuff that he said about members of chambers, and of course the evidence of his sexual advances would be fatal to his engagement. A very handy insurance policy in case ThirdSix doesn't come through against TopFirst on his own.

Monday 9 July 2007
Day 195 (week 41): Ouch

UpTights received a call from a solicitor today. Not just any solicitor, but the senior partner at a massive firm which provides her with a lot of work. Despite this, it would be accurate to say that they have never quite seen eye to eye. Legend has it that this has been since she spurned his advances some twenty years ago. Let's call him OldSoak. UpTights had the phone on loudspeaker and so I heard both sides of the call.

'Hello, OldSoak. How are you?'

'Not bad, UpTights. Not bad. But despite the fact that it's always a pleasure to hear your dulcet tones, I was actually hoping to speak to OldSmoothie.'

'Oh. right. Hmm. Let's see. I'm not terribly good with this new-fangled phone system, you know. I can give it a try though.'

She then pressed a few buttons on her phone and got through to OldSmoothie. 'Hello, OldSmoothie. I have someone on the phone who puts even you in the shade on the loathsome stakes.'

'You're on charming form as ever, UpTights. Now, who could that be?'

'Take a wild guess. He's even older than you, fancies himself even more than you, but unlike you, his dearly beloved wife is having an affair with a young man whom he's just made partner in his firm. Oh, and you can smell him at a distance of a hundred yards.'

'Ooh. Difficult one indeed. You must be referring to our dear friend OldSoak, methinks.'

'Yes, not my favourite person in the world. Pays the bills though, I guess.'

'Well, quite, UpTights. Quite. Priorities and all.'

At which point they were both interrupted from their gossiping.

'Hello? Hello? What on earth are you talking about. UpTights? What's going on?'

It was the voice of OldSoak himself. UpTights had pressed the three-way conference call button.

Ouch.

Wednesday 11 July 2007
Day 197 (week 41): Lucky escape

'Counsel is instructed to do what a man's got to do. To put on his wig and drink his milk.' That was the extent of the instructions which ClichéClanger had sent down with the papers, though to be fair the case pretty much spoke for itself. It was an application in Barnstaple County Court and unfortunately I was slightly late and as I arrived to sign in the usher pointed down the corridor and directed me straight into the courtroom. I went in front of the judge and was relieved to see that the application was unopposed. I started explaining what the case was about.

'And this is an application to vary certain parts of the timetable, isn't it?' he asked.

I confirmed that it was and then spent the next quarter of an hour going through all the facts which led to us making our application. As I came to the end, I looked up hopefully at the judge, somewhat pleased with the clarity with which I had summarised it all. His reply was, 'I'm afraid to say, Mr BabyBarista, that you're in the wrong court. Been going through my list here and there's no mention of your case. Anywhere. Sorry.'

'Oh.'

'Try the next courtroom down.'

Which I did. I knocked on the door and there was a judicial 'enter' from within. I poked my head around the door and asked if he was hearing my case.

'Ah, the applicant arrives. Bit late, don't you think?'

'Sorry, sir. Really, very, very sorry.'

'I'm sure you are. You'll be even more sorry to hear that your opponent has been and gone.'

'Oh.'

'Yes. Luckily for you, he consented to your application in full.'

'Oh.'

'Narrow escape, I'd say.'

'Yes.'

With that, I unpoked my head from around the door and made a sharp exit. Later in the day I had to phone ClichéClanger and somehow explain what had gone on. Started with telling him that the trains were late and that I originally went in front of the wrong judge, when he interrupted me and said, 'Let me stop you there, BabyBarista. I received an email a few minutes ago from the other side giving me the full details of the order.'

'Oh,' I said, unsure where this was going. I figured it'd be better for me to get in my explanation now before he started having a go. Yet as I drew breath to give my little plea in mitigation, ClichéClanger continued, 'Yes. You got everything we asked for. Very well done. A piece of *gâteau* to you no doubt,' he said, emphasising the French. 'You are definitely *le grand fromage* round here today, I can tell you. Well done, BabyBarista. You can expect more where that came from.'

What was I to do? The first solicitor I'd had promising me my own work. Did I correct him? Tell him that I wasn't even at the hearing?

'Look forward to it,' was all I could manage in the heat of the moment.

Well, wouldn't want to ruin his good mood.

Friday 13 July 2007
Day 199 (week 41): Memories

TheBusker was defending a theft today and I was once again following him to court. It all boiled down to whether the prosecution's witness was credible or not. Looked pretty open and shut to me.

'Nothing's ever clear cut, BabyB. Not when it comes to memories. There's no smooth little movie being recorded in that head of yours. It's all a tapestry of jagged images and sounds, stitched together by the imagination. Watch out for those stitches, BabyB. They'll win you case after case.'

So it was today. TheBusker was as friendly as you like to the witness, getting her full story in intimate detail. Then he went back and simply asked, 'And you are absolutely certain that your account is accurate in every detail?'

'Of course,' came the reply.

'Thank you. Now, if we can just go over a few of these details again . . . You say the defendant came from the left?'

'Yes.'

'Did you actually see him come from the left?'

'Er . . .'

'Or did you simply assume it because you heard the shout coming from the left?'

'Er . . .'

One by one he addressed each detail and exposed the little assumptions upon which so many of them were based, reaching into thin air and finding those little stitches added by the imagination.

On such details is a man's liberty determined.

Monday 16 July 2007
Day 200 (week 42): VampCard

UpTights has a big case tomorrow and this afternoon she was told which judge she would be appearing before, which sent her into something of a tizzy.

'He's the most lecherous, chauvinistic pig of a judge in the whole country. Decides by the attractiveness of the legal team rather than the strength of the case.'

'So how do our opponents shape up?' I asked, trying to lighten her mood.

'It's not funny, BabyB, I'm afraid. Not for you anyway. Now that we know he'll be hearing it, I have no alternative but to play a VampCard. You'll be no help whatsoever.'

Oh. Dropped. Just like that. Who cares that I've spent the last few weeks slaving over these papers for her? 'Sorry, BabyB, but you just don't have what we're looking for.'

UpTights called TheVamp down and simply told her that she was needed for a hearing with this particular judge. 'Oh. I see,' she said, in an understanding tone. Not that it'll be much fun for her, but apparently she gets paid twice her usual rate to make her feel better for cases such as these.

'You know what's required,' was all that UpTights said to her about the case. Of course she did.

I was the bag carrier for UpTights and TheVamp today as they arrived at court done up to the nines. They were greeted by OldSmoothie.

'You know, UpTights, each time you lower yourself like this you just feed that little self-hatred monster which gnaws away at your brain each day.'

She ignored him.

'You know that they've changed our judge, I assume?'

She didn't ignore him on that one.

'Yes. Shame really. Feels there's a conflict of interest given that he and I sit on the same golf-club committee. He's passed the case over to his learned colleague.'

UpTights's mouth dropped. Well, it moved as far as it was able. To make it worse, not only was the new judge female but she, like the rest of the legal community, knew the stories about the lascivious nature of her fellow judge and it didn't take much of her female intuition to sniff out what was going on. In fact, going by the pungent smell of expensive perfume coming from UpTights and TheVamp as they entered the courtroom, 'sniff out' would probably be extremely accurate.

'How long has your junior been instructed on this case, Ms UpTights?'

'That is not relevant, Your Honour.'

'Even so. Humour me. How long?'

'Since yesterday afternoon.'

'And when did you find out who would be hearing this case?'

'Er. Yesterday afternoon.'

'And would there, by any chance, be any correlation between these two happenings?'

'Your Honour. M'learned friend is extremely experienced in matters such as this.'

'Yes,' she took a long look at TheVamp before continuing, 'I'm sure she is.'

The case was lost before it had even started and UpTights and TheVamp were left looking like two women out on the pull who'd been turned away at the door of the only nightclub in town.

Wednesday 18 July 2007
Day 202 (week 42): Yo, dude!

It might be the pressure but TopFirst is starting to turn into a parody of himself. He's like the class nerd who's become so full of his own self-importance that he's even started to believe he's cool. There have been a number of affectations over the months but his new catchphrase does him no favours whatsoever. He's started saying, 'Juglandaceous, dude' in the style of Bill and Ted. He immediately follows it up with, 'Great word, huh? Means something to do with walnuts, believe it or not. Thinking of putting it in one of my closing speeches.'

Righteous. Dude.

As for UpTights, she's been working on JudgeJewellery's case. The difficulty is that CheapnNasty, the shop where she was caught, has come back with a load of CCTV evidence showing her stealing all sorts of other jewellery on numerous occasions in the past. They're also threatening to go to their competitors to ask them if they have any similar footage. So for now her only hope is going to be that of the last resort for the desperate, an abuse of process argument. Seems they didn't read her her rights properly after she'd given them the old, 'Do you realise that I'm a member of Her Majesty's judiciary?' line. Thought there was no need. Which of course there wasn't, since she knew full well what her rights were. But if there's a technicality to be had, there'll always be a lawyer there to take it.

Whilst UpTights was in conference with JudgeJewellery I received a call from FakeClaims&Co telling me that they'll need another medical report after which they'll be able to get me some cash for both my injuries. Recorded the call using the loudspeaker on my phone and a small tape recorder and then took it straight round to TheBoss. 'Just the job, BabyB. Can't see how they'll continue in the face of all this evidence.'

I hope he's right for my own sake. Despite the fact that it would be a cowardly, low-down, two-faced thing to do, I have no doubt that he means it when he says that if he goes down, I go with him.

Been checking out TopFirst's network of friends on Facebook. Interesting that he hasn't yet removed Ginny, which made me think that there may be some scope for causing trouble there in the future. That then got me wondering. Tried signing in as TopFirst himself. I already have his personal email address from his dealings with Ginny and so all I needed was his password. Ginny's name failed as did that of his fiancée. Then I tried his football team, his Cambridge college and a few obscure legal terms as it wouldn't have surprised me to find his password was something like 'estoppel' or 'Mareva'. All to no avail. Then it dawned on me. His favourite word of the moment. His naff Bill and Ted bodacious take-off. I typed in 'juglandaceous' – and bingo. Access to his most intimate 459 friends from Cambridge and beyond.

So, just a few small changes to make to his profile. 'Relationship status' was changed from 'engaged' to 'single'. A broken heart next to his name immediately indicated this on the newsfeeds of his friends. Then, I changed his 'looking for' section from 'friends' to 'anything I can get'. Lo and behold, another newsfeed instantly appeared. This I followed up by Googling a paparazzi picture of someone doing a drunken moonie outside a nightclub and uploading it as his profile picture. With his new profile sorted, I set up a group called 'The Great Singles Lurve Shack' and sent out an invitation to join it to all of his friends. After that I thought maybe I'd leave a message on the wall of each of his female friends (excluding his fiancée) saying:

> Hi, I've often regretted having fallen into that 'just good friends' thing and wondered, now that I'm single, whether we should perhaps see if the chemistry's there on a more romantic level? How about a romantic dinner? x

Facebooked. Oh, and just in case anyone tried to trace what had been done, which is admittedly unlikely, I did it all from ThirdSix's computer which he'd left on and available for anyone to use.

Tuesday 24 July 2007
Day 206 (week 43): Damage limitation

As one of TopFirst's Facebook friends I received a message from him late this afternoon both on Facebook itself and also to my Hotmail account.

> Hi, it seems that someone hacked into my Facebook account yesterday. I would like to confirm the following.
> 1. I have not just split up with my fiancée.
> 2. I do not want to have a romantic dinner with all my female friends.
> 3. The photo of a man pulling his trousers down outside a nightclub is not me.
> 4. I did not set up the group 'The Great Singles Lurve Shack'.
> I have instructed defamation lawyers and I hereby give formal notice that I will take legal action against anyone repeating any of this.

And that's supposed to make it better? Anyway, he's trying to get to the bottom of 'The Case of the Facebook Fiend' as he's calling it. Worrier says he suspects it was probably . . . guess who? ThirdSix of course. Who else? Thinks he's getting him back for intercepting his post the other day.

Thursday 26 July 2007
Day 208 (week 43): Battleships

Today I went along to a settlement conference with UpTights. She was representing an insurer who I'll call Sundance and her opponent was once again OldSmoothie. As we were all sitting around a table ready to start FanciesHimself came into the room carrying a box in front of him like it was the crown jewels. I looked more closely. It was a game of Battleships.

'Set 'em up then, OldSmoothie,' said Sundance. 'Your turn to go first, I believe?'

At this point no one had yet explained exactly what was going on, but it was slowly starting to dawn on me. 'Don't worry, BabyB,' said Sundance after it was all up. 'This is no more random than putting your case in front of a judge and it's a heck of a lot cheaper.

214

If OldSmoothie wins, his client gets half a mill in this case. If I win, he only gets a hundred thou. Simple as that, really.'

He noticed that I looked towards UpTights. 'Why brief counsel on our own side, you ask?'

'No, I wasn't wanting to suggest . . .'

'I've known OldSmoothie here for years. Fought hundreds of cases against each other. He only ever agrees to Battleships if UpTights can be the referee.'

OldSmoothie looked very pleased with himself. UpTights on the other hand was less than amused at being paraded around as the most expensive Battleships referee in the world ever.

'If you insist on playing these schoolboy games, the least you can do is to get on with it, don't you think?'

'Oh but UpTights, don't you enjoy the build-up? These settlement conferences are always the highlight of my month.'

'Me too, actually,' said Sundance.

Then they both sat down at the table and stared at each other like a couple of old gunslingers. Silence descended and the duel began. Today it was OldSmoothie who was victorious and he rang his solicitor from the room to report on what a tough negotiation he had been through.

As I was leaving work I noticed in the chambers diary that ThirdSix is booked in on a case against Teflon on Monday and by coincidence he's also in the same court on a different case the next day. He's currently away in Manchester until tomorrow evening and both briefs were waiting for him in his pigeon-hole. I quickly took them out and went back to my room. Satisfied that in both cases he was defending claims which ultimately would be paid by an insurer (as if this somehow made what I was about to do slightly less bad), I made the switch. Actually, it was only the date on the front of each brief which I changed – making the 30th look like the 31st and vice versa. Very simple, but potentially very effective.

We'll see how he gets on.

Monday 30 July 2007
Day 210 (week 44): SuperBlag

The joy of having Teflon as ThirdSix's opponent today was that I could absolutely count on him spreading any malicious gossip that may have arisen as soon as his non-stick little wig landed back in chambers. Sure enough, come 4 p.m., we all received a blow-by-blow account by email:

> If it wasn't enough that our super-clever third six pupil seduced a client at his last chambers, today it got worse. He arrived at court with completely the wrong set of papers. Pretty bad, you might think, but there was more to come. The penny suddenly dropped halfway through the hearing. But rather than stopping and 'fessing up, he only dug his hole deeper. I assume he arrogantly thought he'd be able to blag the whole hearing off the back of the wrong papers. Which he might well have done if he wasn't such a lousy blagger. Now I admit I have no proof of this other than his dreadful performance and the look of realisation on his face when I referred to a particular witness statement. All I can say is that this man is a danger to the public.

Tuesday 31 July 2007
Day 211 (week 44): A quiet word

'HeadofChambers called ThirdSix in for a quiet word this morning.' It was TopFirst gossiping over lunch.

'How did he get on?'

'Denied it all, apparently. Said that Teflon was mischief-making.'

'Perhaps he was.'

'Apparently that's an end to it as there's no proof either way.'

In which case the whole thing needed a helping hand. I knew already that ThirdSix's client had been a Brummie due to Teflon's further reports of the hearing. So, after a little practice with the accent I made the call from a phone box and blocked the identity of the number. 'Hello, can I please speak to the head of chambers?'

It was HeadClerk who answered, which gave me a bit of a fright. 'Please wait whilst I see whether he is available. Who shall I say is calling?'

I gave the name of ThirdSix's client, but it didn't seem to ring any bells.

'And what is your call in relation to?'

'I was represented by ThirdSix yesterday and I am extremely unhappy with the service I received. I am a very busy man and either I speak to the head of chambers immediately and we see if we can resolve this privately or I shall simply send off a complaint to the Bar Standards Board. You choose.'

'I see, Sir. Yes. Please wait a moment.'

Thirty seconds later and I heard the dulcet tones of HeadofChambers. 'Er, hello. Yes. I believe you wish to talk about your case with ThirdSix? How can I help, exactly?'

'I am very sorry to have to say this but he singularly failed in representing me yesterday.'

'In what way, may I ask?'

'He fought the whole thing without having any of the papers in my case.'

'How do you know this?'

'Because I saw the names of the parties on the various sheets of papers and they weren't ours.'

'Did you mention this at the time?'

'I tried interrupting him during the hearing but he told me to be quiet. Afterwards he shook my hand and rushed off before I could say anything else.'

'I see.'

Then I went in for the kill. 'You see, a mistake is one thing. We all make mistakes. But about halfway through it was clear to me that he suddenly realised that he had the wrong papers. Yet still he continued. Such dishonesty reflects badly not only on the professionalism of your own chambers but of the bar as a whole.'

'Yes, quite.'

'Now, just so you know, I'm not at this stage interested in suing him for negligence or anything like that. It's just that I am extremely concerned that this might happen to someone else. You do understand?'

'I understand completely.'

'And in those circumstances it seems I have two choices. The most obvious is to pursue a formal complaint through the Standards Board against both ThirdSix and your chambers. However, personally I would rather not get involved further and would also like to keep my solicitor out of it as he and I have become friends. Therefore, my preferred path would be to hand the matter over to you. You can then call me when it has been dealt with and I can decide whether that puts an end to it or not.'

'That sounds eminently sensible, if I may say so.'

I then gave him the telephone number of my 'pay as you go' mobile phone.

CHAPTER 11
AUGUST: SHOWDOWNS

Use the conquered foe to augment one's own strength.
Sun Tzu, *The Art of War*

Wednesday 1 August 2007
Day 212 (week 44): Owning up

Today ThirdSix was well and truly in the dock. It was Worrier who first told me what had happened.

'It's pretty terrible, BabyB. Apparently, HeadofChambers hauled him in again this morning and in no uncertain terms told him that he'd better explain exactly what went on at the hearing. He also said that if he didn't, the whole of chambers could end up with a complaint being made against it to the Bar Standards Board.'

'And how did he react to that?'

'Well, eventually he owned up and admitted that he had had the wrong papers at court. But when he started suggesting that someone like TopFirst or even the clerks might have switched them, HeadofChambers interrupted him and told him that he should take responsibility for his own actions and pointed out that as soon as he realised they were the wrong papers he should have owned up. Well, as you can imagine, ThirdSix had no answer to this.'

Shame.

After that I received a call from HeadofChambers himself on the 'pay as you go' mobile. 'Er, yes, this is HeadofChambers. I am pleased to say that I have now dealt with our little, er, problem.'

'In what way, may I ask?'

'I have formally disciplined ThirdSix and I can assure you that such an incident will never happen again. In addition, all this will be taken into account when it comes to deciding whether chambers decide to keep him on next month.'

'I see. So you are fully satisfied that this will not be repeated with any other clients?'

'I am.'

'That is all I ask. Consider this an end to the matter. Good day.'

Friday 3 August 2007
Day 214 (week 44): SweatShop

Word has it that despite the fact that the Inns of Court are currently crawling with mini-pupils, there are many candidates who are still struggling to get work placements. Half as a joke, half serious, I decided to post the following on a couple of internet bulletin boards the other day: 'Pupil barrister offers informal mini-pupillage based at Inner Temple library. Good reference guaranteed.' I've already had ten applications and so I'm conducting interviews in the library this evening. Little do they know that I'll take them all on for the next month and get them each to do some research on my behalf for a different member of chambers I am trying to impress.

Best of all, forget the minimum wage. This work comes for free.

Monday 6 August 2007
Day 215 (week 45): RackItUp

When I got up this morning I thought I was destined for a relaxing day trawling through papers. Until, that was, I arrived into chambers to be confronted by HeadClerk looking particularly serious. 'Mr BabyBarista. I need you to get over the road to court six in twenty minutes. Million pound business dispute. Just need you to hold the fort for HeadofChambers.'

Hold the fort? Oh, the art of the understatement. So I arrived at court ten minutes early thinking I might find HeadofChambers there to give me a little background. No such luck and I rang HeadClerk to ask where I could find him. 'That's a good question, Mr BabyBarista.' He paused. 'You see, he has a case in court thirty-two and another in court twenty. Oh, and then let's see . . . there's another in court fifty-six.' He paused again. 'That's in addition to yours.'

Now don't get me wrong. I'd already heard about HeadofChambers's notorious money-making scheme whereby he gets juniors to do all the work and he just turns up for at most an hour a day on each of his cases. Apparently he shows his face, makes a point of looking deep in consultation with his junior and then dashes off to the next case. That's one thing. But what I discovered today was that his scheme falls down when one of those hard-working juniors is ill. That's when the QC should be there to step in. Unless, that is, you're HeadofChambers and you're already juggling too many cases and therefore have to rely on a BabyBarista completely out of his depth. When I finally got hold of him, rushing between two of his courts, the most that I got out of him was, 'Don't worry, BabyB. All you have to do today is to sit tight whilst the other side cross-examine our witness. Just keep a good note. You'll be all right.'

Which would have been OK were it not for the fact that my opponent stopped his cross-examination mid-morning. The judge knew what was going on and was not amused. I asked for an adjournment in order that I might consult with HeadofChambers.

'Mr BabyBarista. Either you are prepared for this case, which would mean that such an adjournment would be unnecessary . . .' He peered at me over his glasses and then continued, 'or you are not sufficiently prepared, in which case you would be in breach of the Code of Conduct for accepting the instructions.' He looked at me and smiled, a cruel, smug kind of smile which said everything. I was skewered. I stood up and tried to buy some time before my career came crashing to a premature end. 'Er, My Lord. Er, if it pleases the court. Er . . .'

'Yes, Mr BabyBarista. What is it to be?'

I stumbled on a little more before my solicitor tapped me on the shoulder. I turned around and he handed me a note which said, 'No further questions. Call the next witness, Mr James.'

'Er, My Lord, I have no further questions for this witness. Unless you have any questions, My Lord, I would like to call the next witness, Mr James.'

Given that I knew absolutely nothing about the case whatsoever, I don't know how I even managed to get through to lunch, particularly with my opponent capitalising on my difficulties by keeping his own questions to a minimum. To make matters worse, all that I got from HeadofChambers at lunchtime when I told him precisely where he could stick his case as far as the afternoon was concerned was, 'There's the spirit, BabyB. I knew I could rely on you. I'll take it from here. Tally ho!'

'Ha!' said OldSmoothie when I told him later. 'He's not called RackItUp for nothing, you know.'

I didn't know.

'And that's not just because he racked up twelve grand today or even that the whole thing's a complete racket. It's his particular skill, like a rack on a train, to hold aloft numerous cases at once which is most impressive.'

'Oh.'

'It's like snakes and ladders, BabyB,' he continued. 'You climb to the top of one ladder only to go hurtling down to the bottom just a short time later. Happens to us all. You may have been a big cheese at university, but as a pupil you go back to being pond life. Same for HeadofChambers. Just wait until he becomes a judge and gets passed all the dud cases. Just snakes and ladders, BabyB. That's all it is.'

Small consolation, I must say, but OldSmoothie wasn't finished as he started to muse, 'You know it's all about marking time, this job. Your year of call and the number of hours you spend on a particular piece of work. It's all that matters. Clock up the hours, clock up the years and the rewards will follow.'

For once he wasn't sounding smug or arrogant. Almost slightly sad. Well, it was as close as OldSmoothie might get to having feelings anyway. 'I just wonder sometimes where those hours have gone. Whether it was all worth it.'

Then it was as if he heard himself saying this and he snapped back to life. With a clearing of his throat and in a particularly deep voice he said, 'But anyway, enough of all that nonsense. Wouldn't have it any other way, BabyB.'

With which he dismissed me with a wave of his hand.

Tuesday 7 August 2007
Day 216 (week 45): Applications for tenancy

BusyBody's started getting up my nose again. Just when I thought she'd finally given up on any chance of a tenancy whatsoever, she starts spreading the word that despite the scandal surrounding her pregnancy, she'll still be applying on the basis that she might start after a few months of maternity leave. The irony is that this decision is probably as a result of my having damaged the other pupils to such an extent that she feels she may be back in with a chance. Anyway, I got an opportunity to mislead her yesterday after all the pupils received a letter from HeadofChambers formally inviting us to apply for tenancy. As I was about to leave in the evening I noticed that BusyBody's letter was still there unopened and with no one around I took it away and spent twenty minutes retyping it.

Dear BusyBody,

In line with our current policy on pupillage, I should like to invite you formally to apply for tenancy. In order to assist us with our application, it would be of great help if you could provide us with an up-to-date CV and a letter explaining why you think you should be taken on, along with copies of three pieces of work you have done for different members of chambers.

We also wish you to undergo a medical examination as part of our formal risk assessment for tenancy. It will consist merely of a brief check-up by a GP. Whilst we assure you that the results will not affect your chances, you are within your rights to refuse any such examination. However, if you are happy to consent to these arrangements, please come to the main chambers conference room at 4.30 p.m. on Wednesday 8th August (i.e. tomorrow) when it will be used as a temporary surgery (chambers tea being moved elsewhere). Please could you bring with you a copy of your application documents along with a urine sample for the GP in a sealed plastic container.

I would ask you to note that your application is absolutely confidential and I would therefore ask that you do not consult with anyone else during the process.

May I take this opportunity to wish you the very best of luck with your application.

Yours sincerely,
HeadofChambers

Wednesday 8 August 2007
Day 217 (week 45): SuperSample

Today I made sure that I was in chambers tea in the conference room bang on time. Ready and waiting. Wondering if BusyBody would have taken the bait. What I'd counted on most was that as someone who aspires to authority, she has never been one to question what such authority might have to say. Well, come 4.30 p.m. there were about twenty members of chambers quietly sipping on their tea when there was an ominous knock at the door. Since barristers don't knock and the clerks never interrupt tea, there was silence. HeadofChambers then boomed 'enter'. At which point BusyBody opened the door holding her urine sample out in front of her. The silence continued and was eventually broken by BusyBody with a stuttering, 'I . . . I . . . I was just after the medical for tenancy. I think I have the wrong room.'

More silence, though you could see lots of pennies dropping in lots of different heads. Eventually HeadofChambers said, 'Er . . . I think you might find, BusyBody, that someone has played a practical joke on you.'

Already bright red and unsuccessfully trying to hide the urine sample under her documents, BusyBody whimpered, 'Oh. Sorry. Sorry. So sorry.' She then turned and scuttled as fast as was possible in the circumstances. After which the room broke down into fits of laughter. Poor BusyBody. Her sexual dilly-dallying had already caused her to be the butt of many jokes in chambers over the past few months. Not only did this make it worse, but it also meant that the list of potential culprits amounted to about a dozen members of chambers. Though it might also be one of the two trouble-making pupils, it was also whispered. Now who could this be, you ask? Why, TopFirst and ThirdSix, of course! So, with too many potential suspects it was generally agreed that the matter would be quietly dropped.

Friday 10 August 2007
Day 219 (week 45): Bride's nightie

UpTights and OldSmoothie. You've gotta love it. They were at it again today. You know it really wouldn't surprise me if one day I came into chambers and discovered that they'd run off together. Decided to settle their differences and go off into the sunset. That love–hate thing. Well, maybe in another life. But today I finally discovered why they are so frequently against each other when I accidentally overheard a conversation between OldSmoothie and his solicitor.

'You're her Achilles heel, OldSmoothie. Any time I hear she's on the other side the papers go straight over to you.'

'Well, I can't say I don't enjoy our little encounters.'

'But that's the beauty of it, you see. The more you do it, the more she hates you and the more she can't help reacting.'

Today was no different and UpTights continued to react to the jibes with a barrage of interruptions. Eventually OldSmoothie said, 'I'm sorry, Your Honour, but my learned friend has been up and down more times than a bride's nightie.'

The judge seemed somewhat distracted by the unfortunate image which OldSmoothie had conjured. Perhaps not realising that he was articulating his thoughts out loud, he said, 'Do you think brides still wear nighties these days?'

This was the last straw for UpTights and she stood up, once again ready to make an objection. At this, the judge snapped out of his reverie and returned to the proceedings.

'Sit down now, Ms UpTights,' he stormed. 'Nighties . . . naughties . . . niceties . . .' He stopped, struggling to bring his mind back to the proceedings. 'I will have none of any of it in my court.' Then he seemed to remember where all of this had come from and calmed down, looked at UpTights and concluded, 'Will you please let your opponent finish without jumping up and down.'

At which point his eyes glazed over and it was obvious his mind had strayed back once again to nighties.

Monday 13 August 2007
Day 220 (week 46): Heart attack

It's a sad admission but late yesterday evening I was in chambers sorting out the numerous sets of papers for my crop of mini-pupils. The chambers phone started ringing and normally I wouldn't have answered. But the number which came up said that the call came from OldRuin's home. I answered immediately.

'Help me,' came a very faint voice. 'Help.'

It was OldRuin, no doubt about that – and yet it was completely out of character for him to be asking for any assistance whatsoever. Something was definitely up.

'OldRuin. It's BabyBarista here. How can I help?'

'Need help.' The voice was hardly coherent. 'Need. Help. Please.'

This was obviously serious.

'Do you need an ambulance?'

'Yes.'

The phone then went dead. Never having rung 999 before, it felt very weird to do so, but I made the call as soon as I had dug out OldRuin's home address from chambers' computer records. 'Yes, ambulance . . . Yes, a friend of mine. Actually I work with him. I don't know what's wrong, but he needs help immediately. It's an emergency . . . No, I don't have any idea what it is. Heart attack, I would imagine. Please get there immediately . . . Thank you. Oh, and please can someone ring me when they have picked him up? Thank you so very much. Goodbye.'

I put the phone down and dashed around the room in something of a panic. My papers were all prepared for the next day and I left them on my desk and simply scooped up the evidence of the work I was setting my mini-pupils in case anyone should stumble upon it. Then I was out of the door and heading for the main road, where I eventually managed to flag down a cab which took me to Waterloo station. There I waited for a train to Winchester, which was where I believed OldRuin would probably be taken to hospital. Thankfully one of the ambulance crew called about twenty minutes later and told me that they were taking him to the Royal Hampshire County Hospital in Winchester. They told me that he'd suffered a heart attack and that if they'd arrived any later he would have died. As it was, it remained touch and go. I eventually got to the hospital around half past midnight and had to wait another six hours before I could see him. He was slipping in and out of consciousness but the doctors seemed confident that he would now pull through. I held his hand and caught a few words from him, though I tried to discourage him from speaking.

'Thank you, BabyB. Very . . . kind . . . Didn't want to tell chambers about heart problems . . .'

'Don't worry, OldRuin. You're going to be all right and chambers will never know. I assure you.'

'But you must go. Get to court.'

'Please don't worry. No case today, thankfully. Day off.'

Which wasn't quite true. Actually, it was a downright lie as I was booked to do a case in Central London at 10.30 a.m. But there was no way I was leaving him in this state. The difficulty was what I was going to have to tell HeadClerk. I couldn't mention OldRuin's condition as this was something he wanted kept private, yet HeadClerk had already voiced his scepticism about people who ring in saying they are 'sick'. I made the call around 8 a.m.

'Very, very sorry but I just feel awful. Can't move. Completely sick.'

'Right, BabyB. I see.' He paused. 'You know how serious this is, don't you?'

'Yes, I do. But I have no choice. No choice at all.' I left it at that.

'You also couldn't have picked worse timing to get sick, BabyB. Doesn't look good at all with a tenancy decision looming.'

'I know.'

'So be it,' he said curtly and ended the call.

That was all he needed to say. Pretty damning. All that effort to get to this point and then to have it all put at risk by circumstance.

The good news is that by the time I left in the evening, the doctors were predicting a good recovery for OldRuin. Wish I could say the same for my tenancy chances.

Tuesday 14 August 2007
Day 221 (week 46): Cold shoulder

I'm definitely getting the cold shoulder from HeadClerk today, and I get the very strong impression that he doesn't believe that I was sick yesterday. He's pretty good at sniffing out the contrived excuse and to be fair to him, he was right on this occasion. The problem is I can't tell him the real reason and so I just have to take my chances which, in the light of his withering look this morning, seem mighty slim. Actually, 'withering' is not a word which does the look justice. It was the kind of look which OldSmoothie once summed up in reference to UpTights when he said (and I won't pass on the full colour of his language), 'You can (empty your bowels) better ways than she looks at people.'

Wednesday 15 August 2007
Day 222 (week 46): Blackmail

'I went to see FakeClaims&Co today to discuss the evidence I'd gathered.' It was TheBoss and what he meant was he'd tried to blackmail them into withdrawing their complaint against him.

'How did it go?' I asked.

'I certainly gave it to them straight. Showed them all the evidence and told them that I was considering sending it to both the Law Society and the police.'

'How did they react?'

'It kicked off. Big time. You should have seen their faces. First there was shocked silence. Then knee-jerk denial. Then indignation and anger and they threatened to call security and kick me out there and then. Luckily one of the two I went to see seemed to have his head screwed on and he calmed the other one down and said that they'd go over what I'd given them and then get back to me.'

'Did you actually demand that they withdraw the complaint?'

'Not in a million years. But let's just say that there was absolutely no doubt as to what I was saying.'

'Well, let's hope they see sense.'

'Yes, BabyB. For your sake as much as mine, wouldn't you say?' Then, just to rub in what he was telling me, he added, 'By the way, I received notice of the Bar Standards Board hearing today. All set for 26th September.'

I no doubt looked shaken by the news as TheBoss continued, 'Which is two days before the tenancy decision, I believe.'

Friday 17 August 2007
Day 224 (week 46): The horror

This morning UpTights settled a five-day case which was due to start on Monday and in the process collected the full brief fee of

£12,000 even though she hadn't even started preparing for trial. Which explains her demob, un-UpTights-type mood when she said breezily, 'Lunch, BabyB? It's been a while since we had a proper catch up.'

Never one to turn down a free lunch, I was whisked off to a different swanky restaurant to the last occasion and when we sat down I was less than surprised when I was asked, 'Champagne, BabyB?'

For a teetotal detox addict, she certainly gets her fair share of alcohol. By 3 p.m. we'd been through two bottles of the expensive stuff and she was on for more. 'No point going back to chambers, BabyB. Not in any state to be billing.'

'Quite so, UpTights.'

'Just one more bottle then, perhaps?'

Oh, go on then! If you must. We continued drinking until about six in the evening after which it suddenly dawned on me that UpTights was starting to flirt. 'You know, BabyB, you can be very clever when you want to be . . . You know, BabyB, you're one step ahead even before you start. Judges will always warm to someone attractive. It's just human nature . . . Oh, BabyB, now don't tell me that you don't have half the female pupil barristers swooning after you.'

Then it started getting even more direct. 'So do you have a girlfriend, BabyB?'

'Er, no, not right at the moment.'

'Not even anything going on with that friend of yours, what's her name?'

'Claire. No, we're friends, that's all.'

'Nothing ever happened with TheVamp? She's always one to make herself available.'

Well that's one way of putting it but I wasn't about to start making any incriminating admissions in that direction.

'No. Certainly not,' I lied.

'But don't you get lonely, BabyB? On those long nights when you're sitting there preparing a brief, with no one to share the little things that make life so special?'

'Er, I guess, maybe occasionally.'

'It comes to us all at some time or other, BabyB. We all crave companionship. Keeps us sane. Gives us meaning. But . . .'

She looked at me and tried to strain her stretched features into an expression I could tell was meant to seem coy, but which actually just looked like she was pulling a face. 'Don't you miss the physical side? Just holding someone close? Waking up next to them?'

The horror. On so many levels, none of which you'd want to dwell on for too long. Then she went on, 'You know, BabyB, if I were twenty years younger . . .'

The image of a female praying mantis devouring the head of her mate sprung into my mind. As I tried to work out how I was going to extricate myself diplomatically, I felt her foot brush my ankle under the table and I almost shot cartoon-like into the air. I was off. 'Er, UpTights. I'm afraid you've just reminded me that I was meant to meet Claire about an hour ago. Have to go now. So sorry. I'll see you Monday. Bye.'

Off. Gone. Out of the lair. There are many things I would do to get tenancy. But that is not one of them.

Monday 20 August 2007
Day 225 (week 47): PupilGeek

Thankfully UpTights has taken today and tomorrow off which will hopefully allow the dust to settle on Friday's little episode. Meanwhile I had the pleasure today of being against PupilGeek, who's created an online game for pupils to play from their phones whilst they are in court. It's basically a fight game between two bewigged barristers and the last one standing wins. Sounds easy enough but the skill is getting the blows in without the judge noticing that you are playing. Today we both had the benefit of lecterns which hid our little consoles from the judge and it would have all gone unnoticed if my opponent hadn't suddenly called me something it wouldn't be appropriate for me to repeat here, never mind to utter in a courtroom, after I'd knocked him onto the canvas. The judge looked up immediately.

'Mr PupilGeek. I've been called many things in my time but never in my whole career have I ever been addressed in such a manner.'

'Er, Your Honour. I'm terribly sorry.'

'Sorry. I should say so. Sorry. You'll be sorry, I assure you.'

Despite the fact that he was my opponent and I wanted to win the case, the injustice of the whole situation rankled even with my competitive spirit, particularly as I'd just smashed his head in online. 'Your Honour, I'm afraid that the comment may have been directed at me.'

Though with hindsight, admitting this was a mistake.

'I see, Mr BabyBarista. What, pray, were you doing to elicit such an extreme reaction? Please enlighten me, do.'

I could think of no innocent explanation.

'Come on, Mr BabyBarista. Let's hear it then.'

'Er, Your Honour, er . . .'

'Yes, yes, young man. Get it out.'

'Well, Your Honour. That was really the problem.'

'What was? What nonsense are you talking now?'

'Getting it out. Wind that is. It's terribly embarrassing really, Your Honour. I was trying desperately not to pass wind but, well, eventually . . .'

There was a titter from my opponent's client behind me.

'Oh. I see. Oh. Well. Quite. I see. I do understand. Well. Perhaps we should move on then.'

Wednesday 22 August 2007
Day 227 (week 47): Back to normal

'BabyB, where's that advice you were going to do for me?'

It was UpTights and she was back with a vengeance today with absolutely no reference to the long lunch.

'Er, I left it on your desk over here,' I walked over to the side of her desk and pointed. I was probably about six feet away from her.

'Please, BabyB. I've told you before. Don't encroach. It's just not polite. Go and sit down. Now, why did you give me a hard copy? What use is that if I want to make changes? Didn't you think to email it?'

'Yes.'

'Well, I haven't received it.'

'Oh. I sent it yesterday. Sorry.'

'Well don't sit there like a lemon, BabyB. Email it over again.'

233

This was pretty much what it was like all day. UpTights's abrasive manner, for the first time ever, became something I welcomed. I just hope my sharp exit last week isn't held against me.

Thursday 23 August 2007
Day 228 (week 47): RobingRoomKiss

It seems that it's the month for blackmail. No sooner had TheBoss threatened FakeClaims&Co with exposing their dodgy designs than it was the turn of ThirdSix to do the dirty. He's been furious with TopFirst ever since the interception of the post and it was only made worse when he got blamed for the Facebook episode. Then of course he jumped to the conclusion that TopFirst had done him over with the switch of the papers. On and on it goes. Except that this time, damaged as he is by the papers switch, ThirdSix has decided to go nuclear.

It all happened at Wandsworth County Court. I'd like to pretend that it was some sort of cruel twist of fate. But it wasn't. Yesterday I overheard FanciesHimself saying that he needed barristers for both sides of a case where an aggressive approach was being demanded each way. Well, not one to miss an opportunity, I whispered that he might want to try putting TopFirst and ThirdSix against each other. FanciesHimself returned my mischievous look as he took on board what I was saying. So it was that this morning they found themselves on the same tube heading towards East Putney station. I know this since I went on to ask FanciesHimself if he could sort me out with a case in the same court just so I'd be able to report the story. I discreetly followed them from chambers and then planted myself near the two of them on the tube, hidden behind a huge copy of the *Financial Times*, Clouseau-style.

'You know, TopFirst, taking my post was one thing – but switching my papers? That was just too far even for someone as ruthless and ambitious as yourself.'

'Yeah, right, like that was me,' TopFirst paused before adding, 'and that's a bit rich after your little game on Facebook.'

'As if, TopFirst, as if. Anyway, it's gone too far. I'm not having any more of it.'

'You're resigning, are you, ThirdSix?' TopFirst smirked before adding sarcastically, 'Shame. We'd all really miss you.'

Now it was ThirdSix's chance to smirk. 'On the contrary, TopFirst. It's you who'll be leaving after you've seen the video I have of you and a certain young lady called Ginny. Wouldn't want the *fiancée*,' he played with the word in his best mockney accent, 'to find out, now, would we?' He paused and held TopFirst's gaze before finishing, 'Which of course she won't, if you agree not to apply for tenancy.'

TopFirst looked shocked and confused. 'What? You have a tape of Ginny and me?' Then he added, 'But if people knew you'd been spying on me you'd kill your own chances.'

'I wasn't spying, I just happened to spot you with her in a bar and conveniently caught your conversation with her on my mobile phone. Anyway, I'd only go down if you could prove it was me.' He smirked. 'Which you couldn't. The footage would be sent anonymously, I can assure you.'

The anger started to mix with something I have never seen in TopFirst before. For a man who always has the answer to everything he started to look almost stumped, and there was no more chat for the rest of the journey or, for that matter, on the short walk to the court. At this point I'd caught them up, having made it look as if I'd just come from another carriage. Imagine their horror when they came to sign in at the door of the court and realised that they were against each other. They both stormed off in different directions, only to find that all the consultation rooms were taken and that they were therefore forced to go and change in the robing room.

I followed a little behind wondering quite how the fight was going to pan out in court. Though when I say fight I mean it somewhat metaphorically. The ancient craft of advocacy taken to its limits. Dry, legalistic put-downs thrown from one side to the other, the judge keeping control with a slight raising of the eyebrows. Which is not what happened at all. No, the robing room of Wandsworth County Court was the scene for a battle in a very real sense. There they were all decked out in their very respectable wigs and gowns, squaring up for a bit of a showdown in court, when TopFirst went over to ThirdSix and pushed him on the shoulder, saying, 'You'll never get away with it. You know that, don't you?'

'Don't push me, you little rat-faced loser, or I'll give you what you really deserve.'

That was asking for it, and TopFirst pushed him harder, after which the whole scene deteriorated into a chaotic mix of fists and robes. Actually, that would glorify what was, in reality, more of a pathetic public-schoolboy-style limp punch-up. Despite being a rugby player, ThirdSix fought like a girl. Flapped around and punched like a mad March hare. Against all the odds, it was TopFirst who showed any real talent, eventually getting stuck in with a slightly mistimed headbutt. Unfortunately for him, and to the delight of the crowd of barristers which had gathered around them, his wig slipped as he made his move, causing him to make a rather mad connection between flesh, bone and horsehair which ended up not only giving ThirdSix a black eye but also leaving TopFirst himself with a nose bleed. Forget the so-called Glasgow kiss. It's a move which is already being described around chambers as the RobingRoomKiss.

All of this needed some explaining when the two of them eventually left the robing room and went to meet their respective clients and then the judge. With more than one victim, it meant that blaming a lamp-post might be difficult and having spent too much time doing personal injury, the best they both came up with was the lame excuse that there was a tripping hazard in the robing room. This really only added to the comedy value as it showed their complete lack of awareness as to the state they were both in. As well as his physical injuries, ThirdSix hadn't noticed that his wig was completely askew on his head. But much better than that was TopFirst who was so flustered that he hadn't noticed that both the back of his gown and the back of his trousers had been torn, revealing a very fetching pair of boxer shorts for all to see which, embarrassingly for him, were emblazoned with the words 'Big Boy' across the back. Personally I had neither the heart nor the inclination to point this out to him and it eventually took a rather embarrassed usher to pass on the information, after which TopFirst blushed and dashed back to the robing room, emerging a few minutes later with a couple of safety pins holding the back of his gown together.

After the dust has settled, TopFirst will have a choice to make. Which conveniently means that for the moment I can hold back on using the mass of evidence I had gathered on him and Ginny.

Friday 24 August 2007
Day 229 (week 47): Hot air

Out for a drink with Claire yesterday evening and she was in good spirits despite the looming tenancy decision.

'Have you noticed recently, BabyB, that whatever alleyway or lane you walk down which has a barristers' chambers in it there's an air-conditioning unit poking its nozzle out of the window?'

'I guess so,' I replied.

'I know it's childish,' she went on, 'but I can't help chuckling at the fact that what they're pumping out, you know, what they're having to expel from the various chambers,' she paused, 'is hot air.'

I laughed. 'How's chambers?' I asked, changing the subject to her prospects of getting taken on. 'Oh, it's all pretty good considering there's only a few weeks until they make a decision. The thing is, there's no one really slipped up like in your chambers so I think it's harder to rule anybody out. How about you?'

I continue to be impressed and not a little ashamed whenever I hear Claire talking about her own experiences of pupillage and the fact that she seems to be thriving without any resort to dirty tricks whatsoever. Not that I felt able to say so.

'Oh, same as ever,' I replied. 'Worrier worrying, BusyBody busybodying and TopFirst and ThirdSix kicking the life out of each other in the robing room.'

'You what? Fighting? That's extraordinary. What happened? Who won?'

I told her the story.

'I didn't think TopFirst had it in him,' she commented.

'I know. I think it's actually helped his reputation in some ways.'

'Well, I wouldn't go that far. Can't wait until I next see him and say, "Hello, Big Boy!" '

Tuesday 28 August 2007
Day 230 (week 48): See you in court

TheBoss received a reply from FakeClaims&Co today. Not, of course, in writing. Not quite the sort of thing that either side would wish to commit to any document. It came in the form of a telephone call, apparently, in which the senior partner told him precisely where he could put his allegations and that if he wanted to start spreading such scurrilous rumours then he'd better be prepared to fund what would be a highly expensive libel action. He then went on to say that whatever the accident management company may have been doing, it had nothing to do with FakeClaims&Co. Anyone within the firm who might have suggested anything to the contrary was simply wrong and would be disciplined and anyone who suggested it outside of the firm would be sued. Got it? See you in court. Oh, and by the way. We don't take kindly to blackmail and so we've decided to add this to our complaint to the Bar Standards Board, along with attempting to pervert the course of justice. The message, as they say, was clear. TheBoss is going down. Big time.

Which is bad news not just for TheBoss, as I could be going down with him.

Wednesday 29 August 2007
Day 231 (week 48): Worry

With all that happened yesterday, I'm having to try very hard not to turn into a caricature of Worrier herself. Got no sleep last night fretting about what might come out at the disciplinary hearing. Now that FakeClaims have widened the net to include the attempted blackmail my role in the whole thing will only be highlighted. Being complicit through my silence was one thing. That might ruin my tenancy chances but would hopefully be unlikely to get me banned from practising as a barrister for ever, particularly given the fact that I was an impressionable pupil being led astray by my pupilmaster. Actively getting involved in the cover-up, though, is far worse. I really am stuffed, and to cap it all I didn't have the best lunch in the world with Claire.

'There's something going on, BabyB. I can tell. It's far more than TheBoss and FakeClaims. What are you up to that you feel you can't tell me?'

'There's nothing, Claire. Really.'

She gave me what OldRuin calls an old-fashioned look, reproving yet kindly.

'Is it TheVamp, BabyB? I know I don't like her but I like even less that we can't talk properly at the moment.'

'It's just stress, Claire. You know, pupillage and all. We're all going through it.'

'Is it maybe your mum? I mean that can get pretty difficult at times?'

I couldn't tell her about TheBoss and all the goings-on there, nor could I mention the various shenanigans with the other pupils, despite the fact that I wanted to. But she could tell I was locking her out. 'Look, BabyB. If you're not prepared to talk to me then I don't see how we can be friends.'

At which point she got up from lunch and left.

Still, despite even this I think that I'm handling the pressure better than BusyBody, at least. The latest I heard was that she was spotted knitting baby clothes in the middle of a court hearing whilst her opponent was making submissions. The judge apparently stopped the proceedings and asked her what she was doing and she told him straight. He was dumbfounded as to what to do about it without causing some sort of offence and so simply let her continue.

Thursday 30 August 2007
Day 232 (week 48): Reassurance

I went to visit OldRuin at his home last night where he is still convalescing. Lovely train journey through the Hampshire countryside and then a five-minute walk through a quiet village to a beautiful old house at the end of a long drive. A nurse greeted me at the entrance and took me via rather a grand hallway and stairway up to his bedroom. The house was a reflection of OldRuin himself, with book-lined walls, ageing furniture and oils on the wall. He was sitting up in bed but looked frail.

'How are you, OldRuin?'

'Oh, they say I'm going to be back and fitter than I've ever been in no time,' he replied.

'I'm so pleased. It's lovely to see you – and what a wonderful house. I particularly liked the stream running through the front garden.'

'Yes, it's always been my favourite part of this place. Used to tickle trout from it as a youngster, you know.'

Despite his condition, OldRuin had invited me over for dinner and had organised for his nurse to serve it to the two of us in his room. 'I wanted to thank you properly for saving my life,' he said.

'I wouldn't go that far, OldRuin, but I was glad to have been able to help.'

I didn't make any mention of the trouble I'd got into with HeadClerk as that would only have made him feel worse. Nor was I going to mention anything about TheBoss and the disciplinary hearing. As I hesitated over what to say, I think he sensed that everything wasn't quite as it should be. 'Is everything all right, BabyB? Tough time at the moment, what with tenancy coming up and everything.'

'All fine, OldRuin. Getting through it.'

'You do look a little tired, if you'll forgive me for saying so.'

I definitely couldn't mention TheBoss and so I simply said, 'Had a bit of an argument with my friend Claire yesterday. All about nothing really. Very silly. Not as if there's anything between us. But I don't like arguing.'

OldRuin had met Claire a few times when she was around in chambers. 'I've always had a soft spot for Claire, you know,' he said. 'Very fond of you she is, I'd say. How is she?' He sounded genuinely concerned.

'Oh, she's all right. Building up a pretty successful practice,' I said, avoiding the real issue.

'Yes, I've no doubt. You know what stands out about her?'

'What's that?'

'Manners, BabyB. Little footprints of the soul and Claire's are impeccable. Understated, modest and kind. I might sound old-fashioned when I say this but in my view they're the key to success at the Bar. With solicitors, with clients and above all with judges.' He mused a little and then continued, 'Many's the time that I've had an opponent who I have to admit to finding more than a little irritating. But if he wanted to interrupt my submission in front of the judge then I would always give way. You know, the arrogant and rude will always stab themselves in the foot so long as you let them. Hoist themselves up on their own petards.'

Then he did what he has often done in the past and alluded to knowing far more than he was letting on. 'Let me take your colleague TopFirst as a counter-example to Claire. Airs and graces galore but no manners.' He paused before continuing. 'She's a bright lady, our Claire. Got a lot to teach us all, BabyB.'

After he had said all of this he gave me one of his kindly looks and whispered, almost as if in private reflection, 'It's love that makes us real, BabyB. Carries us through the difficult times. Without it, we are nothing but shadows. Empty vessels trudging through life.' Again he gave me one of those long, lingering, thoughtful looks before continuing very gently, 'You'll be all right, BabyB. Don't worry.'

Later I gave Claire a call and left a message on her voicemail inviting her out to lunch next week.

CHAPTER 12

September: Tenancy Decision

Pretend to be weak, that [your opponent] may grow arrogant . . . Feign disorder and crush him.
>   Sun Tzu, *The Art of War*

Tuesday 4 September 2007
Day 235 (week 49): BuskerCard

Had the most annoying opponent you could imagine this morning. He was a fellow pupil but as he explained at length he was about ten years older and somewhat overqualified having done a PhD and then taken a medical degree before the Bar. Which made him a doctor, doctor, as far as I could see, though he wasn't impressed by my reference to the jokes.

'It's a nice little warm-up session for me today,' he eventually said.

'Sorry?'

'Our chambers gives us these meaningless cases to limber us up.'

'Oh.'

'Yes, I'm in the Court of Appeal tomorrow, you know.'

Well bully for you. He seemed determined to continue patronising me. After he'd asked me which university I went to and then where I did the Bar course (both of which actually turned out to be better than where he'd been), he then asked, 'Where do you practise?'

I decided to be obtuse just to wind him up. 'Oh no need to practise, me. I just turn up and give it a go. Practise is for girls, I say.'

'No, I meant where are you based?'

'Oh, I see, where am I based?' I feigned ignorance in the face of his extremely unamused response. 'I live in London. How about you?'

'No I meant . . . oh, never mind. What is your Inn?'

'Oh, I'm very much an in one ear and out the other kind of guy myself.'

When we went into court I decided that his nickname should be LatinLover (though if you saw him you'd appreciate the irony) as he just couldn't help overusing that ancient language. All *ex post facto, a fortiori, locus in quo, bona fide*s and the like which in a car case sounded just plain silly and even had the judge raising his eyebrows. As I sat there and listened to him drone on for well over an hour about the value of the case and the various technical arguments it raised, I tried to think what TheBusker would do in these circumstances. When it came to my turn, I drew myself up to my full height and put on my most serious face, which basically meant furrowing my brow. I then said in as deep and slow a voice as I could muster, 'Sir, there are only a few things which it is appropriate for grown men to fight over and the value of whiplash injuries is not one of them. This case is worth £1,500. No more, no less.'

I sat down and cringed to myself. It was the first time I'd actually managed to play a BuskerCard but there was no knowing whether I'd receive the wrath of the judge or perhaps his gratitude for not wasting his time further.

'Thank you, Mr BabyBarista. I agree wholeheartedly and I have to say it is a great shame,' at which point he stared for a little too long at LatinLover, 'that other members of your side of the profession don't approach their cases with the same maturity. £1,500 it is.'

Wednesday 5 September 2007
Day 236 (week 49): ClichéCard

Fresh from playing my first BuskerCard yesterday, I decided that I might try my hand again today. Once more, as I stood up the brow became furrowed, a day older and wiser even than yesterday. 'Sir,' I started, but realised I had forgotten the deep voice of yesterday. I coughed a little and started again, an octave lower. 'Sir.' No, too low this time, but I cracked on. 'Sir, life is but a sparrow's flight through a great hall. It is a will-o-the-wisp. A candle in the wind.'

Ouch. It was so cliché-ridden as to hurt. The voice of TheBusker had deserted me. Run off into the ether, no doubt chuckling at my miserable effort.

'Mr BabyBarista, what on earth are you wittering on about?'

'Er, just taking my run-up, Sir.'

'Well, get on with it. It's turning into the sort of run-up of which even the great Fred Trueman would have been proud.'

'Yes, Sir. Sorry, Sir. Er, all I was trying to say was that life is too short to be arguing about such matters.'

'Mr BabyBarista. At this rate your life, at least at the Bar, will indeed be short. But I'm afraid to say that whilst you may have philosophy to be contemplating, the rest of us mere mortals have jobs to do. For myself, I have spent many happy years arguing over far less interesting and weighty matters than that which now sits before me. I suggest that from now on you play up and play the game.'

The magic BuskerCard, it seems, remains best played by TheBusker himself.

Thursday 6 September 2007
Day 237 (week 49): Apology

'I want to apologise. I'm so very sorry for lying to you the other day.'

Claire had finally agreed to meet me for lunch.

'Go on,' she said.

'There are other things that have gone on this year and I shouldn't have denied it. They're to do with pupillage. I did want to tell you, but I just can't right now.'

'Thank you, BabyB. I'm so relieved to hear you say that. I really thought for a moment that I might have lost you.'

'I thought I might have lost you too.'

There was a long pause as she looked at me, and then she smiled. 'Don't worry, BabyB. I'm not asking to be your confessional. I just wanted to hear you tell the truth.'

'I appreciate that Claire and I also appreciate your standing up to me. More than you can ever imagine. Thank you.'

Friday 7 September 2007
Day 238 (week 49): A favour

Word has it from Worrier that TopFirst is considering telling ThirdSix to stuff the evidence he has threatened to produce about his trying it on with Ginny and then battling on till the tenancy decision. If I can possibly help it this is something I want to avert as TopFirst probably remains the most likely candidate for tenancy right now. With that in mind, I kind of figured it had become necessary to suggest to him that Ginny, the woman with whom he had associated so closely, was in fact a prostitute. Another lie, I know, but hey, who's counting?

> Dear TopFirst,
> I am sorry for being so harsh with you in the past. I'm afraid I have an admission. I am not quite who you think, and I am now in a little trouble. Last night I was arrested for soliciting as well as possession of cocaine and I was wondering if you would defend me? I wouldn't normally ask but given how fond you said you were of me, I thought you might consider it. Clearly I do not intend to tell anyone, least of all your head of chambers, of your association with someone I am sure you would describe as a common escort girl. Perhaps you might return the favour?
> I look forward to hearing from you,
> Ginny (actually my real name is Gina)

No mention of ThirdSix, as that would risk TopFirst presenting him with the email as evidence against him. But it'll hopefully be enough to force him to withdraw from the tenancy race for fear of ThirdSix exposing this illicit connection.

Monday 10 September 2007
Day 239 (week 50): StitchUp

TopFirst came to visit me today. He wanted to go out for a drink after work and so we met in the local wine bar earlier this evening.
'I've got to put an end to this once and for all.'

My heart sank. He'd somehow twigged that I was behind Ginny. Maybe I'd pushed it just one step too far. 'Put an end to what?' I asked. As if I didn't know.

'ThirdSix. Completely and utterly stitched me up. I mean all's fair in love and war and all that, but surely there are boundaries?'

'Do you mean the Facebook thing?'

'Worse even than that, BabyB. He filmed me being chatted up by a girl and now I think he must have set up the whole thing.'

'No.' You don't say.

'Yes. Then to cap it he's threatened to send the film to my fiancée.'

'No.'

'Yes. But there's more. Now I've had the girl herself contact me and reveal that she's in fact a prostitute and she's threatening to tell HeadofChambers about our friendship unless I help her with some legal case.'

'Golly. You're in trouble.'

'I'd say. I just had to pass it by someone. I know we've had our differences, but you're the one person who knows exactly what we've been going through this year. I thought you might understand.'

Part of me wondered whether TopFirst was simply testing to see whether in fact I was involved in all the trouble. But just in case his question was sincere I was happy to oblige. 'Well, if I can help I will. What exactly happened with this call girl?'

'That's the irony of this whole thing. It's a tower of innuendo. I never got anything out of it at all.'

Good old TopFirst. Consistent to the end in his lack of insight and utter shamelessness. He is obviously still smarting at Ginny's rejection.

'Let's look at the options. If you call their bluff what happens?'

'I risk losing the possibility of tenancy and my fiancée.'

'And if you withdraw from the race?'

'Then I probably just lose tenancy this time round. I'm sure they'll let me squat here until I find somewhere else and I doubt this girl will tell HeadofChambers if she knows it can no longer cause me damage.' The word 'squat' was not a reference to some kind of weird yoga position but instead to being allowed to stay on in chambers on an informal basis.

'Well it's your decision. I really wouldn't like to advise you either way.'

'No. You've been a great help. Really. I think it's pretty clear I have no option other than to withdraw. Thank you, BabyBarista.'

'Oh, it was nothing.' Then, before finishing up, I couldn't resist asking, 'So what are you going to do to ThirdSix?'

'Oh, don't worry about that. As if he's not already dead in the water. Rest assured that once I've withdrawn and have no interest in the race, the rumour mill will be rife with made-up stories about our rugby-playing friend.'

Hmm, like it's not already.

Tuesday 11 September 2007
Day 240 (week 50): Losing the war

It's been all go today. First Worrier came to tell me that TopFirst had officially withdrawn from the race for tenancy. She also told me that she'd heard from a friend of a friend that ThirdSix had been caught in possession of cocaine at one of the county courts before joining this chambers. My, TopFirst has been working quickly. I wonder what other malicious gossip he has been spreading. Then ThirdSix came round. Smug in his pyrrhic victory over TopFirst. 'At least I've got him back for stitching me up over all that business with my last chambers.'

Well. Quite.

In the meantime, Ginny received an email from TopFirst telling her where to go, which in the circumstances I kind of admired. He wasn't going down without keeping at least a part of his dignity. I left it at that with no further reply.

So, it would all have been going perfectly were it not for the fact that TheBoss is still spitting blood about FakeClaims and for some reason remains determined to take it all out on me at his forthcoming disciplinary hearing. Here I was, having taken in so many of the lessons he'd taught, having won the battles against my fellow pupils . . . and still about to lose the war.

Wednesday 12 September 2007
Day 241 (week 50): Eh oop

'All right BabyB, you're going to cheer up whether you like it or not.' It was a hungover, caffeine-fuelled, hyperactive Vamp. The last person I wanted to be against this morning.

'What you need is a distraction,' she said. 'Let's play a game. You can either take a northern or a west country accent.'

I gave in and chose northern.

'And bonus points for the words "flat cap", "whippet" and "grim" for you and "cider", "wurzel" and "combine harvester" for me.'

I didn't do too badly with the odd 'eh oop' and 'by 'eck' but TheVamp really excelled herself. The judge, I figure, twigged, but without proof could do nothing. The highlight came when TheVamp put it to a witness that his car was travelling 'slower than a combine harvester being driven by a cider-drinking wurzel'.

Thursday 13 September 2007
Day 242 (week 50): Underbellies

'Ah, UpTights. I see you've had your quarterly refill of botulism. I've always enjoyed the irony of your great desire to fill yourself full of poison.' It was OldSmoothie in chambers tea. It had clearly been a bit of an overdose since despite her anger, UpTights's face hardly changed other than in its complexion.

'And your hair implants are different, I suppose?' she fired back.

'I don't know whether anyone ever warned you about pulling faces and the wind changing but it looks to me that that's exactly what's happened.'

He chortled to himself in a very self-satisfied manner and went to get his cup of tea, leaving UpTights fuming. Conversation then turned to a party being hosted by a north London firm of solicitors whose invitation stated, 'Please bring a party trick'. This led to speculation as to what people would be taking. Innocently, TheCreep turned to UpTights and asked, 'So, have you learnt any new tricks for the party, UpTights?'

Quick as a flash and before she was even able to start an answer, OldSmoothie was in there for the kill and even the less progressive members of chambers winced as he made his strike. 'New tricks? You what? Everyone knows you can't teach an old dog new tricks.'

This time, though, a defiant answer came back from a rather unexpected corner. 'What is it you've got against women, OldSmoothie?' It was BusyBody and she meant business.

'What on earth do you mean? I love all women. Every one of them. Well, except perhaps the fat ones.'

'You see, that's my point. Every time you open your mouth you reveal your misogynistic underbelly.' She looked him up and down. 'And if I may say so, it's rather an over-sized underbelly at that, wouldn't you say? So, go on, what is it? Mother not cuddle you? Too ugly to get a girlfriend before you were rich? Or is it simply that we threaten you?'

For the first time since I have known him, OldSmoothie had no answer to give. After a moment he bowed his head slightly, an expression of utter resignation on his face. BusyBody chose this moment to deliver the killer blow with a smile and a twinkle in her eye: 'One little voice answers back and suddenly he's got the look of a beach donkey.'

There was no escaping the accuracy of her description of his face at that moment. BusyBody turned to UpTights and received a beaming smile. Well, it would have been a beam had her stretched features allowed. She had found the helper she so badly needed in the fight against her foe.

Friday 14 September 2007
Day 243 (week 50): Price of justice

'We've got to win, UpTights. My whole financial future depends on it.' It was JudgeJewellery and today was the hearing of the abuse of process arguments.

'I should say. If you're convicted, you'll be saying goodbye to that cushy judicial salary for a start.'

'No, not that. I've decided I'm going to quit the bench anyway. It's far more important. I've been offered the lead in a huge ad campaign by CheapnNasty along with a television show of my own in which I sit in judgement on various domestic disputes between celebrities. Kind of *Celebrity Judge Judy*. The deal's already done both in this country and the States. Between them they'll pay more than twenty years of sitting on the bench. Oh and I'll be allowed to take whatever I want from any of the CheapnNasty stores for life.'

She seemed more pleased with the offer of free swag than the huge financial deal, but either way it was obvious that UpTights disapproved despite trying to look supportive of her old friend. Then JudgeJewellery added, 'The only problem is that it all falls away if I'm convicted. Then I'll fall foul of the laws against profiting from my own crime. But if you get me off, even with one of your technicalities, then legally speaking, at least, I will be innocent. I will have committed no crime from which I could profit. I will instead be profiting from the crime I didn't commit. If you see my point. Anyway, you can understand my concern.'

Oh, UpTights understood that all right. With their being old friends and all, you'd have thought that JudgeJewellery would have had a little more insight than to put pressure on this highly strung monster at such an inopportune moment. 'Yes, I get the point. Anyway, I think we ought to be getting into court.'

Thankfully for her, the Crown Prosecution Service could not afford to pay for OldSmoothie for such a small case and made do with one of their in-house muppets over whom she ran roughshod. All of which confirmed to me something which has been apparent for the whole of the last year – that you get the result you pay for. Which was good news for JudgeJewellery but as for justice, I think it's time we're honest and simply stick it on eBay and see what it fetches. Sell it down the Swanee river once and for all and be done with it.

Tuesday 18 September 2007
Day 245 (week 51): VirusCard

'Come to beg me not to drop you in it, have you?' It was TheBoss and as usual he was on the money.

'Well it can hardly help your case to be seen to have brought your pupil down with you, can it?'

'I don't think you understand, BabyB. If I go down next week, there'll be no room for mitigating factors. It'll all be over. Finished.

Which leaves me with nothing to lose by getting you involved, and as they say, two minds are always better than one. I've told you enough times, BabyB. It's all there in the magic book. Life itself, BabyB, is war.'

As I was telling Claire over lunch, she said, 'We still do have the virus card, BabyB.'

That was true although neither of us had held out much hope with that one. It had been Claire's idea months ago when TheBoss's own expert had examined chambers's hard disk. An afterthought, really. 'Let's add a virus to the disk so that it'll crash say in a couple of months' time,' she'd said.

This hadn't been too difficult to manage since we'd picked a friendly expert who had given us access to his office and technologically it was pretty basic. The real weakness of it all was that both experts having examined the hard disk, the court wouldn't normally need to see the original.

'It's worth a bit of sabre-rattling at least,' said Claire now. 'Unlikely to get FakeClaims to change their mind about bringing the complaint but it might at least show TheBoss that you've done absolutely everything possible to help him.'

So after lunch I went to TheBoss and suggested that he make a last-minute request for his own expert to re-examine the hard disk this week.

Thursday 20 September 2007
Day 247 (week 51): Almost there

TheBoss did as I suggested on Tuesday and yesterday he received a response from FakeClaims stating that it was too late in the day to be making such a re-examination. TheBoss replied that he insisted. Given the crucial importance of the hearing to his whole career, lateness was not something which would necessarily sway the Bar Standards Board.

Perhaps surprisingly for such a dodgy outfit as FakeClaims, today they've come clean and 'fessed up that in fact the mainstay of their evidence has been destroyed. Though it's extremely unlikely to affect the case, TheBoss was nevertheless delighted. 'You know, BabyB, I don't know how you did it and nor do I really want to know. But it does look like you may well have pulled it out of the bag. Nice one.'

Taking advantage of his rush of over-optimistic hyperbole, I asked whether I could rely upon him not to drop me in his mire at the hearing?

'I'll have to think about that, BabyB. Let's see how it all pans out. I have to say that you haven't done yourself any harm in the last couple of days. Let's see what happens next week.'

Which wasn't quite the answer I'd been hoping for, but was at least a better position than I'd been in earlier in the week.

Friday 21 September 2007
Day 248 (week 51): TheParrot

With all the pressure of tenancy decisions and finance, Worrier has turned into a parrot.

'How's it going, BabyB?' she asked this morning.

'Oh, not bad, considering.'

'Not bad, considering. What have you got on today?'

'Just a small application in Wandsworth.'

'Small application in Wandsworth. Oh.'

'Should only take ten minutes,' I went on.

'Ten minutes, yes.'

'How about you?'

'How about me? Oh, you know.'

Sadly, I do know. Anyway, you get the picture. If it was anyone else, it'd have been tempting to throw in an insult just to hear it repeated back before it registered with the brain. But not with Worrier.

Monday 24 September 2007
Day 249 (week 52): Counter spin

Since he withdrew from the race, TopFirst has been busy wreaking his revenge on ThirdSix. Going round chambers collaring anyone who'll listen and making up a different bit of malicious gossip about ThirdSix for each one. To his credit ThirdSix has shown resilience with his counter-spin. First he painted a picture of TopFirst as a bitter, twisted liar who still hasn't come to terms with the first failure of his life. Given that this is in fact true, it resonated and ThirdSix took on the mantle of official victim. This then allowed him to start suggesting that it was TopFirst who deliberately swapped those papers and set him up to fight the wrong case on the wrong day. Which, ironically, means that ThirdSix remains in the race.

Tuesday 25 September 2007
Day 250 (week 52): SkinsParty

If he hadn't quite managed it so far, TopFirst outdid himself in the revenge stakes last night. He might not have destroyed ThirdSix's tenancy chances but he certainly destroyed his swanky Islington flat. By way of background, he's the only one of us who owns his own flat, and despite his initial unassuming demeanour he's never missed an opportunity to boast. Lording it over the rest of us who are all sharing, even TopFirst. Last night he was hosting a quiet little soirée for a few of his close friends. Drinks and a few of Marks and Spencer's best canapés. You see, despite the fact that he's a rugby player, truth be told, he's actually more an ice and a slice than a ten pints of lager kind of guy and he thought he was having a civilised little get-together. Except it was hardly civilised. Not once TopFirst became involved. If you haven't heard of them before then let me tell you about them now: *Skins* parties. They tend to be held by teenagers whilst their parents are away and they involve smashing up a house beyond even what the Yellow Pages might be able to fix. All this is advertised online and then broadcast to the world via webcam. Well, yesterday TopFirst took the *Skins* party upmarket and advertised ThirdSix's little wine-and-cheese do.

I went with Claire who was celebrating having been taken on in her own chambers. It's something she thoroughly deserves and I'm so pleased for her.

'Let's go and have a final look at your competition before they make the decision, BabyB,' she said. 'From what I've seen they're not a patch on you.'

Well, not at stitching people up, anyway, I thought shamefacedly. As we got near to the flat, I spotted Worrier skulking behind a lamppost, obviously trying not to be seen. Claire saw her too. 'Hello Worrier,' she said. 'Not coming in, then?'

'Not coming in?' She was obviously still parroting. 'Oh, er . . .' She was embarrassed at having been seen.

'Come on,' I said. 'I think we should probably all go for a gander.'

'Er, go for a gander? But I don't want him to think I'm a part of it, BabyB.'

'I don't think there's any risk of that. TopFirst will no doubt be there telling him exactly who's responsible.'

When the three of us arrived at the door, a slightly drunk-looking girl answered and slurred in a South African accent, 'Ah live 'ere,' and extended her hand. She was dressed like a hippy traveller and so I suspected was the first of the *Skins* invitees that I would meet rather than an actual housemate of ThirdSix. I shook her hand and humoured her with, 'That's great. Nice house. My name's BabyB, what's your name?'

'Ah live 'ere.'

'Yes, I know. But what's your name?'

'Ah live 'ere.' It was starting to get silly.

'Sorry, I don't think you heard me properly. I asked what your name is.'

'I heard you perfectly clearly. My name is ah live 'ere.' She then spelt it out, 'O-L-I-V-I-A. Ah live 'ere.'

Oh.

Once inside, the first group I noticed was the pupil skivers, all sipping away at their drinks and looking like they knew they shouldn't really be there but couldn't resist rubbernecking at the damage which was already starting to unfold. Next to them were what looked like a bunch of students playing drinking games which seemed mostly to involve trying to down a pint but spilling half of it on the floor.

It was still only ten o'clock and the house was already starting to show the effects of its uninvited guests. In one corner, bottles of beer had spilled over and were leaking into the carpet. In another, a large and probably very expensive pot plant had been overturned and the soil was slowly getting trodden around the flat. But that was nothing compared to the kitchen which was already full of empty bottles and cans, spilt alcohol and crisps. Then there was the smoke which even with the windows open was so dense that Worrier started to fret about the health implications of passive smoking. I'd say the fire threat was a little greater though and within a few minutes I'd already had to put out one cigarette which was smouldering on his brand new sofa.

But it was early and you could still hear the sound of new guests arriving, one particularly notable crowd singing football songs as they entered. Within the next hour, the whole atmosphere changed from one of mild drunkenness to unadulterated carnage, no doubt exacerbated by the fact that a couple of people had gone round the house forcing vodka shots on everybody. ThirdSix himself was just a blur as he rushed from one group to the next trying unsuccessfully to kick them out and getting more and more stressed in the process. As things started to really go downhill, one of the pupil skivers shouted out over the noise, 'Hey, BabyB. I hear your chambers has been having a bit of infighting between ThirdSix and TopFirst.'

'You could say that.'

At which point, BusyBody came over and started fag-ending on the conversation. Her pregnancy's now showing and she was all decked out in Liberty's finest flowers-and-frills maternity garb.

'Fighting? Not again. Headbutting fellow members of the Bar doesn't exactly enhance our reputation.'

She said this a little too loudly and TopFirst, who had been standing with another group of people, came over to answer his accuser. He was particularly drunk and for some reason he seemed to look even more weaselly than ever. Maybe he's lost weight due to all the worry of recent months. Or maybe it's just how he looks when he's drunk and his pretentious façade starts to slip.

'What, and sleeping with members of chambers, a pupil and a junior clerk does? Get real, BusyBody. We've none of us exactly done ourselves any favours this year.'

Worrier started looking even more nervous than usual and interrupted, 'Look. It'll all be over in a few days. Let's just celebrate that fact this evening and forget everything else.'

'That's all right for you to say,' said TopFirst. 'You've been out of the running ever since you started screaming sex discrimination. You couldn't take the heat right from the beginning and sabotaged yourself just to take the pressure off.'

Worrier was horrified at such direct talk and started stuttering, 'But . . . but . . . that's so unfair. I . . . I . . .' Tears were welling up in her eyes.

TopFirst went in for the kill. 'Oh leave it out, Worrier. You're a loser. It was obvious from the start . . .'

He didn't get any further before Claire came to Worrier's defence.

'At least she's not a smug, arrogant bully, TopFirst.'

'That's a bit rich for Little-Miss-Smug-Oh-I've-Just-Been-Taken-On-As-A-Tenant, don't you think?'

'That's enough, TopFirst,' I said. 'Don't you think you've caused enough damage already?'

'Shut it, BabyB. You really get up my nose the way you're always trying to be friends with everyone. I've had enough of the lot of you.'

With which he turned around and was about to go off in a huff when ThirdSix arrived and poked him in the chest, saying, 'Apparently this is your doing?'

'So what if it is?' slurred TopFirst. 'Not that you could prove it.'

ThirdSix looked like he was about to sock him, when suddenly TheVamp appeared looking particularly appealing in a short black dress which left very little to the imagination and grabbed the attention of both ThirdSix and TopFirst.

'Ain't life just grand,' she said in her best southern drawl, which elicited a response from ThirdSix that contained language that would never pass the lips of a barrister within the confines of a court.

'Well, that's just no way to speak to a lady, young man.' I'd noticed before that the more drunk TheVamp became, the closer she got to almost believing she *was* Scarlett O'Hara.

'What on earth are you all doing here anyway?' he demanded.

'Oh come on, ThirdSix,' said TheVamp. 'Don't be such a spoilsport.' She sidled up and brushed herself against him.

'Look, just because you like having hordes of men round your house doesn't mean the rest of us do,' he jibed.

Never being one to fail to step up to the mark, TheVamp hit the bullseye with her response. 'No. You just bring plastic old hags like UpTights back, don't you.'

But ThirdSix was on a roll. 'Oh, take a look in the mirror yourself. Hardly the picture of youth, with that shrivelled-up, sunburnt old crust. You're so vain you'll be working with UpTights to get bulk discounts in no time, just you see.'

The conversation was interrupted by TopFirst drunkenly turning on his heel, walking straight into a wall and collapsing into a giggling ball. Then, as he went to stand up, he accidentally tripped up one of the many student crashers, who fell forwards pushing a couple more people. There was enough alcohol and different groups of people around that before you knew it, a full-on fight had started. It was time to get out, and despite the fact that Worrier wanted to stay behind and help (I think she still has a crush on ThirdSix), I grabbed both her and Claire and we made a sharp exit, BusyBody and TopFirst following directly behind.

This, it turned out, was fortunate, as within ten minutes we saw police cars arriving. As we walked back to the tube, BusyBody said to TopFirst, 'That's a pretty extreme form of revenge.'

'Oh don't get all goody-goody on me now, BusyBody,' he replied. 'You were only there to watch it happen and don't pretend otherwise.'

He was right, of course. A good dose of *schadenfreude* towards ThirdSix had lifted us from the last miserable seconds of pupillage. Even though it was somewhat unfounded given that, thanks to me, he has copped the blame for so many things that were not even his fault. Nobody said another word until we were on the tube itself. When the other pupils had gone their separate ways, I suggested that Claire and I stop off for a celebratory coffee before going home.

'I'm so pleased you don't have to worry any longer,' I said as we stood outside the café. As I moved to hug her I couldn't help but be aware of how beautiful she was. Maybe it was because the weight of pupillage had been lifted from her, or, I realised at that moment, what was more likely was that I so rarely took the time to notice her beauty. She looked up as we held each other. A few strands of hair had fallen over her left eye and I gently moved them to one side. She smiled and I could see the concern in her eyes. As we sat down next to each other she said, 'But I do have to worry, BabyB. It's a big day tomorrow. I've booked the day out of chambers and I'll be there to support you.'

I touched her face and suddenly, as if it was the most natural thing in the world, she moved her head towards mine. Gently I kissed her cheek and she raised her hand and touched the side of my head. As I moved towards her lips I heard from behind me the most almighty, 'BaaaaabyBeeeeeeee!' It was TopFirst with his arms in the air, a kebab in one hand and a can of Coke in the other. He collapsed forward putting both arms around the two of us.

'You sly dog, BabyB. Keeping that under your hat.'

The moment was lost and this time we finally did go our separate ways home.

Wednesday 26 September 2007
Day 251 (week 52): The hearing

I write this sitting in chambers as we all await the verdict on TheBoss. There's been a certain cathartic pleasure in much of this writing but right now it doesn't help a jot as my future at the Bar is well and truly out of my hands and at the mercy of others. Whatever the verdict may be, I can now report that TheBoss has made every effort to bring me down. In flames. It all kicked off this morning when FakeClaims's barrister asked him the simplest question of all.

'Do you deny that you changed the computer records in your chambers as alleged?'

To which TheBoss replied, 'Absolutely. One hundred per cent. These so-called computer experts have got it wrong. Nothing more to it.'

'In which case,' the barrister addressed the tribunal, 'I seek permission to adduce new evidence which rebuts this testimony in its entirety.'

TheBoss glanced at me and for a moment looked caught off guard before he composed himself once more and said, 'I have nothing to hide,' correctly guessing that the tribunal would probably let the evidence in anyway and that therefore it was better to brazen out whatever was coming.

The prosecuting barrister then produced an iPod and a pair of speakers and proceeded to play the contents. Which were recordings of conversations between TheBoss and me. Secretly made. As soon as TheBoss heard the first few lines, he looked at me and exclaimed, 'They taped us. How did they manage that? They nailed us, BabyB.'

But despite my hopes that at that stage he would finally give me some slack, particularly as I'd helped destroy the physical evidence against him, he went on the counter-offensive.

'I didn't want to say this before and have only held off in order to protect my former pupil, but what this evidence will show is that both the idea for the cover-up and its implementation came from BabyBarista.'

This, of course, was completely untrue, although I had been brought in effectively as an accomplice.

'Yes,' he went on. 'It is BabyBarista who is the technical whizz-kid. I mean, look at me, a middle-aged man with no computer skills at all. How on earth could I even contemplate such a plan without the mastermind of BabyBarista?'

It then got worse.

'In fact, I suppose things could have been a lot easier were it not for the fact that as his pupilmaster I felt in some way responsible. I only discovered what he had done after the event and I accept that to the extent that I didn't report him, I am guilty. But as to my role in the cover-up itself, it was non-existent.'

The barrister for the prosecution listened patiently before going on. 'And this is the truth of the matter? Your final word?'

'It is.'

The prosecutor then made a slightly theatrical pause, enjoying one of those rare moments when cross-examination can quite literally cut someone to shreds. He then continued, 'Well, you might be interested to listen to this, then.'

It was a further recording on which my voice could be heard addressing TheBoss: 'All I did was to keep quiet about seeing that set of papers.'

To which TheBoss replied, 'That may be so, BabyB, but it looks far worse than that now, and you know it. You knew everything about the plan itself and then, even worse for you, you've since officially denied knowing anything about it. You'd better start realising that soon.'

For the first time, TheBoss was well and truly stumped. He stood there in silence for a few seconds before the prosecutor asked, 'You've been lying to us all along, haven't you?'

TheBoss shifted uncomfortably before going back on the offensive.

'I don't know where this tape came from but it's obviously a fake. That conversation simply didn't happen.'

But from then on in TheBoss was well and truly sunk.

So now I wait to see whether I sink with him.

Thursday 27 September 2007
Day 252 (week 52): The verdict

The Standards Board came back and found TheBoss guilty and disbarred him completely. As he came out of the hearing, he was not looking at all happy. I walked down the steps with him and he said, 'I told you, BabyB. If I go down, you're coming with me. FakeClaims&Co will no doubt be raising a complaint against you as we speak.'

I looked him straight in the eye and suddenly it dawned on him. 'You cut a deal. Those were your tapes all along.'

I continued to look at him.

'You must think you're mighty clever, BabyB. But you forget. The Standards Board can raise their own complaint. You're going down whether you like it or not.'

I held his gaze and something about my quiet confidence must have made him realise the full extent of the deceit.

'You've been in on it with them all along. Right from when? The start of the tapes?'

We stared at each other without speaking, before I answered, 'You gave me Sun Tzu and yet failed to remember *Wall Street*. What was it Bud said as Gecko was being led away? "All warfare is based on deception. If your enemy is superior, evade him. If angry, irritate him. If equally matched, fight and if not: split and re-evaluate." '

He was visibly thrown as the full picture finally became clear. As he struggled to regain his composure, I threw in, 'Some might say, "case closed".'

He looked finished, and you could almost see his brain whirring with all the implications. Then, with just a hint of irony, I added, 'This place just ain't big enough for the both of us.'

Slowly his arrogant side whimpered back into life and he gave a wry smile. 'You know, BabyB, this might be the beginning of a beautiful friendship.'

Which just leaves the small matter of a tenancy decision for tomorrow.

Friday 28 September 2007
Day 253 (week 52): Tenancy decision

Having survived the Standards Board, today there was further waiting around as chambers had their annual meeting to decide which of the pupils they were going to take on as a tenant. TopFirst had officially retired from the race, but the others remained in despite their own difficulties. Worrier and her discrimination claim, BusyBody, YouTube and her in-house pregnancy and ThirdSix, his switched papers and fights with TopFirst. Then there were my own difficulties with HeadClerk and, more importantly, my association with TheBoss. I may have cut a deal elsewhere, but not with chambers.

Come the allotted time of five o'clock, my phone went while I was in the library. Except that instead of it being UpTights, it was TopFirst.

'I've worked it out.' My stomach went through my bowels as I heard these words. 'It suddenly dawned on me this afternoon. You were the one who set me up with Ginny. It wasn't ThirdSix at all. You sneaky, backstabbing, conniving . . .' At which point he launched into an impressive tirade of unprintable abuse. As if the pent-up frustration of the last year had all fermented into a bitter reservoir of bile and suddenly the dam was bursting and it was all flooding out.

'I don't know what on earth you're talking about, TopFirst . . .' I was trying to give myself time to think as I saw all of my carefully laid plans collapsing around my ears.

Then TopFirst gave the real reason for his call. 'Listen, you don't have to start putting up a defence to this one, BabyB. We both know I don't have any evidence. I just want you to know that I know. I will never forget, BabyB. Nobody ever beats me at anything and I tell you now that no matter what career you scrape together, you'd better watch your back.' With which he put the phone down.

I couldn't stay in the library after that, so, rather nervously, I called Claire. She agreed to meet me in the pub, but just as we were sitting down, the call I'd actually been expecting came. It was UpTights. They had made their decision.

'You're in. Welcome to chambers.'

I was speechless for a few seconds before I started mumbling incoherently. UpTights helped me out.

'The others have not been taken on though BusyBody will be allowed back for a third six after she's had the baby.'

'Thank you for telling me.'

'You know what really made the difference?'

I didn't.

'OldRuin. Kindness goes a long way, BabyB.'

Claire was the first to congratulate me. 'Well done, BabyB. You've been through a lot this year and I'm so pleased you've made it.'

'Well we both know I couldn't have done it without you.'

'It was nothing.'

'It wasn't nothing to suggest I tape TheBoss's conversations or to help me cut a deal with FakeClaims and the Standards Board.'

We both looked at each other and paused. My thoughts immediately turned to last night and as I struggled to articulate what I was feeling, Claire came to the rescue. 'Hey, come on,' she said. 'You need to celebrate.'

I returned her smile and as we set off I quietly took her hand in mine. As we left lawyerland and walked down the Strand, we passed OldRuin who was slowly walking towards Waterloo. He was again in his Bunburying clothes, although he no longer had reason to catch the earlier train. He stopped and smiled at the sight of the two of us together. After he had greeted Claire, he looked at me and said, 'Very many congratulations, BabyB. Much deserved, if I may say so. I know they don't like us doing this but let me shake your hand and formally welcome you to chambers.'

'Thank you, OldRuin and all the more so for putting in a good word.'

'Oh. They mentioned that, did they? I'd take it with a pinch of salt if I were you. They picked you because they think you'll be a good barrister. Something, for what it's worth, that I also happen to believe.'

Then he noticed that I was carrying TheBoss's magic book. 'Sun Tzu, hmm?' He chuckled and said, 'I've always preferred the art of law to the art of war, myself.'

I got another of his enigmatic looks. 'I know you've had a few difficulties this last year and perhaps even made a few mistakes.' He hesitated, smiled gently and then went on. 'Don't be too hard on yourself. We're all learning. And making mistakes. It's what we do. Right up to our last breath.'

As we parted, I looked up and noticed a familiar face staring back at me from one of the enormous advertising hoardings next to the road. It was none other than JudgeJewellery promoting her latest range for CheapnNasty underneath a slogan which echoed the words of OldRuin.

'Who are we to judge?'

ACKNOWLEDGEMENTS

I'd like to thank the following people in particular for their invaluable help in the making of *BabyBarista*: my agent Euan Thorneycroft of A.M. Heath; the wonderful team at Bloomsbury: Alexandra Pringle, Helen Garnons-Williams, Mary Morris, Jenny Parrott, Erica Jarnes, Sarah Marcus, Penelope Beech and Jude Drake; Alex Spence at *The Times*; Dean Norton and everyone at 1 Temple Gardens for their continued support; cartoonist Alex Williams; writers Mark Evans, Andy Martin, Tom Anderson, James Woolf and Alex Wade; barristers Mark Warby QC, Daniel Barnett, Mark Sefton, Dominic Adamson, Aidan Ellis and Anthony Johnson; Garry Wright at Law Brief Publishing; Di Beste and Jo Pye at CPD Webinars; Andrew Griffin at XPL Publishing; Delia Venables; Tamsin Robinson; Mike Semple-Piggott, David A. Giacalone and the community of 'blawgers'; readers of the blog at *The Times*; Rev. Bill Long, Rev. Dr John Stott and Rev. Barry Priory; Tim Heyland at Tiki; Gus, Ross, Claire and Lisa Thomson at Saltrock; Mikey Corker at Loose-Fit; Jools at Gulf Stream; Graham and Angie at the Black Horse; Emma and Andy at The Corner Bistro; William Sin at Y Ming; Richard Waddams; Jonny Bull; Jay Stirzaker; Fiona Sturrock; Jamie Bott; Simon Skelton; Sandra Dahl; Douglas E. Powell; Tamsin Onslow; Jim and Kath Gardner; Rachel Kyle; Matt, Nora and Jim Waddams; Rita Roup; Dr Basil Singer; Mark and Luke von Herkomer; Andrew Clancey (Clanger); Jon Gilbert; Joe Kenneally; Nathan Roberts; Michael Pritchett; Ben Finn; Madeleine Potter; Valerio Massimo; Alexia Somerville; James Roccelli; Tom Hampson; Pam Sharrock; Richard and Hannah Pool-Jones; Toby Backhouse; Taffa Nice; Rick (Hammer) Yeo; James Yeo; Stuart (Max Steele) and Maggie de la Roche; Paul Irwin (Goat); Gareth Harrison; Miranda Barnett; Peach Wright; Richard Hall; Simon Nixon; Simon Rumley; Kat Algate; Miranda Coberman; Marie Fraser; Dan Rudman; Sunny

Rudman-Male; Neil Ferguson; Russell Briggs; Jo and Dave Williams; Jan and Phil Hall; James and Alison Benning; Billy Cox; Richard Gregory; Chris Preston; Kieron Davies; Wayne McGrail; Ian Wright; Jon Curtis; Vicky Woodward; Les Wolnik; Nick and Ellie Ridler; Lawrence Dick; Elizabeth Renzoni; Katie Langdon; Steve Pye; Sophie Ashcroft; Nick Priddle; Mary Clay; Bruce and Kath Baker; David Andrews; Adam and Kelly Bradford; John, Julia, Lewis, Josie and Joan Kliem; the Best family and Graham and Sandy; Elizabeth, John and Heidi Tempest; Robin Kevan; Sue Chambers; Tina Kevan; Bob Chambers; Lucy, Nick, Toby and Dominic Hawkins; Anna Kevan; Bruce Wilson; Sophie Kevan and all my family; and above all, Dr Michelle Tempest.

A NOTE ON THE AUTHOR

Tim Kevan is a barrister and writer. As well as writing the BabyBarista blog for *The Times*, he practised as a barrister in London for ten years, during which time he wrote or co-wrote ten law books, was described by Chambers UK as 'incredibly talented' and with an 'unsurpassed knowledge of the law' and was a regular legal pundit for television and radio. He is also the co-author, with Dr Michelle Tempest, of *Why Lawyers Should Surf*, which *The Times Online* described as 'a song for the modern age which could well become a cult classic' and the *Independent* said 'makes a strong case for [surfing] being a productive metaphor of our immersion in time and space'. He now lives by the sea in Braunton, North Devon, goes surfing at the merest hint of swell and is a co-founder of two businesses which provide online legal training and publishing respectively: CPD Webinars and Law Brief Publishing. Brought up in Minehead in Somerset, he was educated at Cambridge and was a scholar of the Middle Temple.

www.timkevan.com
timkevan.blogspot.com
timesonline.typepad.com/baby_barista

A NOTE ON THE TYPE

The text of this book is set in Linotype Sabon, named after the type founder, Jacques Sabon. It was designed by Jan Tschichold and jointly developed by Linotype, Monotype and Stempel, in response to a need for a typeface to be available in identical form for mechanical hot metal composition and hand composition using foundry type.

Tschichold based his design for Sabon roman on a font engraved by Garamond, and Sabon italic on a font by Granjon. It was first used in 1966 and has proved an enduring modern classic.